Praise for

Two Brides Too Many

"Mona Hodgson has been charmi[ng] [her reade]-
ries for years, and now she is givi[ng us] [much more in her]
debut novel, *Two Brides Too Many*. Spunky sisters, mail-order brides,
a mining town full of men, but where are the right ones? I was capti-
vated from the first page, wanting to read faster to see what would
happen next and to read slower so the book would not be over. A great
read."

—LAURAINE SNELLING, author of The Red River series
and *Daughters of Blessing*

"From the opening scene to the happily-ever-after ending, Mona
Hodgson's *Two Brides Too Many* puts a fresh spin on the tried-and-
true mail-order-bride story. What happens when you combine two
sisters, two elusive grooms, and the rugged mountain outpost of
Cripple Creek, Colorado? Love, laughter, and one of the best historical novels of this year!"

—KATHLEEN Y'BARBO, author of *The Confidential Life
of Eugenia Cooper* and *Anna Finch and the Hired Gun*

"*Two Brides Too Many* is one good book! Mona Hodgson sweeps the
reader away with Sinclair sisters Nell and Kat and nestles them in the
majesty of Colorado, where a cast of characters eagerly await, to create a home. Hodgson leaves a tasty trail of breadcrumbs ready to lead
us into the next story. Two more sisters…I can't wait!"

—ALLISON PITTMAN, author of *The Bridegrooms*

"Strong characters play out an intricately crafted story across a rich tapestry of setting. Not your usual mail-order-bride story, and I loved the twists and turns. A real page-turner."

—Lena Nelson Dooley, award-winning author
of *Pirate's Prize, Wild Prairie Roses,* and *Love Finds You in Golden, New Mexico*

"A delightful first novel from veteran writer Mona Hodgson. Spunky brides, spirited sisters, and sweet romance add up to a tale the Old West won't soon forget."

— DiAnn Mills, author of *Breach of Trust, Sworn to Protect,* and *A Woman Called Sage*

Two
BRIDES
Too
MANY

Two
BRIDES
Too
MANY

~∞~

A Novel

MONA
HODGSON

WATERBROOK
PRESS

TWO BRIDES TOO MANY
PUBLISHED BY WATERBROOK PRESS
12265 Oracle Boulevard, Suite 200
Colorado Springs, Colorado 80921

All Scripture quotations are taken from the King James Version.

The characters and events in this book are fictional, and any resemblance to actual persons
or events is coincidental.

ISBN 978-0-307-45890-2
ISBN 978-0-307-45891-9 (electronic)

Published in association with the literary agency of Janet Kobobel Grant, Books & Such,
4788 Carissa Avenue, Santa Rosa, CA 95405.

Published in the United States by WaterBrook Multnomah, an imprint of the Crown
Publishing Group, a division of Random House Inc., New York.

WATERBROOK and its deer colophon are registered trademarks of Random House Inc.

Library of Congress Cataloging-in-Publication Data
Hodgson, Mona Gansberg, 1954–
      Two brides too many : a novel / Mona Hodgson.— 1st ed.
         p. cm.
      ISBN 978-0-307-45890-2 — ISBN 978-0-307-45891-9 (electronic)
   1. Sisters—Fiction. I. Title.
      PS3608.O474T86 2009
      813'.6—dc22

                                                        2009029180

Printed in the United States of America
2010

10 9 8 7 6 5 4 3 2

For Cindy, Tammy, and Linda—my very own sisters.

Behold, I will do a new thing;
now it shall spring forth;
shall ye not know it?
I will even make a way in the wilderness,
and rivers in the desert.

ISAIAH 43:19

ONE

1895, Portland, Maine

I have you cornered."

Kat looked up from the writing desk to the table, where Nell was grinning. Nell's match with Ida had been particularly animated on this Sunday afternoon. Both were fiercely competitive, and Kat knew better than to challenge either one of them at checkers, or most any game.

Ida perched on a cushioned chair, face to face with Nell. The oldest of the four Sinclair sisters wasn't accustomed to losing, and it showed in Ida's furrowed brow. She stared at the board, but the pattern of the red and black disks didn't change. When she finally made a move, Nell snatched the red game piece off the board, her blue eyes sparkling.

"That's five out of seven, Ida." Vivian, the youngest at sixteen, called the tournament from the sofa where she lounged with Sassy, her Siamese cat.

"You've been dethroned, sis." Kat closed her journal. "We have a new Sinclair checkers champion."

While Ida lifted an imaginary crown off her head, Nell stood and smoothed her skirt. Ida placed the invisible trophy atop Nell's wheat-blond twist. "I present the new queen of checkers." Ida bowed. All four sisters giggled.

Kat picked up her journal and walked to the window. Fabric ties held tartan curtains open, framing the idyllic outdoor scene. Crimson and golden leaves adorned the maples and oaks outside, and a couple of squirrels frolicked while a handful of leaves twisted and twirled above them like autumn acrobats.

Acrobats in fall colors
Twist and twirl...

Kat hurried back to the writing desk and recorded the words in her journal, her pencil flying over the page. Sunday was the most inspiring day of the week. The Sabbath's time of rest and reflection always left her refreshed and full of new ideas.

Nell cleared her throat. "I don't suppose you're writing about my victory for the *Portland Press Herald.*"

"A recounting of your conquest, as great as it was, isn't Kat's cup of tea." Vivian laughed. The name *Sassy* fit Vivian as well as it did her cat.

"Now if Nell were the writer in the family, we'd all be reading a most romantic love story," Ida said, returning the checkerboard to the bookcase.

"I believe in love." Nell shrugged. "Is that so bad?"

"Believing in love is not at all bad, poppet." Father's warm voice drew their attention to the doorway. He wore a herringbone suit, his auburn mustache and beard neatly trimmed. He leaned against the door frame, his arms crossed over his chest.

"We have a new checkers champion, Father." Nell raised her hands to her head and formed a crown. "Me."

"And such a humble winner." A weak smile turned up one side of Father's mouth, and an uneasiness began to niggle Kat's stomach. Something wasn't right.

While Father joined all four of the girls at the table, Tilda shuffled into the room and set a tea tray down on the mahogany table. She'd served the Sinclair family for ten years, and Kat would never forget how lovingly Tilda had cared for Mother until Mother's death eight years ago. Tilda poured hot apple cider into the china cups and straightened up slowly.

Kat lifted her cup and took in a deep breath, inhaling the fragrant steam, then took a lemon bar from the platter and passed the tray to Ida.

"Her rule will be short-lived." Ida squared her shoulders. "I'll have my title and crown back next Sunday."

"My girls are headstrong, even while being fair flowers." Father lifted his cup with finely kept hands. "That's what helped me survive losing your mother." After a drink of cider, he returned his cup to the table. "I have news, girls, and I'm counting on that independent spirit of yours."

While Kat considered what kind of news would have Father counting on their independence, she swallowed the last bite of lemon cookie.

"What kind of news, Father?" Nell asked the question before Kat could get it out.

"My job here is being terminated in May of the coming year."

"That's awful." Vivian's empty cup clinked against the saucer. "They can't do that!"

Nell frowned at Vivian's pessimism—a battle Nell and Vivian engaged in often. "You'll find something soon, Father," she said. "I'm just sure of it."

"Nell's right." Kat couldn't believe she'd said that. Her father had worked for Wyatt Locomotive for as long as she could remember, and there weren't many other prospects here in Portland. "May is still eight months away. You'll probably find something even better by then." She hoped her voice sounded more optimistic than she felt.

Vivian scooted back her chair and folded her arms in a huff. "It makes no difference how much time they've given you. You've given them much more."

"Well, they haven't let me go entirely," he said, letting out a sigh. "They've offered me a job overseeing their locomotive engineers in Paris."

Nell gasped and Vivian shrieked. Sassy jumped off Vivian's lap and scurried for cover. Kat sat still, stunned.

Father was taking a job in France.

While most writers might find a place like Paris exotic and alluring, Kat didn't. She liked living in Maine. Portland had been their home all her life. This was where Mother lived and died.

Ida pinched the bridge of her nose, signaling one of her headaches was coming on. "I can't leave Portland, Father. I'm only halfway through my secretarial course here."

"Yes," he said. "I've thought about that." The clock began to chime, and Father waited for the fourth and final chime to sound before he continued speaking. "This house belongs to the company," he said, pressing his hand against the arm of his chair. "They are only providing me with a one-room apartment in Paris."

The niggle in Kat's stomach fast became a churning. She couldn't believe that Father was leaving them behind. At nearly nineteen, she should be ready for this, but with their mother gone, he was all they had left.

"You're leaving us here?" Nell asked, her voice shallow.

"I don't get to go to Paris?" Vivian whispered.

Father rose from his chair and strolled to the fireplace. Pulling Mother's picture off the mantel, he stared at it, as if drawing strength from her. "I have to do this," he said. "I don't see any other way."

Her father looked so forlorn that Kat almost stood up to give him a hug. She didn't like it, but she knew the decision to take the job had to be as difficult for him as it was for them. "We'll be fine, Father."

"I know you will, Kat. I have faith in each one of you. Your mother did a fine job of raising you to be exceptional young women." Father returned the photograph to the mantel. "I need to know that you four will be well cared for until I return, so I've arranged for Vivian and Ida to stay with your aunt Alma here in Portland until they finish their schooling. Then they'll join you and Nell in Colorado."

"Colorado?" Nell's voice quivered.

"Yes. I think Colorado will be the best place for you," he said, his eyes sad. "Towns are growing fast there, and the mountains are grand, and I've had many occasions for business there." Father returned to his cup and took a long drink. "There are good, solid men there, and as much as it hurts me to see you go, Colorado is a land of opportunity. That's what I want for my girls."

Questions piled upon questions, leaving Kat feeling a bit queasy.

What was Father talking about? Opportunities for what? And what did men in Colorado have to do with her and Nell? Kat glanced at Ida for answers, but her big sister looked just as dumbfounded as she felt.

"After the war, many men from the East moved out west, where they're making good wages in the mines, railroads, and businesses. Some are even striking it rich. Vivian isn't of the age for a husband yet. The rest of you are, and I'm afraid it's time to start looking." He shook his head. "Ida will finish her studies first, but I want the two of you to wire advertisements to the *Cripple Creek Prospector* in Cripple Creek, Colorado."

"Advertisements?" The one word was all Kat could choke out.

"Yes, poppet. Advertisements for husbands."

Kat pulled her napkin to her face and tried to hide her dismay. Traveling west to look for husbands was one thing. But advertising in a newspaper for one was another matter entirely. It just wasn't something that well-bred ladies did.

But one look at her father's pained face made her realize that everything had changed.

TWO

❧

1896, Cripple Creek, Colorado

Kat tried to block out the *clickety-clack* of the train wheels as she wrote in her journal.

An adventure. That's what I'll call this journey Nell and I are on. It's not so much a romantic tale as it is an adventure story. The story of two sisters—

"My name's Lucille Reger. My mother and I are going to see my aunt."

Kat laid her pencil in her journal and looked up at the girl who sat in the train seat across from her.

"I'm Kat Sinclair," she said, studying the young passenger. Lucille had boarded the train in Colorado Springs with her mother, who now slouched in the seat opposite Nell, sleeping as if she hadn't closed her eyes in days. The girl had had her nose poked in a worn copy of *Grimm's Fairy Tales* for most of the journey, but now the book sat on her lap. "And this is my sister Nell."

Nell looked up from the letter she held and gave the girl a warm nod. "Hello, Lucille."

"Are you writing a book, Miss Kat Sinclair?"

"This is just my journal." Kat closed the soft leather cover. "My sister and I left Maine the better part of a week ago, and I've been writing about our journey."

Pulling another letter from the bundle in her lap, Nell looked over at Kat, a brow raised. "You could write a book, you know, if you set your mind to it."

"Thank you, but—"

"I'd read your book if it had princesses in it," Lucille volunteered. "Or an evil witch." The train snaked around another mountain, and the girl's barley-sugar curls bounced at her shoulders. "Do you write about those things?"

"Sometimes I do write about my sister."

Nell elbowed her. "The good princess."

"I just like to write poetry and record things in my journal. I'm not a real writer."

Nell huffed. "What do you call writing for the *Portland Press Herald*?" Sunlight streaked through the window, highlighting her freckles.

"I call it a thing of the past." She'd written two articles for the paper, and it was not a regular job by any stretch of the imagination. Kat appreciated her sister's encouragement, but now that she was moving out West to marry a miner, journal writing was probably as close as she'd come to being a writer. It was probably best that she concentrate on this new chapter—life in Colorado with Mr. Patrick Maloney. Kat returned the journal to her bag and pulled out her own bundle of letters. It was a much shorter stack than Nell's.

They'd only been corresponding with their grooms-to-be for three months, but they were the most hopeful weeks she and her sisters had enjoyed since Father announced his move to Paris. Kat couldn't believe she was finally going to meet Patrick.

Lucille held up the book in her hand. "I'm reading 'Cinderella.' It's my favorite story. What are you reading?"

"These are letters from my own prince." Nell smiled, her eyes sparkling.

Lucille's blue eyes widened. "You have a prince?"

Nell slid her intended's hand-tinted photograph out of a worn envelope on her lap. "This is my Judson Archer," she said, gazing at his face for probably the twentieth time this week.

"He does look like a prince." Lucille's curls bounced as she nodded.

Nell tapped the bundle in Kat's lap. "My sister has one too."

Lucille looked up at Kat. "Do you have a picture of your prince?"

Kat wasn't inclined to call Patrick Maloney a prince. She'd never so much as met the man, but he was a foreman for a big mine, he wanted a wife, and he had sent her train fare. That had seemed to be enough to ease Father's mind, so Kat tried to be optimistic. She pulled Patrick's photo from the folds of his last letter. She'd received it the day Father announced that Kat and Nell couldn't wait until June to wed the two men who wanted them for wives. The next day she and Nell had boarded the westbound train in Portland.

Kat scooted to the edge of the seat to show the tintype to Lucille. The girl shook her head. "I like his chin, but I don't think a prince wears a hat like that."

This girl was much too precocious for her own good. In the picture, Patrick wore a bowler with the eye of a peacock feather secured in the band. But a man's clothing hardly disqualified him as a prince, or as an appropriate husband. She could think of a dozen quick responses to the child's observation but thought it best to hold her tongue.

"Did you see my Judson's ocean blue eyes?" Nell continued to gaze at her photograph.

"The photographs are hand-tinted, Nell. You can be sure it's an embellished coloring."

"Devotion swirls in their deep pools."

Devotion swirls in their deep pools. Kat sighed. To think, she'd been the one accused of florid prose.

She looked down and studied Patrick's solid Irish face and well-trimmed handlebar mustache. Skimming his jaw with her fingertip, Kat imagined the feel of manly stubble. "Do you know what this cleft in Patrick's chin means?"

"That he's as stubborn as a mule." Nell giggled, and Lucille mimicked her.

"It's the mark of a decisive man." She'd made up the theory, but it did seem likely, given the brevity she'd seen in Patrick's letters. So what if he wasn't as long-winded as Nell's Judson? He had simply made up his mind more quickly. Plus, he worked as a foreman at the Mary McKinney Mine and volunteered with the fire brigade, so he was obviously an industrious man as well.

"Mrs. Judson Archer." Her sister's wistful whisper sounded like a flute in a romantic rhapsody as she picked up one of the letters and began to read. " 'My dearest Nell, I'm counting the days until you arrive in Cripple Creek and become my beloved wife. The fifth of June is far too many days away.' "

Patrick was obviously too busy with work to write incessantly. And probably too shy to go on about such personal feelings, but that was all right with Kat. She could do any writing that needed to be done.

"He said the fifth of June. This is only April twenty-eighth." Lucille stood to reach for the letter, nearly falling on top of them before she sat back down.

"Our father had to leave Maine sooner than expected, so we had to move up our trip." Nell tucked Judson's picture and the letter back into its crumpled envelope and slipped the bundle into her satchel. "We sent telegrams to let them know we were leaving Maine several weeks early." Nell brushed at the soot that spotted her dress sleeve.

"I want to see your princes. Will they be at the depot?"

Kat raised an eyebrow. Lucille sounded much too dreamy for a child her age.

"Yes, they'll be there." Nell studied the empty ring finger on her left hand.

"Are you marrying them tonight?"

A nervous giggle escaped Nell's closed lips.

Kat sighed. Her sister was much too patient with the girl. "No."

"Kat's prince sent us the name of a boardinghouse where we can live until we're married."

Kat gave Nell her look that said enough was enough.

"She's just curious," Nell whispered.

"You're encouraging her to be meddlesome."

The train's rhythm had slowed as it made its final ascent up the narrow track that gripped the edge of the mountainside, like a cat climbing a gnarly tree trunk.

The conductor opened the car door, and a blast of cold air followed him into the compartment and stirred Lucille's mother.

"What?" The woman asked the question of her daughter, who pointed at the pudgy man with the wire-rim spectacles. He hitched his thumb between the buttons on his striped vest. "Fifteen minutes to the Cripple Creek Depot, folks."

Nell glanced down at her soiled calico travel dress. "We're a frightful pair…covered from our curls to our boots with soot. I do wish we had time to freshen up at the boardinghouse before we meet our future husbands."

"We'll just have to do our best with what we have," Kat sighed. "Since they'll be the ones taking us and our trunks to the boardinghouse." She pulled a handkerchief and a mirror from her reticule, and Nell followed her lead.

Once Kat was satisfied that she'd done all she could to look her best for the man she'd soon call her husband, she twisted toward the window for a better view of her new home. The sight stole her breath. Clouds bubbled up over a tree-lined ridge, and the tops of wooden roofs peeked out from under the naked branches. The city was much larger than she expected. Snowcapped mountains surrounded the town like the fluted white edges of Mother's favorite bowl. Pikes Peak loomed to the east, and the sun spread fingers of light across the purple robes that adorned the stand of mountains to the west. Kat wanted to retrieve her journal, but there wasn't time to write much.

"Those are the great Rocky Mountains," Lucille's mother whispered, adjusting the pearl-tipped pin in her hat.

Just then, the train's shrill whistle blew, signaling their arrival. Kat buckled her satchel and positioned her hat, pinning it solidly into place, while Nell pulled her wool coat off her lap and smoothed the velvet collar.

Kat bent toward the window, looking for any sign of a bowler with a peacock feather, but the pressing crowd gathered on the platform made it difficult.

"There's been a fire." Kat sucked in her breath and pointed to the scorched depot building. Nell nodded and looked up at the charred hillsides surrounding the station. "What have we gotten ourselves into?" Kat whispered.

Nell squared her shoulders. "We knew it would be different," she said, trying to sound confident. "We'll be fine. You'll see."

They had to be. Father was thousands of miles away in France, and Ida and Vivian were depending on the two of them to forge a fresh start for all four of the Sinclair sisters.

The train finally screeched and squawked to a stop, and its passengers jumped into motion. Men stuffed newspapers into their bags and donned wide-brimmed felt hats and derbies. The three other women in the car adjusted hairpins and shawls, and reached for the arms of the men who accompanied them.

Clutching their bags, Kat and Nell joined the others in the aisle that would lead them back to solid ground and to their princes.

∾◠◡∾

Nell watched as the young woman ahead of her took her husband's arm. They crossed the threshold and laughed, and a longing for such comforts stirred deep inside her.

Soon it would be her crossing thresholds with Judson Archer.

Passengers near the door at the front of the car pulled their wraps and overcoats off the pegs. As Nell neared the exit, she shrugged into her cape and buttoned it, pulling the fabric tight around herself.

They stepped onto the platform and moved, like sheep, with the crowd. As people branched off, greeting those who came to meet them, the crowd thinned, and Nell looked about for any sign of their intendeds.

There was no one on the platform who resembled Judson, and Mr. Maloney's peacock feather would be hard to miss. "They're not here, Kat."

"I'm sure they'll be here." The tight set of Kat's jaw contradicted her words.

"Where's your prince?" Her eyes wide, Lucille stood in front of her, several steps behind her mother and the woman Nell presumed was her aunt.

Kat was right—she'd said too much to the child. The girl was a stranger, and a young one at that, and now Nell felt obligated to address questions she couldn't answer.

"They were probably delayed at work. After all, we did surprise them with our news of an early arrival." Nell looked at Kat. Her sister's raised eyebrows and closed lips gave no indication of a plan to jump in with help. "Or maybe it was just a missed communication.

It's not all that surprising. So much can go wrong with sending a wire."

"Come along, Lucille," the girl's mother called from the depot door. The girl turned away reluctantly, her shoulders sagging. Nell sighed. She'd learned her lesson—they wouldn't tell anyone else why they had come.

Within minutes, their two trunks were the only baggage left on the platform. Everyone else had gone and they were alone. The late-morning sun glared in Nell's eyes.

Nell plopped down on her trunk. "We wired them. They should be here."

"We'll wait fifteen more minutes." Kat lowered herself down onto her trunk too.

Nobody came.

Half an hour later, Nell searched out a porter, who gave them directions to Hattie's Boardinghouse. She tried to ignore the pity on his face as she made arrangements with him to have their trunks delivered.

The sisters shuffled to the stairs and stepped off the depot platform onto a layer of slushy snow. Icy water seeped into Nell's boot. A stiff wind had them clutching the brims of their hats as they walked to the front of the depot and onto the snow-laced road, but the sun felt warm on her face. She linked arms with Kat for stability as much as for camaraderie.

Nell was happy to be off the train, even if their arrival wasn't exactly what she'd imagined. Perhaps it was better this way anyway. When she did finally meet Judson in person, she would be clean and looking her best.

They walked up the street towards the boardinghouse, past several burned-out businesses, dodging carts and burros and men. So many men. They were everywhere. On horses. Beside donkeys. Behind carts. All of them gawking at the sisters. Nell kept her eyes trained on the ground, but something caught her attention. A man, wearing a familiar hat. She stiffened, jerking Kat and nearly pulling her down.

"Are you all right?" Kat asked, steadying her. "Did you stumble?"

Nell shook her head and then pointed across the street. "That man there in front of the Cash and Carry."

"That's…Patrick's hat," Kat said quietly. The man had his arm around a tiny woman in a red satin bodice. Her long blond hair was pulled to one side, cascading down her shoulder. She whispered something in his ear, and he threw his head back and laughed.

"But it can't be him." Nell wanted to believe it couldn't be Mr. Maloney—not with another woman on his arm. Not with a woman who wore a dress like that.

Kat pulled away from Nell and started to storm across the street.

Nell grabbed hold of Kat's cape and yanked. She couldn't let her sister make a fool of herself. "We need to find our lodging," she said, pulling her sister back toward her. "Besides, you can't be sure it's Patrick. Men in bowler hats are probably a dime a dozen in these camps. You don't want to start your new life here like this."

Nell watched the man open the door to Ollie's Saloon and hold it open for the woman, and they both disappeared inside.

Kat sighed and turned toward the boardinghouse. "I guess I'll find out soon enough, either way."

Nell nodded and started walking up the street, dodging slushy puddles. Kat would find out soon enough. That's what worried Nell.

THREE

Kat sat on the sofa beside Nell in Widow Hattie's parlor, bouncing her knee and fidgeting with the hem of her shirtwaist. Three teacups dotted the table in front of them, and music was playing on a new Edison phonograph in the corner.

Kat was thankful for a comfortable place to stay, especially after she'd seen all the burned-out buildings and makeshift construction in town—much of it didn't look habitable, let alone comfortable. But she wasn't in a frame of mind for idle conversation. She and Nell had arrived at the boardinghouse just ahead of their trunks, with only enough time for a bath before their supper of roasted chicken and wild rice.

Although the food was tasty, the mealtime was long on awkward exchanges with their landlady and the two couples who boarded here. Nell had redirected the conversation anytime Hattie or a fellow boarder broached the subject of the sisters' reasons for coming to Cripple Creek. Everyone in the house knew Kat liked to write poetry and Nell liked to cook. They'd also heard all about Maine, and Ida and Vivian.

The other boarders had disappeared upstairs, and now Kat needed to think. She needed to decide what to do about Mr. Patrick Maloney. Despite Nell's insistence to the contrary, the man outside the grocer's had to have been Kat's intended. Greased brown hair. A handlebar mustache. Irish men sporting handlebar mustaches were probably as plentiful in gold mining camps as flies were in a stable, but Kat doubted that more than one of them wore a bowler cocked to one side with a peacock feather tucked into the band.

Their landlady perched on the edge of a wing-back chair across from them, and Kat couldn't help but expect the chair to topple over. Hattie lifted her cup and saucer from the table and peered at them over her cup. "Now why don't you girls tell me why you're here."

Kat met Nell's wide-eyed gaze.

"You're unattached, am I right?" Hattie lowered her cup and sat back in her chair.

"Nell and I are not married, ma'am." Kat sipped tea. It was hot, but too sweet.

"Well, most *not married* girls who come to Cripple Creek teach school." The woman's gray eyebrows arched in a sort of question mark.

Nell shifted in her chair. "Mrs. Adams—"

"Call me Hattie."

"Hattie, then." Nell glanced at Kat. "During supper you mentioned your husband, George. How did the two of you meet?"

Hattie looked up at the sisters, her eyes sparkling like polished silver. "You two sisters have to be the most tight-lipped folks on the face of the earth."

"We heard how beautiful it was here." Kat said quickly, glancing toward the window. "But the view from the train nearly took my breath away. We have the ocean in Maine, but these mountains are spectacular."

"I say this might be the most fun I've had since my George died," Hattie said, rubbing her hands together. "I love guessing games. Let's see. You're not teachers. Very few *not married* girls come here for business, other than the shady kind conducted on Myers Avenue." Kat felt herself blush, but Hattie didn't even turn pink. "And if they come to do that, they certainly don't stay with me. You girls aren't that sort, so…"

Kat realized the woman wasn't one to give up…ever. "Our father is in the locomotive business and has contacts here," she said, hoping that would be enough to satisfy the woman.

"Your father is here in Cripple Creek?"

"No ma'am," Kat admitted reluctantly. "He's in Paris."

"Paris, France? He must be a real hoity-toity, doing that kind of gadding about."

Kat couldn't help but smile that a woman who owned a house with electric lights, running water, carpeting, and mahogany furnishings was calling her father wealthy. She'd find out the truth soon enough.

Tapping her fleshy chin, Hattie pushed up from the chair and turned off the phonograph. "So, what we have here are two single sisters whose father moved to Paris and left them behind."

Nell set her rattling teacup and saucer on the table and straightened. "Father didn't exactly—"

Hattie wagged her finger at Nell. "Your wire said you only needed the room for a night or two. Is that all you'll be in town?"

Kat couldn't take this guessing game any longer. Never mind that it meant giving up their privacy. "Ma'am, have you ever heard of a man named Patrick Maloney?"

Hattie nodded and sank into the wing-backed chair. Kat's heart sank with her.

"Just about everybody in town has. That one's taken to the drink. 'Pickled Paddy,' they call him. What business do you have with him?"

Kat's eyes filled with tears, and she fought to keep them from spilling over. She'd chosen a drunk for a groom.

"My stars! You said you weren't married, not that you weren't attached…" Hattie cupped her face, her eyes the size of silver dollars. "Mail-order brides—you two girls are mail-order brides!"

Nell pursed her lips and cast a glance at Kat, then bobbed her head.

"Oh." Staring at Kat, the woman shook her head. "Oh no. Not Paddy Maloney?"

Kat nodded, and a tear slipped down her cheek.

"Letters?"

"Yes." Kat took a sip of tea to steady herself. "He failed to mention the drinking, or that he had another woman."

"Another woman?"

"He didn't show up at the train station today, but on the way here, we saw him out in front of the Cash and Carry. He wasn't alone." Whispering the accusation hadn't made the words sting any less.

"You saw him at the grocery with another woman?" Hattie clucked her tongue. "Today is Tuesday." Their landlady shook her head, as if that made everything clear.

"What's wrong with Tuesdays at the grocery?" Kat wasn't sure she wanted to know, but she had to know now.

"You girls are greener than grapes on a vine."

Kat opened her mouth to protest, but the woman was right—Father had protected them from sordid details. She hadn't even realized it before, but now it seemed a cruel curse to be so naive.

"One morning a week here, proper women stay away from town." Hattie crossed her arms over her chest. "Tuesday mornings belong to the others for their shopping and such."

The others?

"Oh." A sudden heat climbed Kat's neck and face. How was she to marry a man she'd seen with a…strumpet?

She didn't want to admit the answer. She couldn't. But if she didn't marry Patrick, what was she going to do?

Two hours later, Kat lay in bed, holding her breath and listening for Nell's soft snore. Their landlady had clicked her door shut and turned out the lights in her room early, but Kat thought her sister would never tire of chattering about their new surroundings and settle down, let alone drift off to sleep. Kat didn't dare tell Nell about her plan. She wouldn't approve, and when Kat didn't back down, Nell would insist on going with her.

Satisfied that everyone in the house had settled in for the night, Kat slid out of bed. She carefully padded over to the chair where she'd laid her clothes. Once Kat was dressed, she pulled on her boots and quietly stepped into the hallway. The staircase creaked with each step, and she wondered why she'd even bothered to tiptoe. She slipped out the front door, pulling it closed softly behind her, and tugged her cape tight against the chilling wind. A full moon lit the street, and she hurried down the hill to Bennett Avenue. Ignoring the calls of the men that she passed, she marched up the boardwalk toward Ollie's Saloon. She'd just passed the Cash and Carry when a grizzled man staggered out of the saloon in front of her.

"Hey, doll, you got some sugar for me?" His words were slurred, and the odor of alcohol was so strong it made Kat's eyes sting. Snickering, the bearded man lurched and grabbed at her bodice.

Kat gasped and slapped the drunk's hand away. He teetered, and she stepped out around him. Squaring her shoulders, she pushed open the door to the saloon.

Smoke billowed from cigars and pipes, and raucous off-key piano music filled the room with noise. Revulsion churned her stomach, and her supper caught in her throat. She swallowed hard and pressed her gloved hand against her stomach. The sooner she left this place, the better, but first she needed to know if Patrick was here.

Kat blinked and willed her eyes to adjust to the dim lighting. Then she wove her way through tables filled with men engaged in games of chance. Ignoring their leering stares and catcalls, she looked at every face and every hat, but none of them belonged to Patrick.

"I said your tab's full, and I meant it." The male voice gained volume with each word. "Pay up or get out, Paddy."

Paddy.

The titters of females drew Kat to the left wall, where a stocky bartender stood face to face with a man hunched on a stool. Two women stood on either side of him. She recognized the one with the blond hair from the Cash and Carry. The other wore a bustle and leaned in close to the man, her hand resting on his arm. Kat didn't want to believe it was Patrick sitting between the women, but the hat with the peacock feather tucked into the band was undeniably his.

"Mr. Maloney?"

The man spun around and studied Kat from boot to bonnet. "Well, if I'm not the luckiest fellow alive. Pretty women are comin' out of the woodwork lookin' for me." A smirk spreading across his whiskered face, he rubbed his chin just below the cleft.

She was looking at the man in the photo, but the one in front of her wasn't the man she'd agreed to marry. Kat pressed her hand to her roiling stomach again. "I am Miss Kat Sinclair."

His mouth dropped open, and he stood, balancing himself with one hand on the bar, nearly upsetting a small vase of posies in front of the blonde.

"This the gal from Maine?" The question came from the bustled woman.

Kat folded her arms, fighting the urge to scream. Why would such a woman know about Patrick's personal business...her private matters? "I sent you a wire saying I'd arrive early, Mr. Maloney. Didn't you receive it?"

Patrick let go of the bar and swayed a little, then stood up and tugged his overalls smooth. "I'm sorry I wasn't at the depot to meet you, ma'am, but you said you'd be here Tuesday."

"This is Tuesday."

His eyes wide, he removed his hat and held it against his chest. "My deepest apologies. Must've gotten my days mixed up. I assure you, Miss Sinclair, if I'da known you were coming, I never would have planned my party for tonight."

"That's what you call this? A party?"

Patrick stuffed his hat back on his head. "Ladies," he said, gesturing toward Kat, "I'd like you to meet my lovely bride, Miss Kat Sinclair."

The woman from the Cash and Carry smiled, her red lips turning up at the corners. "I'd say I done a mighty swell job on them letters," she said.

Kat jerked. She felt like she'd been slapped in the face. "You didn't even write the letters?"

"Had a little help is all." Patrick nodded, and the feather in his cap wagged. "No need to get your stockings tangled."

Kat looked up at him, feeling dazed and humiliated.

"I have a house for you, and you can pretty it up to suit yourself. We can get hitched tomorrow."

"Hitching is something you do with a horse and a wagon, Mr. Maloney." Kat stepped toward Paddy and looped her index finger over the bib of his coveralls, then pulled on it. With her other hand she grabbed the vase off the bar and dumped its contents, posies and all, down his front.

Cheers echoing around her, Kat handed the vase to the woman from the Cash and Carry, then paraded through the crowd and out the door.

FOUR

❧

*L*ewis P. Whibley pulled a pair of denims over his union suit and grabbed a red shirt, a gift from a doe-eyed widow on the opposite side of Denver. Could've been afternoon by now for all he knew. Tucked away in this frosty downstairs room, he couldn't tell morning from midnight. At least the price was right, especially since the old maid who owned this place had taken pity on him. There was something he could be proud of. He'd managed to outclass his daddy in the profession of con artist, although Lewis preferred the term *charmer.*

He pulled a silver pocket watch out of his coat, hanging on the peg by the door, and rolled the timepiece in his hand. He'd charmed it from a Scottish miner last month. He glanced at the hands on the clock. 2:00 a.m.

He'd left the saloon by 1:30 this morning. Had to have been at least 2:00 a.m. before his head hit the pillow. Lewis tried to reset the lazy mechanism. He wound the mainspring, then rapped the face of the watch, much like his mother had thumped his forehead to get him out of bed in the mornings. He stared at the second hand but saw no movement. Like most of the people in his life, the blasted thing refused to show him any charity. He shoved it back into the coat pocket and buttoned his shirt.

Morning…noon…what'd it matter? One sour day rushed in on the heels of another in this hole. The only time of day that did matter to him was the hour his prey showed up and sat at his faro table. He was counting on them this week, since he wasn't quite ready to leave Denver. He needed at least one more miner's payout before he moved on. Two would be best. That is, if he didn't wear out his welcome before then—a veritable hazard in his trade.

Next to boatloads of cash he'd long spent, his favorite win had been a place in Cripple Creek. Almost a year ago. What a haul, and the greenhorn never saw the sting coming. That one had *easy mark* scrawled all over him—from the Easterner's peacoat to the jingle bobs on his spurred work boots. A snicker bubbled up from Lewis's gut. His job was more fun than was socially acceptable. Plus, he could be as lazy in the mornings as he pleased.

Unfortunately, after that grand haul, he'd lost his good sense and failed to walk away in a timely manner. That costly mistake still pained him clear through to his backbone. His daddy had never lost anything that big.

'Course he'd never won as much in one sitting as Lewis had either—three hundred big ones, a mule, a cook, and a place on a hillside. If only he'd quit playing before that lousy drunk stumbled down the sporting stairs to the table. Lewis thrust his fingers through his hair. Grabbing the strop off his washstand, he set his mind to sharpening his razor. He slid the dull razor against the thick leather band, his tension easing a bit with each stroke.

A savory, meaty scent wafted into his room, and Lewis sniffed. He returned the razor to its place beside the washbowl. Shaving could wait till tomorrow evening, when he'd go out to find his next mark. His lady friend Widow Sanchez wouldn't mind a little scruff on his jaw. She might even find it appealing this evening.

The aroma from the kitchen made his mouth water. Lewis could imagine the spread the old maid upstairs was setting out for her boarders. Ham. Biscuits with honey. Fried eggs. Hashed potatoes. The rumble in his gut begged him to leave his room and take the stairs two at a time, but he didn't dare show that woman his face today. He'd made too many promises and kept none of them. He'd best give her a couple of days to set something else on her mind. He pulled a piece of jerked beef from a sack on the table and bit off a tough end. This would do until supper. Widow Sanchez had turned out to be a good seamstress and a good cook if you had a taste for tamales and chili peppers, which he did. Anything was better than the fusty stuff he was trying to appease his hunger with now.

He heard footfalls on the steps outside his door. He stopped chewing. They were coming closer. Lewis moved to the table and opened his valise, which held the most important tool of his trade. But when he recognized the shuffle on the steps as the mousy old maid's gait, he relaxed. The steps he'd need his two-shot for wouldn't be that cautious and slow. The mouse was probably coming down to invite him to breakfast. After all, it was Wednesday, prayer meeting day.

"Mr. Whibley." A sharp pound on the door followed the woman's clipped call. Sounded like she still had his debt stuck in her craw, and he wasn't of a mind to quibble with her. "Mr. Whibley, I know you're in there. And you had best open this door." Another pound.

This was no invitation to a hearty breakfast. The woman seemed set on pitching a conniption. Fine. He was a professional, and he could handle her outbursts. He knew just the trick that would tilt her.

Lewis unbuttoned the top four buttons on his shirt and roughed up his chest hairs. He held a deep breath, trying to produce the effects of a blush before he yanked open the door. "Why, Miss Landers." Fumbling with the buttons, he tried to appear discomfited by her intrusion.

Her eyes widened, and her jaw sagged. His ploy was a success. "Are you all right, Miss Landers?"

Her face and neck the color of raspberry pie, the old maid stared at a paint stain on the floor beside his stocking feet. He'd touched up a scuffed spot on his table and had apparently gotten sloppy with the red paint.

"I…I am fine, Mr. Whibley."

"That's good news. You worried me with your curt inquiry."

Her nose twitched. "If you do not have my rent money ready, Mr. Whibley, it will not be good news for you. Of that you can be sure."

Prattle. Prattle. Prattle. The woman's favorite pastime. This was proving to be more difficult than he'd given her credit for. He needed to step up his game. "How can you be so offhand, Miss Landers, on prayer meeting day?" He reached for her work-worn hand but only brushed it before she snatched it away from him.

"Wednesday or not, Mr. Whibley, you owe me three weeks' rent. That is fifteen dollars. And let me remind you that fifteen dollars is due right this very minute." She shoved her hand at him, palm up.

"A man can't get his hands on his money on an empty stomach, Miss—"

"Then you had best find your bag and pack it."

She was kicking him out, or at least she intended to. He'd had the money last week, but his exit timing was still off a bit. Never guessed that itinerant preacher would be so skilled at faro—an imposing charmer, that one. Lewis knew he was only in a patch of bad luck. In a slump is all. It happened to the best of 'em. Happened to his daddy more times than Lewis could count. But his daddy had always turned it around, and he would too. His big break would come soon.

Lewis moved close enough to her to smell the bacon fryings on her flour-sack apron. Failing to meet his gaze, the mousy spinster lowered her hands to her apron pockets. She wasn't one to carry a weapon, so it had to be a stance of surrender. He had finally worn her down. That's what he believed until the woman pulled a small supper bell out of a pocket and wagged it in front of his face like a schoolmarm. He reared his head back. The tiny thing sure could make a lot of noise.

Lewis covered his ears, unsure of how to best counter her childish action. "Really, Miss—" A couple of clomps on the steps outside his door paralyzed Lewis's tongue and set his heart racing.

Miss Landers stilled her bell. "That would be Karson."

Lewis backed away from the door. "Karson?"

Clomp. Clomp.

"My brother." She dropped the bell into her pocket.

Clomp. Clomp.

"I never mentioned him?"

Lewis shook his head, wishing like never before for a window in this downstairs cell.

Clomp. Clomp.

It seemed like this was as good a time as any to return to Cripple Creek and win back his lucky silver flask and his home, and see where things went from there.

FIVE

he sisters spent most of Wednesday morning washing eight
days' worth of soiled travel clothes. After fighting a stiff wind
to hang their garments on the line at Hattie's, Kat fully expected that
their laundry would be dry by the time she and Nell returned from
town this afternoon. Finished with that chore, Kat drafted a quick
telegram to send to her two sisters and Aunt Alma. She and Nell
wanted to let them know they'd arrived safely, but both agreed to keep
the details of their abrupt introduction to Cripple Creek to themselves
for now.

After lunch with Hattie and the other boarders, Kat and Nell
slipped into their capes and stepped out onto Hattie's porch, but Kat
couldn't forget the memories of last night's visit to the saloon. She had
come all this way to please Father—to put his mind at ease, and for
what? She didn't have the heart to tell him that the solution to his fi-
nancial concerns for her was nothing more than a complication. And
the confrontation with her intended had only compounded the problem. She couldn't "get hitched" to Maloney, and Nell hadn't yet heard

from Judson Archer. Kat wanted to believe the man who had won her sister's heart through his letters wasn't cut from the same cloth, that there were respectable, trustworthy men here, but why hadn't he been at the station waiting?

Please, Lord, don't let him be like Patrick.

Father had limited funds, and what Kat and Nell had left would cover only five more days at the boardinghouse. Nell needed Judson to be a man of his word. She needed him to marry her soon. And Kat needed to find some way to support herself.

Rounding the corner at Hayden, the sisters dodged a wagon full of lumber and started down the hill to the telegraph office, both of them holding their wraps tight.

"How can you be so patient?" Nell's question carried a sigh. "Aren't you dying to find out about Patrick?"

Kat felt a twinge of guilt, and she swallowed hard against it.

"Why haven't we heard anything from them?" Nell said, ducking her head against the gusty wind. "They sent us train fare. We sent them wires about our arrival, and then not a word."

Kat's skin crawled. Nell needed to know about her escapades last night. They usually told each other most everything, but ladies—even sisters—didn't normally discuss such places, let alone frequent them.

Stopping at Bennett Avenue, Nell looked both ways. "Which way did Hattie say to go at the corner?"

"Left." While Kat stepped up onto the boardwalk, she looked down at her sister. "I'm not patient, Nell," she said quietly. "I saw Patrick."

"We don't know that was him." Nell joined her on the boardwalk, her blue eyes soft with compassion. "We have no proof—"

"No. I mean I talked to him last night."

"You couldn't have. I was with you, and then we were sleeping."

Kat shook her head and stopped in front of the telegraph office.

"You snuck out?" Nell's brow furrowed.

"To go to the saloon next to the Cash and Carry."

"Kat!" Nell's eyebrows shot up. "I can't believe you'd do such a thing." She shook her head. "All alone?"

"I had to see him." Kat stepped to one side to let a couple pass. "I couldn't pretend it wasn't him we saw with that woman," she said, trying to figure out a way to make her sister understand. "And I knew I couldn't marry him if it was."

"You found him there?"

Kat frowned, nodding. "With a woman on each side."

"Oh, Kat." Nell let out a breath. "I'm so sorry. What did you say to him?"

"I was too busy pouring a vase full of flowers down his front to say much of anything."

"You didn't!"

Kat demonstrated her action, and they both giggled.

"I can't marry the man," she said.

"Of course you can't!"

"But what'll we do? The money Father gave us isn't going to last long."

"I don't know." Nell straightened her shoulders and turned toward the door of the telegraph office. "But let's start by finding out if the telegram I sent to Judson was delivered."

A bell jingled when they stepped into the small office, and a tall man holding a half-spent cigar rose from his chair behind a desk.

"Ladies, how may I help you?" His raspy voice made it sound as if he'd been smoking most all his life.

"Good day, sir." Nell dipped her chin. "My sister and I have come to send a telegram, but first I'd like to check on the arrival of one I sent from Maine last week."

Setting his cigar in an ashtray on a desk, the man pulled a ledger out of a drawer and walked toward the counter between them. "Last week, you say?"

"Yes sir. Mon—" Kat caught herself speaking ahead of Nell and looked over at her sister, who gave her a crooked but gracious smile.

"Last Monday to a Mr. Judson Archer at the Mary McKinney Mine." Nell's voice still sounded dreamy when she said his name.

The man pulled spectacles out of his vest pocket and then flipped pages in his ledger. "Ah. Here it is." He scanned a page. "I received it Monday afternoon, and my boy delivered it that same day to the mine. Bucky Holt signed for it. He's the paymaster out there."

Nell looked at Kat, brows raised. "But that doesn't mean it got to him. We don't know if Judson read my telegram."

"Ma'am, the paymaster told my boy he'd see that Mr. Archer got it. That's as good as I can do. Only Holt knows what happened after that."

"Yes, thank you."

The man closed his ledger and picked up his cigar.

Kat reached into her pocket for the note she and Nell had composed. "We'd like to wire Miss Alma Shindlebower in Maine." As Kat spoke the name, she couldn't help but wonder if she herself would end up a spinster like Aunt Alma.

"Of course." He returned his cigar to the tray and crossed the room to the telegraph machine. "Whenever you're ready."

A shot rang out before Kat finished repeating her aunt's name for him. Another shot followed, and then a third in rapid succession.

"Fire!" The man scurried toward the counter that stood between him and the sisters. "It's another fire!" He pulled buckets out from behind the cabinet, clanging them together, and then held two buckets out to each of the sisters.

Kat stuffed the note into her cape pocket, unsure of what he expected them to do with the containers.

"Don't just stand there." The man shoved the pails at them. "There's work to be done. We nearly lost our town Saturday. We have to save it now."

"Us?" Nell looked as if she'd just swallowed a mouse.

"We don't have any idea how to fight a fire." Kat reluctantly took the buckets from his outstretched hand.

He dashed to the door and threw it open, looking to the right. "Myers Avenue again. Looks like the Portland Hotel. Women work the bucket brigade." Two nuns in full habit ran past them down the street, carrying empty buckets. "Follow the sisters up to the reservoir. Go!" He gestured for them to head out the door. "I gotta get my stuff out of here."

"Come on, Nell," Kat said, craning her neck to see up the street. "This is our home now. We have to help save it." Kat walked out the door, and Nell followed. Smoke billowed from the hotel several blocks away. Wagons and carts jammed the street, and throngs of people rushed out of nearby businesses, shouting and carrying goods. Kat rushed up the road with Nell at her side, trying to keep the nuns in her line of sight.

Nell pointed as the sisters and a crowd of women and children turned north at Hayden and scrambled up the hill.

Kat and Nell had climbed a block or two past Golden Avenue, Hattie's street, when Kat began to feel the effect of the high elevation. Her chest began to ache, and she stopped at the side of the road to try to catch her breath.

"I wasn't prepared for climbing these hills." Nell's words came out in huffs and puffs, and she set her pails down and placed her hands on her knees. "Especially at that pace."

Kat moistened her lips. She'd heard about fires in Portland, even seen evidence of them, but never been involved like this. She'd never seen anything like this before.

"You all right?" Nell's voice had evened out some, but she still gasped a bit.

"I am if you are." She tried to sound brave.

Lord, please help us be all right. Please help these townspeople.

Nell nodded, lifting her buckets from the ground, and they resumed their trek to the top of the hill. Clusters of women were gathered around the reservoir. It looked more like a pond to Kat. The older nun, sprigs of white hair sticking out from her headpiece, helped fill buckets and pots, while the younger nun dashed over to a woman with a squalling baby.

Kat dipped her buckets into the cold water and pulled them up. After Nell did the same, they ran to join the women and older children, who had formed a line down the hill. Below them, red-orange flames flicked up through a heavy cloud of smoke. A deep roar echoed all around them. When they reached the business district, flames hissed and explosions shook the air. Kat's breath caught as buildings groaned and surrendered to ravenous flames. The putrid stench of burning rugs and horsehair mattresses clogged her nostrils, and she coughed.

Joining the end of the line, the sisters began passing buckets of sloshing water down the hill. Dynamite blasts weakened Kat's knees. Shouts and pleas directed folks who fluttered about like sparrows in a gale. Some wheeled baby buggies and wheelbarrows full of ammunition boxes and clothing out of burning buildings. Two men carried barber chairs that were still attached to broken floorboards.

The younger nun rushed over to the line, her face pinched. "I need a woman to come with me."

"I'll go with you." Nell stepped forward.

"Leave your buckets," the nun called, already running back up the hill.

Nell set her buckets on the ground and gave Kat a quick hug. "I'll meet up with you at Hattie's."

"Take care," Kat called as she watched Nell disappear into the crowd. Kat stood only three blocks from the hotel where the fire had started, passing buckets in the line along Bennett Avenue. A low, hollow boom behind her made her jump.

"The Portland's roof done caved in." Random shouts and screams drifted in the air, along with the smoke and ash. Embers took flight, falling silently on surrounding businesses and on the houses that dotted the slopes. Several blasts followed soon after. Now horses and burros ran wild in the streets. Moving with an almost intelligent fury, the fire raged.

Kat glanced around, wishing she'd gone with Nell, praying her sister was all right. Out of the corner of her eye, she saw a little girl running up the street. She was headed directly for a burning building.

Kat's temples pounded out a wild rhythm with her heartbeat. Shaking herself out of a daze, she dropped her buckets and raced after the girl. "Stop!" she cried. "Stop!"

"Mama!" The child stopped in the middle of the street, her eyes wide, staring at a wooden structure just down from Kat. Flames lapped at its second-story porches.

Kat had just reached the little girl when windows above them shattered. Kat encircled the girl with her arms and rolled to the middle of the road. They scrambled to their feet, and the little one backed away from Kat, her arms crossed.

"You not a Sunny girl. Where's Mama?"

Kat reached for her, but the child swung her arms, hiding her hands behind her back.

"I want Mama!"

"I'll help you find your mama, but we need to stay away from the fire." Kat didn't know how she would find the woman, but she couldn't leave the child alone on the streets. "You need to stay with me until we find her. Will you do that?"

"You find Mama?" The girl's face looked so hopeful, Kat didn't know what else to do.

She nodded. "Yes." Kat held her hands out to her.

"Rosita promise." The little girl crossed her heart, staring up at Kat. "Now you."

Kat crossed her heart, praying she could live up to her promise to find the child's mother. She glanced around, hoping to see the woman dashing toward them. No one came. But if folks had had time to pull boxes and beds and cases of whiskey out of buildings ahead of the fire, surely everyone had time to escape the buildings. Perhaps this girl's mother was one of the women at the reservoir.

"Rosita, we need to get you up the hill, away from town," Kat said, peering past the long line of women still passing buckets up the steep slope, toward the reservoir. The little girl reached for her, and Kat started to hoist Rosita to her waist, but as soon as she did, the child pushed away from her. "You bleeding." She stared at Kat's back.

Kat swiped at her left shoulder blade, and her fingers brushed against something hard. She tried to ignore the warm, sticky blood and felt something hard digging into her skin. She wrapped her hand around it, pulling out a piece of glass. She gasped and closed her eyes, then took a deep breath. She tried to get air into her lungs, but within seconds, she felt Rosita's weight pressing into her skirt, and the girl slid to the ground. Kat's ears roared, and then there was an unnatural hush.

And then…blackness.

Six

I will do a new thing.… I will even make a way in the wilderness. Morgan had read the passage from Isaiah in his hotel room in Divide last night. And now as his coupé climbed up the slushy road to Cripple Creek, he had no doubts that a new chapter in his life had begun. Boston's graded, sea-level roads had not prepared him for Colorado's Rocky Mountains.

Two weeks ago, he'd been in line for the position of research scientist at the Medical Research Institute. Today, following his response to an advertisement in the *Boston Herald,* he was on his way to work with a Dr. Paul Hanson at the Sisters of Mercy Hospital in Cripple Creek. The hooves of his new horse created a muffled *clip-clop* on the slushy path before him. At this high elevation, the brisk wind was chilling even with the bright sunshine, and he pulled his derby down to meet the scarf at his ears.

Morgan watched an eagle soar against a craggy backdrop and prayed that he would soon be soaring above his past. For now, he was awed by the majestic mountains and regal rock formations of his new home, and he was glad to be free of the bustling city streets of Boston and the political entanglements there. He would continue to look for the Lord's way here in the West.

After traversing a couple more miles, his coupé peaked a hill, and Morgan stopped to stretch his legs. According to the map he'd studied, the vast valley he looked out across would be his new home. But smoke billowed to the southwest, right where he expected Cripple Creek to be.

A fire.

A fire meant injuries. Morgan climbed back up into the seat and grabbed the reins.

He'd made it halfway down the hill when his physician's coupé reared back, dropping its bucket to the right. As the seat spring slammed against the wood frame, Morgan pulled up on the reins. His horse jerked to a stop. The axle ground against rock, and he twisted and watched a wheel careen down the hill past him. It rolled about twenty feet, then flopped onto the ground.

His heart still racing, Morgan jumped out and retrieved the wayward wheel. What was he thinking, leaving the comforts of Boston to head to parts unknown? Now what? Fixing this mess was a two-man job, and that was after he found the nut that had come off the hub.

"That was one wild ride there, mister."

Morgan looked up into a face as rough hewn as the peaks behind him.

"This here's one time I'm thankful for Sal's sluggish nature. Any faster, and I could've been in the middle of your mess."

By the looks of things, Morgan didn't suppose the jenny could've gotten riled if she'd wanted to. Picks, shovels, and whatnot hung from every inch of the rigging that weighed her down.

"Boney Hughes." It was a fitting moniker for the rail-thin man who spit a brown streak onto the snow. "You look like an easterner, all right. Must be Cripple Creek's new doc?"

"Yes, Dr. Morgan Cutshaw." He stuck out his hand and tried to remember that manners were different here in Colorado. "I've come to work with Dr. Hanson."

Boney wandered up the road behind Morgan, his knee-patched overalls rustling like autumn leaves. "I heard you were comin' on the train." The man twisted and shot Morgan a look, his brows raised. "Woulda been a better choice for you."

Given that I'm a greenhorn easterner and all. Boney didn't have to say it.

Keeping his frustration to himself, Morgan followed the man back to the coupé. "This thing wouldn't fit on the train in Divide. The rest of my belongings will arrive tomorrow from Colorado Springs." He could already tell he should've waited with them. Except for the smoke that billowed up below them in large black plumes. "Where that smoke is down there," he said, pointing to the valley. "Is that Cripple Creek?"

The wiry man clicked his tongue. "Sure is. A big fire. Second in only a handful of days."

Stopping about twenty yards behind the coupé, Boney pointed to a black-enamel nut about the size of a dinner roll. "We'll be needin' that if we're to get you back on the road."

Morgan retrieved the nut and dropped it into his coat pocket.

"Doc Hanson'll be mighty glad you didn't wait till tomorrow to get there."

"How long has it been burning?"

"Chief Allen fired the shot around 1:45. Was finally dyin' down some when I left, but we have a mess the size of Mount Pisgah to clean up." He gestured toward a snowcapped hill to the west that was outlined in a smoky haze. "Homes burned. Lots of injured folks. Even some dead ones. But the hospital's still standin', thanks to the fire chief and his men."

"I'd be obliged if you'd help me so I can be on my way."

Pushing his canvas hat down on his head, Boney backed up to the coupé and lifted it off the ground. "Stick it on there, Doc."

Once Morgan set the wheel in place, Boney lowered the buggy. Morgan pulled the nut from his coat pocket and threaded it finger tight.

"Not more than a couple of miles down into town now. I'd have Jesse at the livery give it a good look. From there, I'd take Fifth up to Eaton and over to the hospital so you don't get tangled up in town."

"I'll do that, Mr. Hughes."

"Doc, Mr. Hughes was my daddy. I'm Boney."

"I appreciate your help, Boney." Morgan reached into his coat pocket. "What do I owe you for your services?"

"My services," Boney muttered, shaking his shaggy head. "Nothin'. It's what we do 'round here. Unless you're tryin' to poach a claim." Boney gestured a hanging, and chuckled.

"Thank you. I'll remember that."

Boney turned to his mule and pulled the end of the knotted rope off her back. "See you around, Doc."

After he watched the man lead Sal up the hill past him, Morgan climbed up into the seat and grabbed the reins. The coupé survived the harrowing descent of several hundred yards on rocky, slushy road. His nerves thanked him when the path leveled out, and soon he rounded the corner where the depot for the Midland Terminal Railroad stood at Bennett Avenue. Jesse's Livery came into view, and so did the effects of the fire. It looked as though the blaze had pretty much burned out, but only a smattering of buildings still stood in the center of town.

Donkeys pulled carts full of belongings and supplies through town, and workers scrambled about with shovels and buckets. As Morgan approached the livery, he scanned the devastation that lay only a couple of blocks down the street. Piles of ash, broken glass, and charred boards stood where people had done business just yesterday. Everything from barber chairs to candy cases formed a wavy line down the center of the muddy road. Most of the businesses and homes at this end of town had been spared, and he was sure there were folks asking why some had lost everything while others had been protected. That had been his question for the past three years.

No doubt the wards and hallways of the hospital were lined with people. The sooner he got there to help them, the better. Morgan guided his dapple gray through the opening at Jesse's Livery. He'd see that his horse ate and drank while Jesse tightened the nut on the wheel.

After Jesse finished with the coupé and his dapple was satisfied, Morgan headed up Fifth and over to Eaton Avenue as Boney had directed him. He managed to avoid much of the chaos, but wagons and folks on foot still clogged the north-south streets as Morgan made his way to the Sisters of Mercy Hospital, a nondescript building about halfway up the block.

He secured his horse to the hitching rail and drew in a fortifying breath, then crossed the hospital's threshold. A stifling wave of smells washed over him. Burned hair. Camphor. Dirty linens. Shouts and wails echoed off of dingy walls. About a dozen men and a couple of women lined the perimeter of a room the size of his father's parlor. Some sagged on deacon's benches, but most leaned against walls or slouched on the floor.

Three women stood behind a table ripping sheets, and he guessed those were the bandages he'd be using. The youngest of the workers wore a pale blue gown and a hat elaborately trimmed with feathers and flowers. She appeared better suited for a Sunday in Boston than for hospital work. Looking up at him, she straightened her shoulders. "You must be our new doctor from the East."

"Yes ma'am." He removed his derby. "I'm Dr. Morgan Cutshaw."

"We're glad to see you, and Sister Mary Claver Coleman will be too." The young woman's smile was pleasant. "She's the reverend mother here, and she's been working in the burn ward since the fire." Removing her apron, she stepped out around the table and then extended her hand to him. "I'm Miss Darla Taggart."

Her soft hands told him she rarely did much labor, if ripping old sheets could be considered such. "Miss Taggart." Shifting his attention to the other women, he dipped his chin. "Ladies, it looks like you are doing a kind service, providing bandages for the wounded."

After Miss Taggart introduced the other two women, she scooped up an armful of fabric. "If you'll follow me, I'll show you to the burn ward."

The young woman sauntered down the hallway ahead of him, her fancy boot heels drumming against the wooden floor. A highly impractical female, and a bit too friendly for Morgan's liking. But he was overly sensitive about such matters.

She stopped in front of a closed door, peering up at him. Morgan opened it and followed her into a room about the size of his mother's kitchen—small for a burn ward, given the extent of the fire.

Eight cots packed the room. It looked more like a logjam than a hospital ward. Male patients screamed and cried. A nun with tufts of white hair sticking out of her headpiece stood over a man whose pants had been burned off of both legs, exposing blackened flesh.

"Sister Coleman, this is Dr. Morgan Cutshaw," Miss Taggart said, her gaze averting from the horrific scene in front of her. "I'll leave you to your work, Dr. Cutshaw."

"Thank you for your assistance, Miss Taggart."

She nodded, her lips pinched together, and fled the room.

"You're a godsend, Doctor," the sister told him. "They keep bringing them in. All the supplies are there in that cupboard, and you can start with Mr. Yu down there at the end."

The sound of men shouting in the hallway drew Sister Coleman out of the room.

"Doctor, come quick."

At the sound of the sister's frantic call, Morgan slammed the cupboard door closed and rushed into the hallway where two miners carried an injured man, his leg a confusing mess of blood and grime.

"Doc, this here's Ethan Goeke," said the tallest of the soot-covered men.

Morgan saw that a belt had been wrapped around Mr. Goeke's mangled limb. "We were using dynamite to clear a building from the fire, and his leg's hurt pretty bad."

"Follow me to the surgery room," said Sister Coleman, spinning around and taking long strides down the hallway. As Morgan followed behind her and the men, he heard her murmuring a prayer. He hoped he could be God's answer to the sister's petition, and maybe he could finally make a difference.

SEVEN

❧

*N*ell found herself surrounded by chaos. Pews were stacked on top of one another around the edge of the room to maximize the floor space inside the church. Babies cried, and mothers called for their toddlers, who were running around the sanctuary. Hundreds, maybe even thousands, of people had been displaced by the fire, their homes and belongings lost to the hungry flames, and Father Volpe had opened up the St. Peter's Catholic Church as temporary housing for displaced women and children. Pallets of bed sheets and blankets covered its floors, but still more women came, seeking shelter.

Nell glanced around the room at the weary mothers. She couldn't imagine their heartache—their husbands in the center of danger, fighting the fire, their children to care for, and no home. Lucille, who had ridden into Cripple Creek on the train with Kat and Nell, was there with her mother, aunt, and baby cousin.

Church folks whose homes had been spared had brought extra blankets and clothing, and food was on its way, but Nell's heart ached for the children huddled around the room. She tried to remember what used to help her when she was scared. Sometimes Father would gather her and her sisters for a story. Nell looked around the room, but she didn't see any books. Well, she knew a few stories. Nell moistened her lips and whistled, drawing the children's attention.

"It's story time, everyone. Come sit down." Nell sat in the middle of the pallets and motioned for the children to join her.

"Does anyone want to hear a story?"

"I like the purple cow one." The request came from a boy who was missing a front tooth.

"That sounds like a good place to start." Father had read Gelett Burgess's poems from the newspaper just weeks before he announced his news about Paris, and Nell knew the short poem by heart. Nell recited the first three lines, and the children joined in on the last one.

" 'I'd rather see than be one!' " The little girls giggled and the boys laughed. One little guy with a cowlick mooed like a cow, spurring them on.

The scene reminded Nell of a verse from Proverbs. Something about laughter being good medicine. She knew it was good for her, and she could see in the faces of the children that it was, at least, a healthy distraction from the fear that had held them in its grasp only an hour earlier.

"You're good with children, Miss Nell." Lucille's aunt rocked her infant son.

"Thank you, ma'am." She'd hoped the Lord would bless her and Judson with many children. Now that seemed little more than a childish dream. He'd received her wire more than a week ago, and now that she was here, she'd not heard a word from him.

"Miss Nell." Lucille stood over by a mountain of pews, reaching into her valise. "I have my book. You could read a story from *Grimm's Fairy Tales.*" She pulled the worn book out and walked back over to Nell. "As long as it's not 'Cinderella.'" Soot smudged the girl's face as surely as the fire had sullied her romantic spirit.

Nell took the book from Lucille, vowing to keep her own ideals alive. She knew her prince was real and his letters true.

Please, Lord.

❧

Kat opened her eyes, trying to orient herself. A dim light mottled the tattered curtain that surrounded her cot. She tried to figure out where she was. Voices swirled around her, but she didn't hear Nell's among them. Then she remembered. Nell was off helping the Sisters of Mercy, or back at Hattie's. Father was working in Paris, and Vivian and Ida were with Aunt Alma in Maine. And here she was lying in a hospital in a town that held nothing but heartache for her.

Feeling a bit lightheaded, Kat blinked back the tears that pricked her eyes. She raised herself up into a sitting position. When a twinge of pain pinched her shoulder and traveled down her left arm, she rolled onto her right side instead. The piece of glass must have done more than just cut her skin. She shouldn't be surprised. Nothing about life in Cripple Creek had been easy so far.

Why, Lord, why?

She'd done all she knew to do. She'd even rescued a little girl from the fire. Rosita was probably reunited with her mother by now, while she lay here all alone, wearing a ripped dress that smelled of smoke and dried blood. Drawing her knees to her chest, Kat let the tears fall.

"You waked up."

Sniffling, Kat dried her face on the sheet and rolled to her left side, wincing against the ache in her shoulder. The little girl she'd found sat up on a blanket against the wall. "What are you doing here?"

Rosita crossed her heart. "You 'member?"

Kat sighed. She remembered everything, but why was the girl still here?

"Now we find Mama."

Why hadn't someone reunited this child with her mother?

"Rosita, have you seen my sister?" Kat said, trying to peer around the curtain. "Her name is Nell. She's about my size, but with blond hair."

The little girl shook her head, sending a drape of black hair over her narrow eyes. "I only seen Doc and the Black Sack Sisters."

The Black Sack Sisters. Kat felt a smile tug at her. Apparently that was Rosita's name for the nuns.

Rosita toddled over to the bed. "You better. We find Mama now?"

Before Kat could respond, she heard footsteps approaching and turned onto her back, hoping to see Nell walk in. Instead, a tall man pulled on the curtain and stood at the foot of her bed while Rosita scurried back to the blanket.

"I'm Doc Hanson." He fiddled with the stethoscope curled around his neck. "It's good to see you're awake."

"Thank you. Kat Sinclair." Kat rolled to her right side, then sat up. A much less painful feat from that angle. "I know a piece of glass cut me, but why am I so sore and groggy?"

"Ma'am, it was a pretty good-sized piece that dove into the deep tissue near your shoulder blade. I used six sutures. You lost some blood, so we gave you a sedative to help you rest for a couple of hours."

Kat rubbed her brow. "That explains my lightheadedness."

He scratched his bald head. "The fire wiped out thirty acres and left thousands of folks homeless." He glanced over at Rosita, who had her thumb in her mouth. "I'd count yourself among the lucky, Miss Sinclair. You'll be fine."

The man was right. The injury could've been a lot worse, and here poor Rosita was stuck with some stranger when all she wanted was to find her mother.

"Doctor, I found Rosita looking for her mother during the fire."

A shadow crossed his face, deepening a scar above his right eye.

"I thought she might be—"

"Her mother's name was Carmen." He'd whispered it, and Kat wasn't sure she'd heard him right, but before she could say anything, he'd turned toward Rosita. "Come here, child." He opened his arms to her, but the little girl shook her head and turned to the wall.

"Was?"

The man nodded, and Kat's throat tightened.

"Sister Coleman found Carmen's body just twenty feet out behind Sunny's brothel where she worked," he said, his eyes sad. "Had weak lungs, and the smoke was too much."

Acid burned Kat's throat, and she swallowed hard. "Her father?"

"Don't know anything about him. Nobody left here 'cept the other girls."

"Surely they could—" Kat gestured at Rosita.

"With their building gone, might be a while before they could do anything."

"The sisters?"

His chuckle sardonic, the doctor shook his head. "Ma'am, we're all going to be tied up caring for the injured for a long time. You'll have to find someone else."

Kat felt like she was going to be sick. How could she be the only one available? She'd have to find a place to take Rosita. That's all she could do. But first she had to tell the little one her mama was gone.

Sliding her legs over the side of the cot, Kat looked down at the child. "Rosita, I need to talk to you about your mama, but I need you to come here." She patted the cot, and when Rosita inched toward it, the doctor hoisted her up beside Kat.

"Miss Sinclair, I have to get about my business. More and more patients are pouring in."

"Yes, of course. Thank you."

"The sisters left you a cotton frock to change into." He glanced at a hook behind the cot where a housedress hung beside Kat's cape. "When you feel up to it, you can go home."

Home. That was Maine.

But even as the thought blew across her mind like a wayward wind, she knew Maine was no longer her home. She wasn't sure where home was now.

"Come back in a week to get your stitches out," Dr. Hanson said. "Sooner if you have any redness or swelling."

He was already on the other side of the curtain when she mumbled, "I will." Kat had no idea how she would manage to find someone to care for Rosita on top of finding Judson Archer for her sister and finding a means to support herself. And dealing with Patrick Maloney was another matter entirely.

Moments later, Kat had told Rosita they weren't going to find her mama, that her mother had died. The little girl sat in the middle of the cot, facing her.

"Mama gets better. Doc makes her better."

Kat folded her hands over Rosita's. "Not this time."

The child pulled her hands back, her eyes welling up. "I want Mama!"

"I'm sorry."

The child's bottom lip quivered as tears poured in rivulets over her cheeks, and an ache the size of Pikes Peak gripped Kat's heart.

What was she to do now? What was either of them to do? She couldn't leave the girl here to fend for herself. There had to be someone who could care for her. She'd start with Miss Sunny tomorrow. For now, she needed to get them both to Hattie's for a bath and some supper. She pulled the smock off the peg.

"I'll change my clothes, and then we'll go to Hattie's Boardinghouse. You can stay the night with me and my sister."

Rosita nodded.

Once she'd changed into the smock, Kat retrieved her cape and wrapped it around Rosita. "When we get to Hattie's, we can take baths and have something to eat." Tomorrow she'd find Sunny and see if she knew any more about Rosita's family.

Draped in the wool cape, Rosita shadowed Kat through the ward and into narrow hallways where men and women waited for treatment. Before she and the little one could reach the hospital door, a scream from down the hallway pierced the putrid air.

"Somebody please help me!"

No one rushed to the woman's aid. Kat knew she had to see what was wrong. She reached for Rosita's hand. The child at her side, she hurried toward the pleas and wrenched open a door.

The woman on the bed, who had the roundest middle Kat had ever seen, was alone and devoid of even a single stitch of clothing. She looked like a knotted rope that had been dragged through a muddy wash, then plunked on the cot and left to unravel. Soggy red hair was plastered to her bobbing head. Kat remembered when Mother had gone into labor with Vivian, and the experience still seared her memory. She knew enough to know she wasn't qualified to help this woman. Besides, a birthing room was no place for a child, and Rosita had been t...ough enough today.

"I'll go find a doctor."

"No." Rocking in lopsided circles, the woman motioned for Kat to come close. "You have to help me." She arched her back and grabbed her knees.

Kat motioned Rosita toward a chair by the door and crept toward the bed.

Neither of them belonged here. She should've been at home in Maine playing checkers with one of her sisters in front of a warm fire, not in some wild mountain town with a naked woman on the verge of giving birth.

EIGHT

ollowing the surgery on Mr. Goeke's leg, Morgan returned
to the burn ward. He craved fresh air, but he couldn't leave
the side of the man with the charred arm. Sister Coleman had been
called away from the hospital, so he was tending to the last burn vic-
tim on his own. He finished treating the scorched skin and dropped
his instruments into an enamel pan. After he scrubbed his hands over
the sink, he pulled a sterile petroleum jelly dressing out of the con-
tainer. Once he'd finished wrapping the arm, he returned to the water
bowl.

"We need a doctor. Now!" The woman's shout had come from
down the hallway, and the fear in her voice zinged Morgan's spine.

He darted out of the room and followed guttural cries to an open
doorway where a small Mexican girl waved him inside. Rushing past
the child, Morgan stopped at the foot of the bed where a young
woman hunched over the knees of a loud, writhing patient in the
midst of labor. The midwife glanced toward the girl, who now sat in
a chair near the door, then at him, her eyes wide.

"I'm Dr. Cutshaw, ma'am. Is this her first baby?"

The woman in the bed kicked the air. "Only baby! And if I ever see—"

"First babies can take a day and night or more to deliver." He shifted his attention to the midwife, who looked as if she was about to cry. "I'll send someone to look in on you in a while."

The patient reared up, muttering curses.

"That won't do." The midwife clenched his shirt sleeve, pulling him toward the woman. "See for yourself."

Morgan opened his mouth to rebuke her, but then he saw the tiny blue foot that dangled out of the patient. The sight stole his breath.

He sighed, whispered a soul-deep prayer, and rolled his shirtsleeves to his elbows. Ignoring the mother's curses and screams, he reached inside her. When he felt the baby's other foot, he grabbed and pulled until he had both legs out.

But the baby's head remained inside his mother. He needed to get the child out.

Haunting memories surfaced and threatened to undo Morgan as he reached back inside the mother and secured one hand on the infant's spine. He wouldn't let another baby die.

"Why won't the baby come out?"

Morgan fought his growing frustration with the midwife. She should have known what's wrong.

"Breech." And its breathing may already be cut off.

Morgan's heart pounded. He couldn't let this happen.

He placed his other hand on the woman's pelvis and twisted, flipping the baby face down. Then he slipped two fingers inside the baby's mouth and pulled. It was still stuck, and time was running out. Struggling for a better grip, he rocked the baby back and forth and then pulled harder until the head began to emerge. The mother's shrieks only got louder as he slowly eased the child out. He pulled the baby clear of the mother, and for a moment, the only sounds were the mother's shuddering breaths and the midwife's shaky announcement that it was a boy. The mother wasn't screaming anymore. Neither was her infant son.

He wasn't breathing. The baby had to breathe.

Lord, he has to breathe.

Holding the baby's feet secure, Morgan dangled the newborn and gave him a quick whack on the back. "Cry. Come on, boy, you have to cry."

The slightest of whimpers tickled Morgan's ears. He slapped the baby's back again. "Come on, fella. I know you have more to say than that."

Miniature arms flailed and legs kicked. A hearty wail followed, and then a steady tirade. The boy's chest heaved and his body quaked. His ears pinked up. And Morgan thought his own legs would collapse beneath him. Sighs of relief filled the room, instead of the groans of sorrow that still echoed in his dreams.

Thank You, God. He had done a new thing.

Morgan handed the baby off to the midwife, who awkwardly enfolded him in the dry towel. She handled the newborn as if he were a china vase. This could be her first midwifery, he reasoned. But had she slept through the training? Her hesitation to reach in and manipulate the infant could have endangered this mother and her son. If he hadn't come when he had—

"What now?" The midwife glanced hither and thither, everywhere but at the newborn in her uneasy arms.

"You can lay him on his mother. Then please find a clean sheet and cover her."

Inexperience was no excuse. Not when you had lives in your hands. After Morgan clamped the cord, he snipped it. Then he motioned the midwife away from the bed and the little girl, who now played patty-cake with the plaster wall.

"This woman and her baby could've died because you were too timid to take action."

Her jaw dropped. Had the woman never been corrected? No matter. Someone needed to instruct her and then watch her in an actual birth. Someone other than him.

"I'm reporting you to Dr. Hanson. You have no mind for being a midwife."

"And you, sir, have no mind for being a gentleman." The young woman dashed out the door, with the little girl running to catch up with her.

❧

Hand in hand, Kat and Rosita walked out of the hospital and turned the corner to climb the hill to Golden Avenue. The wind had cleared out the smoke, and the sun had given way to a nearly full moon. Kat breathed in deep swallows of the fresh, crisp air. It was the first relief she'd had from the stench of smoke in several hours. She and Rosita both needed a good cleaning and a fresh change of clothes. The whole town could use a nice long bath.

Nightfall cloaked the devastation below, but the darkness hadn't brought silence. Search and cleanup efforts continued in spotty moonlight and lamplight, and desperate voices echoed off the ring of hillocks that cradled Cripple Creek. In startling contrast, a chorus of cheers drew Kat's attention to the reservoir two blocks above them. Swinging lanterns flashed light like fireflies on a summer evening. Then in the eastern hills, Kat glimpsed the glow of the train charging toward town, bringing relief supplies. Tears stung her eyes. The destruction was swift and merciless, and the need dire, but help was on the way.

Please, Lord, let that be true for me and Nell too.

Surely they'd find Judson Archer soon, and he'd take Nell to be his wife. And Kat had to believe that even though trusting Patrick Maloney had turned out to be a mistake, she'd be all right.

"I like ba-bies." Rosita said, though she wasn't much more than a baby herself.

"I do too." It was true as long as she didn't have to push or pull one out, or watch it being done. And the child should not have been in the room, watching. She and Rosita should both have their ears cleansed of that woman's bawdy ranting.

"But you no like the baby man."

"I don't know him, Rosita." But Kat didn't have to know the man for his words to hound her. *"This woman and her baby could've died because you were too timid to take action."*

He'd thought she was a midwife. She had met men like this one before, wearing fancy herringbone vests with shiny watch chains dangling from their pockets, believing they knew everything. Some of those men wore handlebar mustaches and bowlers with peacock feathers. That doctor didn't know her any more than Patrick Maloney did. She wasn't timid. Eight days ago, she'd left the comforts of Maine—the only life she'd known—to live in the unknown. Why, she'd even been in a saloon just last night. But she was no midwife, he was right about that. The birthing room was no place for her or for a child. All she'd wanted was to be a writer. Then her father's company turned their world upside down, and she'd given up her dream to forge a life for her and her sisters.

More cheers from the reservoir crowd pulled Kat out of her stewing and told her the train had rounded another curve, and food and supplies would be here soon.

Turning onto Golden Avenue toward Hattie's, Kat thought about what she'd say to Nell and the woman who housed them. Hattie. Kat didn't want to worry Nell, but a child hadn't been part of their arrangement with their landlady. She'd have to reassure them it was only for the night.

The two-story clapboard house looked especially inviting tonight. Lights glowed in the windows and the chimney belched smoke as they approached.

She looked down at the child, who peered up at her, sadness etched in her coal black eyes. "This is where Nell and I live right now."

"And me?"

"Yes, until we can get you back with Miss Sunny and her...uh, girls." They walked up the steps while Kat prayed that the reunion would be tomorrow.

A mouth-watering whiff of a hearty soup and fresh bread greeted Kat as she opened the door, and so did the squeal of children. The two couples boarding here had expected to return to Colorado Springs on the afternoon train, but even if their plans had changed, they were both childless.

Taking Rosita's hand, she stepped inside and led the little girl to the parlor doorway. Hattie's phonograph played while a mother rocked and nursed a baby, her eyes closed. A little boy stacked wooden blocks in the corner while two little girls giggled over dolls on the sofa.

Rosita tugged Kat's arm, hiding behind her skirts. "Your Nell?"

Kat shook her head and whispered, "No, I don't know who that is." She guessed Nell was helping Hattie in the kitchen, working to feed these unexpected guests. "But let's go find Nell."

The hallway opened up into a large dining room where two women set plates and soup bowls on the table. Kat recognized one of them from the train—she was Lucille's mother. Had they fallen prey to the fire too?

Lucille's mother looked up at Kat, a hint of recognition lighting her eyes and inspiring a smile. "Hello. I was so exhausted on the train, I don't think we even exchanged names. I'm Edith Reger."

Kat returned the woman's smile and gestured toward the other woman. "Is this your sister?"

"No. She's the one in the parlor, feeding my nephew. Their house is gone, and so is Thelma's here." Edith squeezed the shorter woman's hand.

"I'm so sorry." Kat's heart sunk. Her troubles paled in comparison. "I'm Kat Sinclair."

"Nell's sister." Thelma's voice was as thin as her soot-smudged face.

"I am." Kat took a step toward the source of all the stomach-stirring aromas, her wee shadow clinging to her skirt. "Is Nell in the house?"

Edith shook her head. "She went back over to the church, but she shouldn't be long."

Nell wasn't here? A lump formed in Kat's throat. She needed her sister. Just to see her. To touch her to know for sure that she was all right. To talk to her about all that had gone on. Kat moistened her lips, hoping to soften her anxiety.

"Your sister was concerned about you." Edith glanced down at Rosita. "I see you've been busy too."

"Yes." Kat didn't want to get into her experience right now. She would tell the story once. "Nell's at the church?"

"She and Sister Veronica took food over to the woman and children staying at St. Peter's." Thelma spoke as she set the bowls on the plates. "I don't know what we would've done without her. She's so good with the children. Had them calmed down and laughing in no time."

That sounded like Nell. She'd always been good with children, and helping others seemed to feed Nell's soul.

Edith set spoons beside the plates. "When St. Peter's started running out of room, Nell brought us here to Hattie's."

Sister Veronica must have been the one who came to them in the bucket line, looking for help. Just as Kat began piecing the puzzle together, Lucille whooshed into the room carrying a bread basket and a crock of butter. "Miss Kat! There you are! Where have you been?"

Kat sighed. "It's a long story." Glancing down at the little girl at her side, she rubbed her temple where a headache had suddenly lodged. "This is Rosita."

"I want my house." Rosita hung back, burying her face in Kat's skirt. "I want my mama."

"Oh, honey, I want my mama too." Hattie rushed into the dining room, carrying a pink tureen with steam rising from it. "And my stars, am I glad to see you. Nell will be too."

"You have a mama?" Rosita's shoulders relaxed a bit as she peered up at the gray-haired woman in front of her.

"I did." Hattie set the dish on the table, smiling at the child. "But she's gone now." She cocked an eyebrow in Kat's direction.

"This is Rosita." Kat wondered if the woman knew the child's mother was gone too, and if so, how? "She's…she's with me. Just until tomorrow," she added.

"My mama gone too." Rosita's lip began to quiver again.

Tears filled Hattie's eyes. "Oh, child." She patted Rosita's raven black hair and looked over at Kat. "Today?"

Nodding, Kat wiped at the tears that began to spill over her own eyelids.

"Well then, Rosita, you and I have a lot to talk about. I'll put you in the chair right beside me for supper. Is that all right with you?"

The child nodded, and then followed Hattie to the table. Soon, five children, including Rosita, and five women gathered around the food set before them. Rosita sat between Hattie and Kat. The chair on Kat's other side remained empty, and she fought the urge to go to St. Peter's Church and bring her sister home.

"Let's talk to the good Lord, shall we?" Hattie reached for Rosita's hand on one side and Lucille's on the other. Taking her lead, they all joined hands.

Just as Hattie was about to say amen, the front door burst open and Kat jumped up from her seat.

"Kat? Are you here?" Nell ran into the room, rambling on about bucket brigades, burning houses, and women and children needing cared for. Kat met her halfway, just as Nell started to cry.

"I'm here."

She wrapped her sister in a warm embrace, ignoring the ache in her shoulder. When they'd dried their tears, Kat led Nell to the table where the other women thanked Nell for all she'd done for them and for so many others.

Nell looked a mess—her clothes soiled and smoky and her hair mussed—but as she sat down, her eyes sparkled with a kind of satisfaction that Kat didn't feel. Helping others seemed as natural to Nell as blossoms were to spring. Nell had found her place here.

Kat sighed. Now all she had to do was to figure out where she belonged in this new territory.

NINE

 ❧

*M*organ finished scrubbing his hands in the washbowl and grabbed the only towel he could find. He tried to block out the mews and coos of the newborn and his mother. Some doctors weren't meant to birth babies.

And neither were some midwives. He scrubbed the rough cotton against his hands, thinking of the helpless woman. She was a pretty girl, he remembered, but clearly scatterbrained.

"You done real good, Doc." At least the new mother wasn't swearing at him anymore. "You saved my boy."

Thank You, Lord.

"By the grace of God." Morgan balled up the towel. If only he understood why His grace helped some and not others.

"Don't know nothin' about that, but me and my boy are alive, and us women are lucky to have a doc like you 'round here."

"Thank you, ma'am."

She let out a guffaw, and her son whimpered. "I look like a ma'am to you?"

Not one iota. Morgan turned away from the bare leg that curled out around the sheet.

"Didn't think so."

She also didn't look like a woman who should be mothering a baby. Opal, on the other hand, would've made a fine mother. The world was upside down.

"Name's Iris. And you're much too stuffy for the miners and the cowboys around here."

"If behaving in a proper and respectful manner is stuffy, then I'm guilty. I'll thank you to cover yourself proper-like. We run a respectable hospital." At least he hoped they did. How would he know? He'd tended to burns and delivered a baby, but he still hadn't met anyone in charge.

She flipped the thin sheet over her leg.

"Thank you." This culture of familiarity and impropriety would take some getting used to.

"You'll get used to things around here soon," Iris said, adjusting her son in her arms. "Even learn to like it."

He wasn't sure he possessed enough imagination to believe that.

"I need to check on my patients in the burn ward." He laid the towel over the back of a chair and headed for the door. "I'll send someone in to help you clean up."

As soon as Morgan stepped into the hallway, a beak-nosed man planted himself in front of him. "Well, aren't you something?" The man's imperious look told Morgan that *being something* in his eyes was more reprimand than praise.

"Sir?" Morgan unrolled his shirt sleeves. He wished he had the suit coat he'd left in the burn ward.

"*Sir?*" The deep grooves above the bridge of the man's nose formed a permanent scowl. "Folks around here call me Doc Hanson."

"Morgan Cutshaw." Morgan stretched out his arm for a handshake, but when his new boss didn't reciprocate, he withdrew it and stuffed it into his pocket.

"I presume you met Miss Sinclair."

"I only got her given name, but she and her son seem well."

Hanson chuckled. "That was Iris, one of Blanche Barton's girls. Miss Sinclair is the young woman who nearly knocked me down in her rush to get away from you."

"The midwife. I wanted to talk to you about her."

"Save your rant." Hanson raised a gnarled hand. "Miss Sinclair isn't a midwife."

"But she was—"

"Here as a patient."

Morgan flinched. A patient? Why didn't she say something? Not that he'd given her much of a chance.

"She saved a little Mexican girl from a spray of glass, and a piece dug into her shoulder. She was here recovering."

No wonder she'd looked so shocked at his reprimand. He'd barked at a good Samaritan. Remorse knotted Morgan's stomach.

"I didn't know—"

Dr. Hanson interrupted him. "You a gambler, Dr. Morgan Cutshaw?"

Morgan watched Dr. Hanson for a moment, trying to read his new boss.

"Apparently so." He'd gone all in, leaving everything and everyone he knew to pursue the unknown. An act of faith or a gamble? He couldn't say for sure. He'd already played his cards wrong. He had meant to avoid entanglements with women, but thus far he'd hit a swarm of them. The fair Miss Taggart. Miss Iris, who was most comfortable without a stitch of clothing on, no matter the company. And Miss Sinclair—to whom he owed an apology. "Why do you ask?"

"'Cause I'm betting you had no idea what you were in for when you decided to move out here to the wild and woolly West."

No idea at all.

TEN

❧

Nell lifted Rosita off the bed she and Kat shared, and carried her across the small room. Kat looked up from the dressing table, but Nell shook her head to let her sister know she had it under control. After the child's belly was full and Hattie had given her a bath, Rosita had climbed under the quilt and fallen fast asleep. Now the little one's breath warmed Nell's face, stirring her deep longing to mother children. That's all she'd ever wanted—to have a family of her own.

Until she began receiving Judson Archer's letters nearly four months ago, Nell didn't have a name or a face to attach to the prince of her dreams...her one true love. But now that she did, her heart ached for him all the more.

Judson, where are you?

She'd studied every man's face in town this morning, and while she was helping during the fire. According to the man at the telegraph office, Judson had received her telegram. Why hadn't he come looking for her?

Had she been a fool to fall for Judson Archer?

Shaking her head, Nell bent over to lay the little girl on the makeshift pallet set out for her in the corner. She settled Rosita on the mat, and the child groaned and rolled to her side, curling into a ball. A twinge of guilt niggled at Nell. Only four years old, this little girl was motherless and homeless, and here Nell was feeling sorry for herself.

Nell pulled the quilt over the little one and tucked her in, just like she would her own someday, and kissed her soft cheek.

Bless this poor child, Father.

That's what she needed to be doing, praying for all the hurting people she'd seen and heard tonight. Especially those in the room with her. Her own sister had suffered much in the past two days.

"I'm at twenty strokes." Kat sat on the bed, holding her tortoise-shell hairbrush in her right hand. "I'm not going to make it to one hundred tonight."

Nell crossed over to the bed. Taking the brush from Kat, she knelt behind her on the bed and started brushing her sister's pretty auburn curls. When she lifted the layer of hair, Nell could see the bulky bandage through her sister's dressing gown. "Does your shoulder hurt much?"

"Not too bad unless I try to lift a stack of plates, or a child." Kat twisted and grinned, her brown eyes shining like polished tiger's-eye gems.

"I'm sorry I wasn't at the hospital with you." Nell gently combed the bristles through Kat's hair. "You must have been frightened."

"I especially missed you in the birthing room." Kat laughed. "The doctor really thought you were a midwife?"

"That's what he said. 'You have no mind for being a midwife.'"

"Didn't you tell him you were a patient?" Nell laid the brush down on the dressing table.

"In a hundred varied and witty ways. Once I left the hospital."

They both giggled, then fell silent.

"What a strange day." Nell glanced over at the pallet.

"Not at all what we expected to find in Cripple Creek, is it?"

Nell bit her lip. No, it was not at all what they expected to find here. "I'm so proud of you for saving Rosita," she said, fighting back the tears that welled up. "What will you do about her?"

"I plan to find her family tomorrow."

"But her mother is gone, and you told us the doctor didn't know anything about her father."

"She and her mother didn't live alone, Nell." Kat worried a thread at a seam in her nightgown. "It may not be a family like we knew growing up, but—"

"You said you found her calling for her mama on Myers Avenue." Nell stood up. She moved to the glass window, pulled back the lace curtain, and peered into the darkness. "You can't mean to give her to those other women."

"That's precisely what I mean. She knows them. She's comfortable with them."

"You mean they're comfortable with her."

"I can't just—"

"Mama!" Rosita's mournful cry silenced them both. The little girl sat up, crying and blinking. Nell thought to turn out the light, but the darkness would probably only frighten her more. Rosita shuddered, her sobs wrenching Nell's heart. "I want Mama!"

"We're here, little one. We can't bring your mama back." Sitting on the pallet, Kat cupped the child's wet face in her hands. "You're not alone, Rosita, and…I know someone very special that I think you'll like." Kat tiptoed theatrically to her trunk and knelt down in front of it.

Nell walked over to Rosita and sat down beside her. They watched Kat open the lid of her trunk and slide her hand inside. The little girl's whimpers began to subside, and she tipped her face up to Nell, her eyes wide.

Nell shrugged and returned her attention to Kat. They both watched as an embroidered face with whiskers and button eyes peered out over the edge of the trunk. Two long cloth ears flopped over the hand that held it. In a falsetto voice, Kat said, "Greetings, Rosita. I'm HopHop, and I want to be your friend."

Rosita giggled, and Nell couldn't help but join her.

Her eyebrows raised and her eyes wide open, Kat waddled toward Rosita, bouncing the white cotton bunny in the air. The little girl scrambled to her feet and reached for HopHop.

"Rosita, my mother made this bunny for me when she was sick. After she died, whenever I was feeling sad, I'd hold HopHop tight."

"I remember that." Nell nodded, blinking back her tears.

"I almost didn't bring HopHop across the country, thinking it was a childish thing to carry into a new life. Now I know why I brought him."

Nell gave Kat a big smile, and then a gentle hug.

Less than ten minutes later, Rosita snuggled HopHop under her quilt. Kat rotated the switch on the wall, shutting off the bare light bulb hanging from the ceiling above them. Nell crawled into bed, letting her weary body sink into the soft cradle of the mattress.

Please, God, comfort Rosita. Please be with my Judson, and bring him to me. And, God, please bring a man to Kat who will cherish her as she so deserves.

ELEVEN

Thursday after lunch, Kat watched the parade of boarders that filed into Hattie's kitchen, carrying their soiled plates and cups. Fortunately, Lucille had helped steady the little ones who toddled through with their dishes and the salt and pepper shakers. Now, the mothers and their children, along with Hattie and Rosita, had all gone up to their rooms for an afternoon rest. Kat was ready to do the same, once she and Nell finished cleaning up the kitchen.

Lucille's baby cousin had cried about every two hours last night, waking the whole house, and sometime in the wee hours of the morning, Rosita awakened with a bad dream. She, Nell, Kat, and the cloth bunny ended up sharing the bed, which was a tight fit to begin with.

While Nell pinned Kat's hair up before breakfast, the landlady came to their room seeking their help. Extra mouths to feed meant more kitchen work, and as a result, Hattie offered the sisters discounted rent in exchange for their help in the kitchen. Nell had agreed on the condition that Kat do "light duty" until her shoulder healed. Consequently, she'd been relegated the job of washing dishes, and that's why she stood at the cupboard now, looking at the stacks of dirty dishes and wondering where to start. The sooner she finished her task, the sooner she could rest, so she reached to lift the stack of plates. Her shoulder rebelled, and Kat flinched, while her sister clucked her tongue.

"Oh, no you don't. I'll get those." Nell wagged her finger, rushing to Kat's side. "No lifting, remember?"

Nodding, Kat stepped out of Nell's way. "Thank you."

Nell set the stack of plates in the tub of hot water, and Kat watched pungent lye suds poof and rise, then fade.

Rise and fade.

That's what had happened to her life as Mrs. Patrick Maloney.

That's what had happened to Rosita's mother.

Kat couldn't let it happen to her. Her time here on earth…in Cripple Creek…had to count for something.

"I don't think you should go out today." Nell scooted the cups and flatware toward the wash basin. "You need to rest."

"Instead of going to look for Rosita's 'family'?"

"Yes. Hattie said having her here isn't a problem, and there are other children for her to play with. You saw her this morning with Thelma's little girl. She seems to be warming up to her."

Kat scrubbed a plate, rubbing her dishcloth across its face, even after it was clean. "We can't keep her here indefinitely. We have other things to do." She handed the dish to Nell. "Our room is crowded."

"I know, but we can manage another day or two."

The iron door knocker rapped on the front door, and Kat dried her hands on her apron. She hoped it wasn't more people needing a place to stay.

Since Hattie was upstairs with Rosita, the sisters went to the door. Kat pulled it open to find the younger nun from the reservoir and a tall, lanky man on the porch. Both of them looked as though they'd been chewing on lemons.

"Sister Veronica?" Concern etched Nell's brow. "Is everyone at St. Peter's all right? Do you need my help?"

"They're doing fine, thank you." The sister looked at the man beside her. Clumps of gray hair ringed the sides of his otherwise bald head. "Nell, this is Wayne Snelling. He's our sheriff, and he needs to speak to your sister."

That's when Kat noticed the badge at the collar of his canvas coat.

"Me?" What would he need to see her about? She'd heard a fight break out in the saloon as she'd walked out the other night, but he couldn't blame her for that, could her?

Nodding a greeting, the man looked down at the hat he held, then glanced around. "Is there a place where we can sit down and talk?"

Nell laced her arm in Kat's. Her blue eyes were suddenly cloudy, and Kat looked away. "Yes, the parlor," Nell said, and led the way, then sat down on the sofa beside Kat.

"Sheriff," she said, her voice thin. "Does this concern our father, or our sisters?"

"No ma'am, it doesn't." The sheriff reached into his coat pocket and pulled out a scorched flask. His face long and drawn, he handed it to Kat. "We found this inside a burned-out building, ma'am."

Kat grasped it with two fingertips and held it away from her, then nodded, at a loss to know what else to do. Yes, she'd been inside a saloon, but she didn't own a whiskey flask, and until now, she'd never even touched one. What could that nasty thing have to do with her?

"We don't drink, Sheriff." Nell tightened her grip on Kat's arm.

"It was Paddy Maloney's, ma'am."

"Patrick's?"

"Sister Veronica told me you were his intended."

Kat held the flask out, but the sheriff didn't take it back. "He's not here, Sheriff."

"I know, ma'am. I'm right sorry, but Paddy…" The man cleared his throat. "Patrick Maloney was killed in the fire."

Sucking in a gasp of air, Kat jerked up stick-straight on the sofa and dropped the flask. It bounced off the area rug and clanged onto the hardwood floor. She saw Nell wipe tears from her face, but Kat didn't shed any of her own.

Anytime a person died, a good Christian should feel the loss… should mourn the death. She should feel grief for the man, but it was guilt that knotted Kat's stomach. She'd poured flowers down his front. Although she'd initially found the act satisfying, now it seemed like a childish and petty transgression against a pitiful man. Patrick Maloney had made counterfeit promises, and she'd believed him. She'd said good-bye to her family and journeyed long and hard to marry Patrick, to start a new life here with him. She had stitches in her shoulder because of him, and a motherless child in her charge, but regardless of the man's dishonesty and decadence, he didn't deserve to die.

Still, try as she might to grieve his death, Kat couldn't feel anything but relief.

Forgive me, Lord.

TWELVE

⁓⤜⤛⁓

Friday morning, Kat added a period to her last sentence and, laying her journal in her lap, shut her eyes and leaned back in the rocker. She swayed in slow, steady sweeps, breathing in rhythm with the chair's light creaks.

She had the room to herself for a few moments, and she wasn't quite finished taking full advantage of it. Kat had come upstairs to "get ready" for her walk into town after they finished the breakfast cleanup, and Rosita was down playing with the other children.

She'd taken advantage of the quiet to write in her journal. Since she'd left Maine, her writing had less to do with poetry than it did prayers. More like pleas, really. Petitions for herself and for others— Nell and Rosita, Father, Vivian and Ida, Edith and Lucille, and Thelma and her three children. Kat found herself especially diligent about praying for Nell's Judson Archer. Nell wanted him and needed him. Kat prayed Judson was a good man who would take care of her sister and cherish her. And that he'd show up soon.

As Kat went down her list of people to pray for, she said a special prayer for Patrick's family, wherever they were. A squeal from downstairs pulled Kat out of her reverie. Opening her eyes, she stilled the rocker and carried her journal over to the trunk. She had better get moving. There were things she needed to tend to, and right now, finding a home for Rosita topped her list.

Sliding her book of writings down the inside edge of the trunk, she bumped up against the flask and the dishtowel she'd wrapped around it. She didn't know why she'd even kept it. She buried the flask beneath the tea towels Ida had embroidered for her, squared her shoulders, and walked over to the wardrobe.

Kat pulled her hat off the shelf and tied its ribbons firmly under her chin. Then she walked down the stairs, where waves of laughter rolled out of the parlor.

Two button eyes peered over the back of the sofa. HopHop's long ears flopped over Rosita's little brown hand, and a strand of raven black hair streaked the bunny's expressionless face.

"Greeting, Miss Hattie. I'm HopHop the bunny." A toothy smile widened the little girl's face. Hattie tittered. Kat giggled, and so did the others.

Nell rose from a chair and joined Kat in the doorway. "Look how happy you made her," she said under her breath.

"I just gave her the rabbit."

Nell pinched her lips together and shook her head. "You gave Rosita hope."

Hope in the form of a rabbit? Kat smiled. Perhaps she had made a difference, even if it was only a small one, for a short time.

"While you were upstairs, Thelma's husband took a break from the work and stopped by." The smile left Nell's eyes. "He's found them a place to live."

"That's great." Kat forced herself to smile. "So they'll all be leaving? When?"

"Tomorrow."

The news added even more urgency to Kat's errand. Once the other women and children were gone, Rosita wouldn't have anyone here to play with. Then what would she do?

"I'd better get going." Kat glanced over at Rosita. She clutched HopHop, watching one of the other little girls play puppet with a sock monkey Hattie had found in her things. "I'll be back in plenty of time to help you with lunch."

"Are you sure you're up to this?"

"I'm sure, and the walk will do me good." Kat smoothed the lace collar on her two-pieced dress.

"I should go with you," Nell said, moving to follow her sister.

"You're needed here." Kat gestured toward the children. "And Judson could call for you at any moment."

Nell shook her head. "I hope so."

"I do too. Just because Patrick turned out to be a…God rest his drunken, two-timing soul, it doesn't mean you shouldn't find Judson and marry him."

Kat gave her sister a quick hug, then strolled down Hattie's front porch steps. In truth, she was thankful for a little more time to herself. The sun felt good on her patched shoulder, and she liked the local practice of only wearing one petticoat. A simpler, more comfortable way of dressing suited her just fine. She took careful strides down the hill to the core of Cripple Creek. What ground wasn't slushy from the melting snow was littered with the ash that still filled the air with a choking dryness.

The town was abuzz with activity. Some men loaded piles of rubbish into carts and wagons, while others worked on the water pipes or erected tents or other makeshift buildings. Kat strolled east on the sunny north side of Bennett, her boot heels clacking on the boardwalk. Farther up, the First National Bank of Cripple Creek had hung a shingle on a charred warehouse. She stepped out around the folks lined up out in front of it. Passing the burned-out Cash and Carry gave her pause. As she walked out around the ten-by-twelve-foot frame box that sat on the street, she read the sign: OLLIE'S SALOON. Kat's breaths grew shallow and her knees weak.

She shook her head.

She couldn't think about Patrick. Not about any of it. Not now. She needed to concentrate on finding a home for Rosita.

At Bennett and Third Street, Kat turned south past the Mush and Milk House to Myers Avenue, and turned right.

Keeping her head high and her gaze straight on, she walked at a clipped pace toward the burned-out area where she'd first seen Rosita. She had a job to do: find Rosita's family. There had to be more to her family than a deceased mother. Maybe a father somewhere. Aunts. Uncles. Grandparents. Someone had to be looking for the child. And if her only family was the Sunny girls, as the child referred to them, then so be it.

"Hello, little lady."

Kat started, and spun around. She saw the mule first, then a wiry man in grubby overalls on the other side of the animal.

"Boney's the name. Boney Hughes."

"Kat…Katherine Sinclair."

"Well, Miss Sinclair, you look about as out of place here as udders on a bull." He spit a stream of brown on the snowy street behind him.

Kat forced down a gag before she spoke. "I'm looking for Sunny. I know her…uh, building is gone, but I thought she might be here for the reconstruction."

"Men are taking care of that. Sunny's workin' out of Lola's Parlor till they can get her new buildin' up." He looked down the street, where a handful of tents stood. "Lola's is that brick building at the end."

"Thank you kindly, Mr. Hughes." Kat headed down the street and stopped outside the two-story house. The fire had scorched one side of it, but etched flower bouquets still decorated the glass windows on the front, obscuring the view to the inside.

Kat straightened her spine and opened the door. Her boots sank into a plush carpet. A grandfather clock stood between two Queen Anne chairs. Flocked wallpaper. Mirrors. It wasn't how she'd expected the inside of a brothel to look. Not that she'd given it much thought. But it was no wonder that some women would turn their heads this way. Lofty living. Fine gowns. A man's attention.

Patrick's attention.

The sound of a rustling gown drew Kat's attention to the velvet drapes at the back of the room. A curvy woman in a silk dress sauntered through them. At the sight of Kat, the woman's smile melted.

"Not a client, I see." She slapped her lace fan shut against her other hand. "You a missionary, come to save us?"

A slow burn crept up Kat's neck and over her jaw. "Uh…I'm looking for Sunny."

"That's me." Wavy blond hair streaked the woman's bare shoulders.

When Kat was nervous, her gloves made her hands sweat, so she tugged them off. "I'm Kat Sinclair, and I'm not a missionary, ma'am. I just wanted to talk to you about Rosita."

"Carmen's girl. None of us have seen her since the fire that took her mama."

"I found Rosita during the fire. My sister and I have been caring for her, but we can't continue to do so. I came to ask about her family. If you or any of your…uh, workers know anything about Rosita's father or—"

"Most of the girls don't say much about family, and I don't ask. We have an understanding."

"But surely you must have heard something. Did she see any visitors besides the—"

"Rosita did mention a grandmother once. At least I think that's what the child was talking about. Tell you what…" Sunny tapped her made-up cheek with her fan. "I could take the girl in. She's used to us, and there are enough of us around here that we could see to her."

Nell wouldn't like it, but Kat had to consider what was best. The little girl wasn't entirely comfortable with the sisters, and they were ill prepared to care for her. Patrick was gone. Judson had yet to turn up. It was best that the little girl have a stable, if not respectable, place to live. Kat was about to accept the woman's offer when a whiskered man stumbled down the stairs, adjusting his belt.

Sunny smiled in his direction. "I could put the girl to work in the kitchen or with the laundry…something for another twelve years or so. Then she'll be old enough to earn some real money."

Kat flushed beneath her collar, and her shoulder wound began to burn. Sunny planned to… "You will do no such thing."

"Have it your way, miss. But we're all working girls, and I need to get Jeb here squared away." Sunny raised her hands, flaunting her painted nails. "So unless you're planning on rosying up your cheeks and lowering that hidebound neckline of yours, I suggest you scat."

"Thank you for your time." Thanks to Mother's early influence, Kat was able to give a gentle answer, but she turned quickly and put her energy into opening the heavy leaded-glass door. Nell wouldn't take to seeing the sheriff again so soon, especially if he'd come to report her sister rotting in jail for a fight in a brothel. Kat held her head high and walked out.

THIRTEEN

M organ left his coupé at the hospital. He needed to stretch his legs a bit, and he took long strides down the hill to Bennett Avenue. He'd been on his feet much of the night, but the train ride across this country and the mountainous buggy ride had left his legs restless. Besides, the house he was to have moved into upon his arrival in Cripple Creek had burned to the ground, and the clear and inviting afternoon air offered him a reprieve from his temporary housing in the hospital's dingy basement.

He knew he was ahead of the train's scheduled arrival, so he decided to take a circuitous route to the depot. He would get his blood pumping while he made a mental list of some of his tasks.

He needed to send a telegraph to let his mother know he'd arrived safely.

To arrange transport for his belongings.

And secure a place to store them until he found proper housing.

Morgan hadn't finished his list when he caught sight of a familiar face. Across the street, Miss Sinclair stepped out of one of the most scandalous enterprises on Myers Avenue. A man stumbled out the door behind her.

"Not so fast, you pretty gal, you." The drunk waved a glove in the air then sniffed it and touched it to Miss Sinclair's cheek. Scowling, she grabbed her glove, and the man toyed with her, bobbing it up and down like bait.

As Morgan turned onto Bennett Avenue, he couldn't help but wonder if he'd ever see Miss Sinclair among polite company, or if all of her friends were of questionable character. With so much to do before dusk, he best get back to his list. If his things were on the midday train, he'd need to tend to them straightaway, before work tonight.

Morgan resumed his walk to the Midland Terminal at the east end of town. He was still considering his observation of Miss Sinclair when he heard piano music, a fair-to-middling rendition of "Swanee River." The rich notes reminded him of Opal's concert piano. It couldn't be— He quickened his steps to the depot.

There on the landing, Miss Taggart, the woman he'd met at the hospital the day he arrived in town, perched on the bench in front of his square grand piano.

"What do you think you're doing?" He marched toward Miss Taggart, not stopping until he was standing directly over her.

She lifted her hands off the keys as if they'd suddenly become hot. Lowering her rounded chin, she peered up at Morgan, her eyebrows raised. "Doc-tor." She scooted off the end of the bench, stood, and pulled gloves from her pocket.

"Miss Taggart?"

"Due to the ongoing deliveries of relief items for our fire victims, your belongings arrived at the depot early today, and the piano was just sitting here begging to be played."

"I see." That explained why Opal's piano and his other furnishings sat outside exposed to the elements, but it didn't explain why this woman whom he'd only briefly met had availed herself of his possessions. The perfectly coiffed and finely adorned woman reminded him of Penelope Covington back in Boston, and he couldn't help but glance around expecting to see Penelope's beady-eyed father charging toward him with his ultimatum. That image didn't help his disposition toward Miss Taggart.

"When I heard the train whistle this morning, I came to help direct the delivery of some of the supplies." She pulled the gloves over her small hands. "My father is Reverend Taggart, the parson at the First Congregational Church of Cripple Creek. The buildings there are being used to house the homeless and to serve as a sort of depot for clothing and bedding, and such things."

"It seems as if you do a fair bit of volunteering."

She straightened, tugging on the hem of her jacket. "I do, but everyone here does in a tragedy."

Tragedy was the word that best described the devastation he'd witnessed in the aftermath of the recent fires. And here he was concerned about someone enjoying his piano.

"It seemed shameful to let such a fine piano sit here unattended." Miss Taggart caressed the ivory with her gloved hand. "I apologize if I was presumptuous."

She pursed her lips, and Morgan sighed, wondering if he'd ever learn to stop and think before he jumped to conclusions. Miss Taggart didn't know that seeing a woman sitting at the piano would send a hundred jabbing memories straight to his heart. She was a bit presumptuous, but she cared about her community, and he couldn't fault her for wanting to enjoy the piano.

He removed his hat and cleared his throat. "I apologize, Miss Taggart. Of course, it's good that you were here to watch over my belongings. Thank you."

"I accept your apology."

"Now, if you'll excuse me, I need to make storage arrangements until I have a house."

Her green eyes widened. "There isn't any extra room at the church right now, but I know of the perfect place."

Morgan glanced from the piano to the two trunks and the bookcase on the depot platform.

"Hattie's Boardinghouse. The widow has plenty of room there, and it's just up Hayden from the hospital, on Golden Avenue."

"That sounds like a good possibility." Morgan lowered the lid over the piano keys and pulled the blanket over it.

"Splendid. It's settled then, and I'll take you there."

And before Morgan knew what was happening, Miss Taggart had hold of his arm and they were walking, together, to the boardinghouse.

FOURTEEN

◦◦◦◦

Kat climbed the stairs to her room, her arms full of clothes, Rosita on her heels. The house was quiet except for the light sounds of Nell puttering in the kitchen. Hattie had taken the others to see the house Thelma's husband had found for them. Kat laid the laundry on the bed and reached for Rosita's clean dress.

"I do this." Rosita pulled her dress off the pile before Kat could.

Kat grabbed a bath towel from the bed and shook it out. "You helped with the clothes at your old house?"

Focused on her task, Rosita nodded and carefully laid the dress out flat, then smoothed the blue sleeves over the bodice. Apparently, Miss Sunny had already put the child to work. The woman's inference that she would someday employ Rosita for *that* kind of vocation still made Kat's skin crawl. But she couldn't provide for Rosita either. Lucille and her family were leaving Hattie's tomorrow, and the landlady would no longer need the sisters' help in exchange for their rent. And Judson Archer had yet to call on Nell.

Lord, help me. What will we do?

She had to do something. Someone in Rosita's family had to be concerned about her whereabouts. That's when Kat remembered the hint of hope Miss Sunny had wedged into her ugly comments. Miss Sunny had heard Rosita mention a grandmother.

The child was still folding her dress when Kat pulled her unmentionables from the pile. "Do you remember your grandmother?"

"*Abuela.*" Her eyes fill with tears. "I miss Abuela. I miss Mama."

Kat guessed the word meant "grandmother." "I'm sorry, Rosita. I'm trying to help you. I want to try to find her."

Rosita wiped her wet cheeks, then folded in the sides of her skirt.

Blinking back her own tears, Kat sat on the bed. This wasn't just about avoiding her duty to care for the child. She really did want what was best for Rosita. She had to hope the child's grandmother was alive; she'd do everything she could to find the woman.

Her bottom lip quivering, Rosita carefully folded the bodice of her dress over the skirt.

"Did she live in Cripple Creek?" It seemed unlikely, but Kat didn't want to leave any stone unturned.

"Not Abuela. Me and Mama moved."

"Do you remember where she lived?"

"Far away."

Sighing, Kat swallowed her frustration and continued folding clothes.

"Did your grandmother ever come here to Cripple Creek to see you?"

Rosita shook her head, her eyes brimming with sadness. "Too far, Mama said."

Kat's heart ached for the grandmother and her granddaughter. The woman may not even know where they'd moved to, or that her daughter was dead and Rosita needed her.

Kat didn't even know the little girl's family name, let alone the grandmother's given name.

"Do you have another name? I am Miss Kat Sinclair, and you are Miss Rosita…"

"Just Rosita."

Kat bit her lip. It wasn't the child's fault. Kat was frustrated, and she needed someone to blame.

Patrick Maloney.

She was here because of his promises. Kat flopped back on the bed, and Rosita giggled.

"All done with work, HopHop." The little girl toddled over to her pallet and sat down with the cotton bunny.

Kat rose from the bed and put the various stacks of clean clothes in their proper places while Rosita played with HopHop. After Kat set her unmentionables inside her trunk, she pulled out the bundle of Patrick's letters. She should burn them all. But first, she felt the desire to read them again. There had to have been clues to his deception in them—something that could teach her not to make the same mistake again. She'd start with the first letter—the one where he'd said just enough to sound like a good man. Leaning against the chest, she slid the letter from its envelope.

Dear Miss Sinclair,

I read your note in the Cripple Creek Times with rapt attention.

I am a foreman at the Mary McKinney Mine here in
gold country.

I am a single man in search of the right woman.

But not a single-woman man, waiting for the right woman. Kat
studied the penmanship. It was now obvious it was a woman's hand.

It would please me to know you.

I will wait ever so impatiently for your letter.

With high regards,

Patrick Maloney

She had answered his first letter with her stomach in knots. She'd
apparently mistaken qualms for keenness. Kat pulled the most recent
correspondence from her short stack.

Dearest Katherine,

My heart has not stilled since your last letter.

Your acceptance of my promise of marriage is all I think
about.

My impatience is growing.

I long to see your face and to feel your warm embrace.

To that end, I have sent payment for your train fare.

I only wish I didn't have to wait until the 5th of June.

He didn't wait. Not for her.

All empty promises. And, no doubt, most of them came from the
mind of the other woman. How could she have been so gullible?

She picked up another letter. After she'd looked at this one, she'd take them all down to Hattie's stove and put her lost dreams behind her. She needed to move on. She needed the Lord to be her light. She needed to trust Him.

Kat opened another envelope.

Dear Miss Sinclair,
    Thank you for your forthwith letter.
    You have the penmanship of an angel.

The letters were full of this kind of sticky-sweet syrup. Those weren't the words of the man she'd heard in the saloon talking about "getting hitched."

    I am hopeful that our correspondence will continue.
    I am also hopeful that we may have a future together.
    You'll be happy to know that I am a man of means.

Means for other women, that is.

    I own a fine horse and a comfortable home that would be yours if you agree to marry me.

Did she dare believe the man actually had a house? *I have a house for you.* That's what he'd said in the saloon. The man had to have lived somewhere, and if he did have a house, it was hers. She had to tell Nell.

"I need to go downstairs." Kat jumped up from her nest on the floor and glanced over at the pallet where Rosita lay curled around

HopHop, her eyes closed. She laid a quilt over the little one and then descended the stairs two at a time. She found Nell sitting at the dining room table, filling the salt cellars.

Her sister stared up at her, a frown on her face. "You're supposed to be resting."

"Listen to Patrick's letter." She lifted the page to read, lengthening her neck for dramatic emphasis. " 'You'll be happy to know that I am a man of means. I own a fine horse and a comfortable home that would be yours if you agree to marry me.' He's gone. We were planning to be married. He promised it to me, and now it's mine."

"You said he didn't even write—"

"I know, but the man had to have lived somewhere. What if he—"

"You're grasping at thin air."

"It's all I have. It may be foolish, but I'd like to look into it."

The front door opened, and the sound of children's voices and shuffling footsteps echoed from the stairway.

Nell had just finished filling the last salt cellar when Hattie rushed into the room. "Is Rosita asleep?"

Kat tucked the envelope into the back of her skirt. "Yes, she's upstairs."

"Now if only those little ones would follow her lead." At the kitchen door, Hattie looked over her shoulder. "Oh, I almost forgot. We have visitors in the parlor. I started the music, but could you see to them while I get us all some tea?"

Nodding, Nell stood and then turned to Kat. "We'll talk about this later."

Kat wanted to talk about it now, but instead she followed her sister to the parlor. The moment she saw the couple sitting on the sofa, Kat felt her mouth fall open and her face flush. Dr. Morgan Cutshaw jumped to his feet, looking just as stunned to see her.

His wife remained seated.

Morgan leaped off the sofa at the sight of Miss Sinclair. A strange regret niggled at him as they stared at each other. He shouldn't have given in to Miss Taggart's insistence that she come with him. He couldn't say why it bothered him that Miss Sinclair saw them together, but it did.

"Miss Sinclair."

Another woman he hadn't met studied him and then glanced at Miss Sinclair. "Is this the doctor from the hospital?"

Miss Sinclair nodded. She looked toward him, but not at him when she spoke. "Dr. Cutshaw, this is my sister, Miss Nell Sinclair."

Now he noticed the resemblance. Their hair and eye colors didn't match, but both had high cheekbones and pronounced chins. And they obviously had shared at least one story about a mean doctor who scolded good Samaritans for being bad midwives.

"I'm pleased to meet you, Miss Sinclair."

"And you, Dr. Cutshaw."

Miss Taggart stood beside him now, peering at the original Miss Sinclair. "You know Dr. Cutshaw from the hospital?"

Miss Sinclair's face flushed the color of a ripe plum. "Mrs. Adams is making some tea and will be with you shortly. If you'll excuse me and my sister, we have business to attend to." She dipped her chin in a tight but polite acknowledgment. "Dr. Cutshaw. Mrs. Cutshaw."

Miss Taggart blushed. "We're not married."

"Oh." Her brow raised, Miss Sinclair looked at him like he'd done something wrong. "I see. You…I just assumed—"

"Pardon me, ladies." He gestured toward his companion. "This is Miss Darla Taggart. We are…uh…her father is the minister at the First Congregational Church here in Cripple Creek. She was kind enough to accompany me to see Miss Hattie about a matter." His heart pounding, Morgan paused to draw in a breath. "In the meantime, may I have a word with you?"

After a quick glance at her sister, Miss Kat Sinclair nodded in his direction. "A moment."

Miss Nell Sinclair extended her hand to Miss Taggart. "You and I can go see about helping Miss Hattie." When Miss Taggart didn't move, Miss Sinclair moved toward her. "Follow me."

When they left the room, the sister with the auburn hair walked to the hearth and turned to face him, a storm brewing in her brown eyes. "You wanted to speak to me?"

"About our first meeting, I want to apologize for our misunderstanding."

"It was not my misunderstanding, Doctor."

She wasn't going to make this easy, and he didn't blame her.

"It was completely my fault. I made a mistaken assumption. I later learned that you yourself had been a patient. Dr. Hanson said you have stitches. How is your shoulder faring?" He hoped that wasn't too personal a question.

"I'm—"

Suddenly he pictured Miss Sinclair standing on the porch on Myers Avenue, and a rolling heat singed his ears.

"My shoulder is fine. Thank you."

"You'll have the sutures removed on Wednesday?"

"Is that all, Doctor?"

Morgan cleared his throat. "Miss Sinclair, I am truly sorry about our misunderstanding. But as a Christian person, I feel it's my duty to warn you of the evils of certain men in this town—the type who might frequent establishments ladies of your apparent caliber shouldn't fall prey to, no matter what kinds of frills they display." Morgan looked away and took a deep breath before continuing. "I was walking past Myers Avenue today, and saw you speaking with such a man."

The force of her gasp nearly knocked him off his feet. "You, Dr. Cutshaw, think I was talking to that man on purpose?" She stepped back. "You are an infuriating man. A mistaken, assuming, maddening man. I am not a fool. Nor am I drawn in by satin and lace and…free liquor! Believe me when I tell you, sir, that I know what kind of *certain* men live in this town."

"Kat?" Her sister rushed into the room, carrying a full tea tray. "Is something wrong?"

Kat looked over at him, her jaw set in a tight frown. "This…man saw me this morning and had the audacity to…just never mind." She turned, her skirt swishing in the rush, and stomped out of the room.

Listening to the young woman's deliberate steps up the stairs, Morgan couldn't help but wonder what life would be like if the two of them got along.

FIFTEEN

Lewis P. Whibley tucked the folded faro table under his arm and strutted down the hallway to the narrow stairs above Japanese Charlie's Saloon in Colorado Springs. Three days had passed since that mousy old maid in Denver sent him packing, penniless. He'd barely escaped her robust brother.

Squaring his shoulders now, Lewis straightened his bolo tie. The sound of chinking glasses and bottles brightened his spirits. It meant a crowd was gathering below. He had an adequate take here last night, but he needed a few good nights for train fare and a hearty pot of seed money. A night or two at the table with that daft miner in Cripple Creek, and his luck would change. He'd win back his silver flask and his home. Why, he might even settle down and take himself a wife.

Lewis felt his blood boil. In one stupid night, he'd doled out everything he had to that cheat Paddy—all his winnings. That louse had even lured the saucy redhead away from him. Still made his gut burn.

His daddy was fond of saying that greed was like a dark pit full of angry snakes. Well, it wouldn't bite him again. He would outwit the miner this time. Outlast him too, until he had won back what was his. Might even see about that redhead again, if he had a mind to.

Tonight would be good practice—that is, if he could get to the table. Two upstairs girls stood between him and his seed pot.

"Ladies." He tipped his hat. The one with the ruby red lips and long legs was tempting.

But it was the other one who sidled up to him and pressed a weighty hand on his arm. "Hey, handsome, you look much too serious tonight for your own good." Batting heavy lashes, she patted her bare collarbone. "I have a place where we could see to that serious ailment of yours." Her laugh was raw.

"As tempting as that is, I'm all about business tonight, ladies. After all, a man has to earn his keep."

The woman pulled away and turned back toward her friend.

They weren't so different from him. He knew when a mark wasn't going to pan out, and so did they. Waving him off, they turned toward the next prospect. Lewis needed to do the same thing. Focus. That's what had worked for his daddy.

At the edge of the hazy room, he assembled his faro table with a showman's finesse. Like bees to honey, a buzz of gamblers landed at his table. A couple of cowboys. One he guessed to be a lawyer or a newspaper man. A fourth man stood across from Lewis. He'd seen horses with smaller noses than the one on this guy. He'd been at this faro table before, although Lewis couldn't say where. Lewis had drifted far too much the last couple of years.

Stacking his chips, Lewis made eye contact with each player. "Shall we, gentlemen?"

"You were in Cripple Creek last year, weren't ya, mister?" The guy's voice was familiar. It sounded like he'd been chewing rocks.

His natural instinct was to run, in case he'd cheated the man with the big nose, but since he had a fist full of bills, Lewis stayed put and shuffled his deck. Something jogged in Lewis's memory.

"Name's Whibley." He laid the deck facedown on the table. "We had a good game, as I recall. Ollie's place in Cripple Creek, wasn't it?"

"Yeah. I'm the paymaster over there at the Mary McKinney Mine." He pulled a cigar from his jacket and lit it.

Lewis traded chips for cash from the other players. "I'm headed back to Cripple Creek in a few days."

"Heard you all had a couple of nasty fires up in Cripple Creek last month." The cowboy to Lewis's left shoved a wad of tobacco in his cheek and arranged his chips in neat stacks.

"Two big ones in four days. A bartender started the first one, fightin' with his…woman." The paymaster sneered at the leggy gal hanging on one of the cowboys. "The second one in the kitchen at the Portland Hotel. Six people died. One of 'em was a no-good high-grader, hauling ore out in his lunch bucket, stealing from my mine." He fanned out his cards. "Found out afterward. The devil welcomed Paddy Maloney with a round of drinks, you can be sure."

Lewis dropped a stack of chips, sending them rattling to the floor. Paddy Maloney was dead? Well, that changed things. His return to Cripple Creek was going to be easier than he thought. With Paddy dead, all he had to do was move back into his place. His luck was certainly changing.

But first things first—his train fare.

"Enough chatter, fellas. Let's get down to business."

Sixteen

fter breakfast Saturday morning, Nell embraced Edith out on Hattie's front porch. Then she hugged Thelma and kissed the baby cradled on her hip. Having the sisters and their children in the house had kept Nell busy in the kitchen. She'd miss them, and the activity that made waiting for Judson a little less worrisome. Unlike her sister, Nell didn't like being alone, especially now.

"We'll be praying for all of you." Thelma followed Lucille and the other children down the walkway.

"God bless you all!" Hattie waved from the doorway. "You be sure to come back and see me anytime."

Kat had already said her good-byes and taken Rosita upstairs to get ready for their trip to the mine and into town to send the telegram she didn't get sent the day of the fire. Her sister was wise to distract the little girl right now. Rosita had warmed up to having other children around, and she was bound to miss them as much as Nell did. Once Thelma and her family had turned the corner at Hayden, she went inside and closed the door behind them.

Tears pooled in Hattie's eyes.

"I'll see if Kat's ready to go," Nell said, turning away before her landlady saw the tears in her own eyes.

"Did your sister say what it was that made her mad at the doctor this time?" Hattie asked.

Nell knew what Hattie was doing, and she guessed they all needed a distraction, but she wasn't going to discuss Kat's private matters. "I'm sure they'll work it out." At least, Nell hoped they would. Admittedly, the doctor had yet to converse with her sister without exasperating her, but that didn't make him a bad man. He had, after all, saved that prostitute and her baby before Kat's very own eyes.

And he was unmarried. Kat would never admit it, but she did need a man.

So did Nell. *Judson Archer.* The difference was that Nell knew it. Now if she could only find him. Nell turned and climbed the stairs, and heard the phonograph start playing downstairs. She wished she had money to shop for a new music cylinder or two. Hattie's three were becoming quite familiar.

Nell walked into the room just as Kat slid a yellow ribbon over Rosita's curls.

"Time for my wagon ride?" Deep dimples punctuated the little girl's question.

Nell nodded, and Rosita slid off the bed and darted out the door with HopHop in her hand. Kat stood and pulled her bonnet off the bed.

As they descended the stairs, neither one of them spoke. Nell pulled her mantle off the brass hook and stepped out the door. It wasn't especially cold out, but Nell wanted to protect her dress from dust on the happenstance that Judson was actually there.

Less than an hour later, Nell held the reins as Hattie's wagon bumped down a hill, across mine tailings, and into a cloud of rock dust. Rosita was wedged between her and Kat, and Nell could barely hear her own cough for the deafening sound of machinery.

Nell pulled back on the reins to slow Hattie's mare. Although Kat's shoulder didn't seem to trouble her much now, Nell had insisted on driving. She leaned forward in the seat, straining to see through all the dust. Dirty men scuttled about like worker ants. "Any ideas on where we might find the paymaster's office?"

Kat pushed stray hairs back from her face and straightened her hat. "Let's start with that small tin shed." She pointed to a corrugated shack with bars on the windows. "It looks to be some sort of office."

Nell directed the horse toward the small shed off to the right of a much larger one. When she stepped out of the wagon, she noticed the sign on the front of the building: PAYMASTER. Her heart quickened. As foolish as it may be, she and Kat both held high hopes for this visit. They both needed answers.

Nell reached for Rosita and lifted her to the ground. "You are to stay right beside me or Miss Kat. Understood?"

Nodding, the child clutched Nell's hand, her dark eyes mirroring the anxiety that knotted Nell's stomach.

Kat wrapped the reins over a railing out front, then joined them at the door. As the three of them stepped inside, dust mixed with body odor and cigar smoke to create an immediate threat to the breakfast

Nell had eaten. She pressed her lips together to avoid gagging. Kat's pallor signaled that she was doing the same.

Two men with cigars hanging from their mouths looked at them from behind a desk covered with papers and books. The larger man removed his spectacles and slanted a menacing look Rosita's direction.

Straightening, the smaller man rose to his feet and pulled his cigar out of his mouth. "Don't get too many women around here."

Nell squeezed the little girl's hand, hoping to reassure her.

"Which of you is Mr. Holt, the paymaster for the mine?" Kat had shouted the question, trying to be heard over the pistons in the stamp mill.

"That's me." Still scowling at Rosita, the man with the bulbous nose flicked ashes into a can.

Mules had better manners.

"I'm here about Patrick…Paddy Maloney."

He set his cigar across the top of the can and stood. "The rat is dead."

Kat started but quickly squared her shoulders. "Yes. I'm aware of that, sir."

"Now why on God's green earth would a proper lady like you come out here lookin' for a cad like him?"

"Did Mr. Maloney work here?"

"Pickled Paddy worked here, all right. When he remembered he had a job. He was a mucker." The smaller man snickered. "Cleaned up after everybody else. That's how important he was."

Nell sighed, and Kat shook her head. Patrick's letters said he was a foreman. So far, the only grain of truth to any of it was that the man had lived and worked in Cripple Creek. The house was most likely a lie too, but Nell understood why Kat had to know the truth. She'd save her questions about Judson until Kat had her say.

"Sir, did Mr. Maloney have any family in Colorado?"

"No. Wasn't anyone who would have him for more than a—"

"I have a letter that states his promise of marriage." Kat pulled Patrick's letters from her pocket.

Mr. Holt stepped out around the desk and planted himself against the front of it. "Well, I'll be. He'd gotten himself a mail-order bride." He shook his head and turned to the smaller man, who laughed, his eyes wide. "But that doesn't tell me why you're here."

"I also have a letter that says we have a house."

"Let me see those letters of his." He put out his hand, his greedy palm up.

Kat showed him the letters. Nell prayed that her sister would receive good news.

"Doesn't mean much to me." He skimmed the letters and retrieved his cigar from the top of the can. "I don't know anything about Paddy having a house. Wouldn't believe it, if I were you."

Kat looked over at Nell, her eyes watering.

Mr. Holt stepped behind the desk and pulled a tin box from a drawer. "As slack as Paddy was in his work, he still had some pay coming. Three days at three dollars a day." He counted out nine dollars. "In my book, it's the least the man owed ya." He handed the bills to Kat.

"Mr. Holt." Nell had tried to be patient, but she'd waited three days to talk to him. "A week ago this Monday past, you received a telegram for Mr. Judson Archer."

His eyes widened and his fuzzy brows twitched. "You the one that came from Maine?"

Nodding, Nell let go of Rosita's hand and stepped toward the desk. "Did you give it to him?"

"I would've, but he wasn't here."

"Oh." That's all Nell could manage to force out around the lump in her throat. Judson had worked here, but now he was gone.

"Ma'am, that one's a different story." The smaller man puffed on his cigar. "As upstanding as the working day is long. Went to Manitou Springs on family business. He'll be back this coming week."

"Oh, that's good news." Nell's spirits lifted. "Thank you, sir."

Judson Archer wasn't a liar like Patrick Maloney turned out to be. And as soon as he returned, he'd read her telegram and call on her straightaway.

He will. Won't he, Lord?

SEVENTEEN

The wagon bumped down the hill toward town. Kat stared at one particular white cloud off by itself in a mostly blue sky. Separated from the other clouds, this one seemed adrift. Directionless. Aimless.

Why, Lord, why am I adrift?

Kat reached into her pocket and fingered the nine dollars the paymaster had given her. The money would help, and she was thankful for it. Certainly, the man didn't have to give it to her. But it wasn't a house, and it wouldn't buy one. At best, it would buy her and Nell and Rosita a few more days at Hattie's.

Of course Patrick had lied about having a home. That's all he'd done from the beginning. Even the handwriting was a lie. She should've known better than to let anything in those letters build her hope.

Now what?

Weary of her own self-pity, Kat sighed. She was seeing her prayers for Nell answered, and that should be enough. Nell hadn't stopped smiling since the paymaster's endorsement of Judson Archer. The man had a good reputation, and that counted for a lot. The best news was that the other man in Mr. Holt's office said he'd return to town this coming week. Since this was Saturday, that could be as early as tomorrow.

As the horse clip-clopped down the hill and toward the depot, Kat took in a deep breath, drawing strength from Nell's good news. She would set her own disappointments aside and concentrate on Nell's imminent happiness and Rosita's needs.

Lord, help me.

Hammers pounded in the center of town and on the surrounding slopes as the cleanup continued. Horse hooves clomped and wagon wheels screeched against the rocky roadbeds. Men carried boxes and crates into wood sheds and tents that stood where piles of smoldering ashes lay just days ago. Others had stacked brick and mortar, rebuilding their barber shops and saloons with hardy materials, like the few original buildings left standing in the fire's path.

As Kat watched Cripple Creek being rebuilt, renewed, and transformed, she asked that the Lord do the same in her.

"Girls! Over here, girls!" Kat recognized the singsongy voice as Hattie's and glanced over at the makeshift boardwalk. The landlady waved from outside the combination mercantile and post office tent that had been set up during reconstruction.

Kat and Rosita returned her wave while Nell pulled the wagon over to the side of the road.

"We can walk to the telegraph office from here." Nell climbed down from the wagon and lifted Rosita out.

Kat stepped up onto the boardwalk while Rosita helped Nell secure the horse to the hitching post.

"That house is pin-drop quiet with everybody gone." Hattie

walked toward them. "Got so lonely I wrote a nice long letter to my brother and brought it right down to the post office."

Kat pulled the telegram for Aunt Alma out of her pocket. "We're headed to the telegraph office. If you'd like to take your wagon, we can walk home from there."

"I just might take you up on that offer, but not before you girls tell me what you found out at the mine."

"Judson didn't get my wire because he is out of town," Nell practically sang.

"How long will he be gone?"

"He's returning this week." Nell's smile lit the sprinkling of freckles across her nose.

"That would explain the shine in your eyes." Hattie turned toward Kat. "And you?"

Kat sighed. "He doesn't know anything about Patrick having a house. I should've known the man was lying about that too. I suppose I just—"

"And what about Paddy's horse?"

"I didn't ask. I'm sure he—or the woman who wrote the letters, I should say—lied about that too."

"He did have a horse." Hattie nodded. "A sorrel. I saw Paddy with it at Jesse's Livery early last week."

Kat cocked her head. "You're sure it was his?"

"Oh yes. Jesse was in a mood to talk, and said Paddy owned the horse."

More like Hattie was in the mood to talk and wouldn't let the man be, but that didn't matter to Kat.

"I guess it couldn't hurt to stop at Jesse's Livery and ask about it."

She turned to Nell. "We can go by there when we're finished at the telegraph office."

She might not have a husband or his house, but she might have the man's horse. For right now, that would have to do.

⤜⟋⟍⤏

Nell and Rosita followed Kat through the gaping barn door into the dark stable. Kat was a woman on a mission, and Nell tried to stay out of her way. Nell admired her persistence and desperately wished for good news for her, even if it was only a horse she could sell.

The livery smelled of manure. Nell pulled her handkerchief from her pocket and covered her mouth.

"You ladies need a wagon, do you?" The man tossing hay into a stall was huge—tall, and almost as wide around.

"Hattie Adams over at the boardinghouse told me to talk to Jesse."

"That's me." He leaned his pitchfork against a post and hooked his thumbs on the bib of his dirty overalls. "I own the livery. If Miss Hattie sent you, I'll give you the best I have available."

"Thank you, but I'm not looking for a wagon. She said Patrick…er, Paddy Maloney may have left his horse here Wednesday before the fire."

"He did."

"I've come to claim it."

"I'd like to oblige you, miss, but Ollie come by yesterday and claimed Paddy's horse for payment. The man had a saloon tab longer than my arm."

Kat's shoulders slumped.

Poor Kat—another disappointment. How many would her sister have to endure? Nell reached for Kat's hand. "Thank you, sir." Tugging on Kat's arm, she looked around for Rosita and turned toward the door, but they both stopped cold when they saw the man who traipsed through the open doorway. He was the dirtiest man Nell had ever seen—from his mud-caked boots to a shaggy beard that looked to have been white. A mule followed him inside, carrying a whole shed's worth of tools on its back.

He looked at Kat, then slapped his crusty overalls, sending a cloud of dust into the steamy air. "Well, I'll be an ant's eyebrow if it isn't the little lady I seen on—"

"Mr. Hughes." Kat dipped her head.

"You know this man?" Nell couldn't imagine how her sister knew him.

"You've got pretty company today." He laughed.

Nell felt a warm flush move up her face. Rosita darted out from behind a hay bale and ran to him. "Mr. Bo-ney."

"My Rosita." He pulled her into his arms and twirled her around, producing the most delightful giggles with each spin. "I've been worried mindless over you since I heard about your mama. Sick all the way to my dirty toenails about her, I am."

"Me too." Rosita leaned her head against the man's shoulder. "'Cept I got clean ones. Miss Kat gave me a bath."

He looked at Kat, his bushy eyebrows hiked. "You takin' care of Rosita now?"

"For now. I'm trying to find her family."

"That explains why you was lookin' for Miss Sunny." He nodded. "Mighty good of you to see to her."

Kat nodded and gestured toward Nell.

"Nell, this is Mr. Boney Hughes."

Nell dipped her chin in a greeting.

"This is my sister, Miss Nell Sinclair."

"Pleased to meet you, ma'am." Removing his hat, the man bent in a half bow.

At least he knew better than to try and shake her hand. "Thank you, Mr. Hughes." She wanted to say that she was pleased to meet him, but she wasn't given to lying. "You were friends, you and Rosita's mother?"

Chuckling, the man leaned toward the sisters and shielded his whiskered mouth. "Not that kind of friends, ma'am. Rosita's like a granddaughter to me, though we're not blood family."

"Mr. Bon-ey? Can I sit on ol' Sal?"

He tugged the mule over next to him and swung Rosita up onto the bedroll on its back.

"Mr. Hughes, do you know anything about Rosita's grandmother?" Kat asked. "Did Carmen ever talk to you about her family?"

"Carmen mentioned having a mother in…uh. Now, where was it?" He scratched his head. "Santa Fe, I think it was."

Nell's heart quickened. The name of a town was at least something. "Where's that?"

"New Mexico, ma'am. A couple hundred miles from here by rail."

"Oh." She stepped back. "That's a long way away."

"Yeah, but I can wire the sheriff over there for ya, if you'd like, and he can help us find her."

"Yes, thank you."

He placed his hat back on his heat at a cockeyed angle. "My pleasure. Now you two here lookin' for a horse? Ollie's got a real fine one for sale."

"We came here to ask about that horse," Kat said quietly. "It was Paddy Maloney's."

His eyes wide, the man glanced at Kat. "He was one of them that died."

Nodding, Kat drew in a deep breath, and so did Nell. "I came here as his intended."

Mr. Hughes shook his head. "I'm awful sorry, ma'am." He studied Nell. "And you, miss? You came to marry too?"

She felt her cheeks flush. "Mr. Judson Archer."

"Can't say as I know him."

"Did you know Paddy?"

"I did." He spit a brown streak into the straw flooring. "I was in Ollie's Saloon the night he won his place."

"His place?" Kat straightened up.

Nell glanced at Kat and then back at the man. "Patrick does have a house?"

"Up in the foothills above town."

"I have his letters stating he intended to marry me." Kat reached into her pocket. "And one that says we have a home. I asked the paymaster out at the mine but he said he knew nothing about it."

"Well, I know exactly where it is." Boney finger-combed his beard. "And seein's how he promised it to ya, it oughta be yours."

"Can you take us there?" Kat asked, her eyes eager.

"Cain't do it today. Gotta get back to my claim after my business with Jesse, but I can take you there Tuesday mornin'."

"That'd be wonderful."

Although Nell didn't share her sister's enthusiasm, she was grateful for the hope on Kat's face.

Smiling, Mr. Hughes lifted Rosita off the mule. "Will you bring Rosita? Me and Sal love seein' her."

Kat nodded. "We'll meet you here at the livery at 10:00 a.m."

Nell found herself warming to the man. His particular variety of Wild West mannerisms was mysteriously endearing. And if God wanted to use him to help Kat, Nell would be there to cheer him on.

EIGHTEEN

A thumping sound woke Morgan Sunday night. He rolled over and rubbed his eyes, trying to orient himself to his new surroundings. A faint glow from the stove cast shadows that danced across the pipes on the low ceiling. Wheelchairs and gurneys were piled in the corner, next to the door.

More thumping. Who would be knocking at this hour?

"I need to speak with you, Dr. Cutshaw." The voice had a familiar lilt to it, but he couldn't place it. What in the name of common sense was a woman doing out at this hour?

"Give me a moment." Morgan rolled out of bed and grabbed his clothes from the back of a plain pine chair. He dressed quickly and opened the door to a surprising blast of frigid air. It chilled his face and stole his breath. A young woman, holding a lantern, rocked back and forth in a hooded mantle. Her gloved hands held a wool scarf across her nose and mouth, leaving only worried blue eyes uncovered.

"Miss Sinclair?" He didn't see anyone with her. "What are you doing out alone? Are you ill?"

She lowered the scarf. "I'm sorry for the late hour, but we need you at Hattie's."

His pulse quickening, Morgan grabbed his coat off a peg and his doctoring bag from the table. "Your sister? Is it her shoulder wound?"

"Kat is fine, Doctor. It's Rosita. The little girl she's caring for."

Morgan remembered the girl from the birthing room. No place for a child. He also remembered that the woman detested him. "Does she know you've come for me?"

"She knows."

Morgan grabbed his bag and followed Nell out the hospital door and up the road to the boardinghouse, praying for wisdom. As he glanced up at the sliver of moon high above them, he couldn't help but wonder if this was the new thing God had in mind for him— doctoring women and children. It wasn't at all what he came to do in Cripple Creek.

"She was a might puny most of the morning," Nell said, walking beside him in the cool night air.

"Do you know if she has a fever?"

"She felt pretty warm to me." She pulled her wrap tighter around her shoulders. "She'd perked up some this afternoon, but then an hour ago, she awoke crying." The young woman turned up a walkway in front of the yellow house and walked in the front door.

Morgan followed Nell up the creaky wooden stairs to a small room on the right. Kat Sinclair sat on the bed while Rosita wiggled in her arms, crying and clutching a fabric bunny.

He stepped up to the foot of the bed. "Miss Sinclair."

Kat looked up at him, her eyes warm and weary. "She has a fever. I think it's her ears."

He set his medical bag on the floor and sat on the bed beside them.

Rosita looked a little older than William would have been. Morgan studied his young patient. Her gaze dull, she swiped at her right ear. "Hello, Rosita. You saw me at the hospital."

Shaking her head and whimpering, she glared at Miss Sinclair. "The baby doctor."

"Yes, it is, but it's all right. He's a nice man." Kat looked up at him with her brow lifted in a question mark. "He saved that woman and her baby. You need to let him help you get better too." Kat looked his way, giving him a slight nod.

Morgan brushed his thumb and forefinger along the little girl's high forehead. The fluting iron his mother used to press the ruffles on her dresses wouldn't be this hot.

"Do your ears hurt?" He crouched down and looked into the girl's eyes.

Nodding, Rosita tugged at her left ear. Kat swept straight black hair back from the child's temples with a tender touch, much the way Morgan imagined Opal would have. Attentive. Gentle. Tender.

"I agree with you. It's most likely an ear infection." Morgan pulled his bag up from the rug and unlatched the silver clasp. "I'll check them to be certain." He pulled the otoscope out of a gray felt sack. Rosita's mouth dropped open, and she retreated into the crook of Kat's arm.

Morgan lifted the fabric bunny and patted its ears. "Is this your friend?"

"HopHop." Sniffing, Rosita squeezed the stuffed bunny with one hand and swiped at her damp cheeks with the back of the other. "Miss Kat gave him to me."

Morgan held the glass lens of the otoscope to his eye. "This is the special tool I'll use to peek into your ears to see if they're sick." Morgan held the instrument out to her. "Would you like to hold it?"

The child's posture softened. Nodding, she exchanged the bunny for the otoscope and folded both hands around it.

"You can check HopHop's ears for me."

Rosita lifted the lens to her eye as Morgan had done—as his son, William, might have done. Morgan swallowed the bittersweet image and lifted the flat bunny in front of Rosita. "Gently put that pointed end into his ear. Then look through the lens." Morgan pointed to it.

Tilting her head and pinching her lips together, the little girl placed the tip at the seam on the bunny's head and examined a make-believe ear.

"Do you see any infection in HopHop's ear? Any red like you see on an apple?"

She shook her head. "Just thread."

A smile momentarily chased away the weary lines that framed the sisters' faces.

Morgan grinned. She was a bright little girl. "Now, it's my turn to look at your ears. You make sure HopHop doesn't hop away, okay?"

Rosita returned the instrument and took the stuffed rabbit from Morgan. Then she laid her head on a pillow on Kat's lap.

"You're good with children," Kat said, holding his gaze.

"Thank you." *Thank You, Lord.* Morgan pulled a clean handkerchief from his vest pocket and wiped the instrument tip. "Rosita, you hold real still, as HopHop did." Holding Rosita's head steady with one hand and the otoscope with the other, Morgan first looked at the drum in the left ear. It was red and bulging like a frog's throat. Oil might not be enough. It might need to be drained. He had his myringotomy knife with him, but he didn't dare try to lance the eardrum here. If he had to do it at all, he wanted a sterile environment. "This doesn't look good."

Kat blinked back tears. This was why Rosita needed her family. The girl's mother would have noticed the infection sooner, been better able to help. There had to be someone else who could care for her. This was too hard. She'd cared for her little sisters, but this was different. A child needed a mother, and it couldn't be her.

"Time to turn over, little one." Dr. Cutshaw knew how to talk to children. His voice sounded like butter melting on fresh bread.

Rosita rolled over, right ear up, tucking her hand around Kat's middle.

"This one's red, but not bulging. I have some sweet oil with me." He returned the scope to his bag then pulled out the vial of oil and two clean handkerchiefs.

"I'll warm it." Nell took the vial and pattered down the stairs.

Dr. Cutshaw laid his hand on Kat's good shoulder, sending a shiver down her spine. "Kat, Rosita will be all right."

She could feel the warmth of his hand through her cotton dress. He was being too familiar, touching her shoulder and using her given name, but this felt personal—Rosita sick, the three of them sitting on the bed. She hadn't noticed his eyes before: spring grass green.

"The oil should do enough to get you through the night." He set his bag on the floor. "The left eardrum might need to be lanced, but it can wait until tomorrow. Let me know if she's not feeling much better by then."

Nell returned, cradling the oil jar in a tea towel.

"Rosita, I'm going to put the oil in now to make your ears better." Dr. Cutshaw cupped her little chin. When the oil dropped into her ear, she shuddered, but remained quiet while he gently kneaded her ear.

Holding HopHop tight, Rosita scooted and rolled over. After Dr. Cutshaw repeated the treatment in the right ear, he capped the vial and set it in his bag.

"Thank you, Dr. Cutshaw."

"I hope it helps."

Kat eased the little girl into a sitting position and cradled her. She had been taught to treat others how she wanted to be treated, and being cradled and cared for sounded real good to her right now.

The doctor pulled a small paper sack from his satchel and looked at Kat. She didn't see any misunderstanding in them this time. "May I give Rosita a candy?"

Kat realized that the man couldn't be all bad if he saved babies, healed little girls, and handed out candy. She nodded. "One piece."

Yes, the good doctor knew how to endear himself to little ones, and to sisters. Nell was smiling for the first time tonight.

Dr. Cutshaw held the sack open for her Rosita. Kat couldn't help but peer over Rosita's shoulder. Nell looked every bit as interested in the assortment. Caramels. Licorice. Horehounds. Peppermints. Kat hadn't had any candy since she'd left Maine.

Rosita tugged the wrapper off a piece of licorice, and Dr. Cutshaw held the candy bag in front of Kat and Nell. When they didn't reach for it, he pulled out a few pieces and opened his hand. It wasn't the hand of a dandy city doctor who never saw sun or real work. But then nothing about Dr. Cutshaw was conventional, or expected.

After Nell picked a horehound, Kat chose a caramel. The doctor returned the rest to his medical bag, save a licorice that he unwrapped and popped into his mouth. He was twisting the latch on his satchel when Hattie stepped into the room with her hand open.

"Just a minute there, good Doctor. Where's my candy?"

He pulled an assortment from his sack and set them in her hand, then curled her fingers over them. "All yours."

Kat didn't want to like the man, but she did.

"Miss Sinclair?" Dr. Cutshaw was looking at Kat.

"Yes?" Until now, she hadn't noticed the dimple just to the right of his upper lip.

"I've offended you, not once but at least twice that I know of, and I'd like to make it up to you."

"Oh?" Kat's voice was one in a chorus of three women.

"Once Rosita is feeling better, I'd like to treat all four of you to a special evening."

Kat shook her head. She was grateful for his help with the girl, but…

"What kind of treat, Doctor?" Hattie said around the licorice in her mouth.

"That's a surprise."

"I don't think—"

"We accept." Nell slanted a coy grin Kat's direction.

"Thursday then? Providing that Rosita is over her infection, of course."

Hattie and Nell both stared at Kat, their heads bobbing. "With the fire and…all, I suppose we could use a treat," she finally said.

"Perfect."

Kat wasn't so sure it would be perfect, but then, she was beginning to question a lot of her impressions of the man.

NINETEEN

*I*t had been two days, and Morgan hadn't heard any more about Rosita's ears, and neither had Dr. Hanson. He assumed that meant the little girl was faring well, but it wouldn't hurt to check on her.

He grabbed his hat and his medical bag and stepped outside his basement accommodations to a cool spring afternoon.

"Oh, Doc-tor Cutshaw!"

Morgan recognized the operatic voice and drew in a deep breath before he turned. Miss Taggart waved a gloved hand, her smile wide as she sashayed toward him from the corner. The wind ruffled her skirt. She smoothed it down with her hand.

"I was hoping to speak to you."

He tipped his derby in greeting. "Miss Taggart."

"Please call me Darla." She fingered the locket at her neck. "I looked for you after church Sunday, but you'd dashed off before I could make it down the aisle from the piano."

He stepped back. "You wanted to speak to me?"

"I did indeed. At the depot last week, I told you my father's church housed some of those who lost their homes in the fire."

He nodded, wondering where she was going with this.

"Even though they've all found housing elsewhere by now, my father still wants to keep in touch with them."

"It sounds like a good idea." Morgan switched his bag from one hand to the other and waited for her to go on, his eyebrow raised.

"I knew you'd think so." Darla beamed at him.

"What exactly did you need me to do?"

"I'm getting to that, Doctor."

Morgan resisted the urge to check the watch in his vest pocket.

"We're setting up a monthly meeting. That's where you come in."

Morgan still had no idea *where* he came in, but he swallowed his frustration. The woman obviously cared about her town and had a heart for hurting people. He appreciated that about her, but she could take a lesson in succinctness from Miss Kat Sinclair, who didn't mince words. It would save him a lot of time.

"We—Father and I—thought it would be good to have you speak at our first meeting." She nodded. "It's this week."

"I see."

"Each meeting will be a combination of spiritual encouragement and instruction."

He could use a little spiritual encouragement about now.

"The night of the fire was so frantic, and folks have been so busy trying to salvage what they could and start over, that we're concerned they aren't taking proper care of themselves."

"Good thinking, Miss Taggart. In crises, people usually will tend to others and to business matters, and neglect their own needs."

"Exactly. And so many were bruised or burned or cut. I was thinking it would be good if you could prepare a brief talk about wounds and caring for them."

"That's a good idea. Afterward, I could check anyone there with wounds that haven't been seen by a doctor."

"Oh, that would be wonderful!" Darla clapped her hands together. "We'll see you Thursday evening at 6:00 then."

"Oh. But—" He shook his head. "I already have plans for Thursday evening." He had four females looking forward to his mysterious treat. Well, three out of four.

Darla pressed her lips together, pouting.

"But I could do it another time," he said reluctantly.

"Well, maybe we could do it Wednesday after prayer meeting?" she said, her eyes hopeful.

"All right. Tomorrow then."

Darla smiled again. "I'll let father know. Eight o'clock, Wednesday night."

"I'll see you there." He turned to leave but noticed that she hadn't moved or said good-bye. "Was there something else?"

"I was just wondering if storing your things at the boardinghouse is working out for you. At the time, I didn't know those sisters were living there. It isn't too crowded?"

"It's working out just fine. Thank you again for introducing me to Miss Hattie."

"My pleasure," she said, but something in her eyes made him doubt her words. "You know, Doctor, I've been thinking...I play the piano, and you play the piano."

Morgan opened his jacket and glanced at his watch pocket.

"You do play, don't you? It is your piano, isn't it?"

"It was my wife's, but—"

"Oh!" Miss Taggart set her gloved hand on her cheek. "You are married?"

Morgan felt his shoulders sag. He hadn't meant to mention any of it, but now that he had, he owed Miss Taggart an explanation. "My wife died, and I can't fathom ever being married again." It came out in a rush, his candor surprising him. "And yes… I do play the piano." He glanced down at his bag.

She followed his gaze and then peered up at him. "Here I am keeping you from your work. I hadn't even seen that you had your doctoring bag with you. My apologies."

"And mine, if you'll excuse me."

"Of course."

"I'll see you tomorrow evening then." He angled his derby her direction.

"Indeed you shall."

Miss Taggart turned to walk back to the corner at Eaton, and Morgan walked up the hill to Golden Avenue and over to Miss Hattie's. Just before he knocked on the front door, a woman's singing met his ears. It certainly wasn't anything like Opal's sweet and pure vocals, but it was a heartfelt version of "Blessed Assurance" nonetheless. When he knocked a second time, Miss Hattie opened the door, fanning herself with a dirty cloth.

"Happy Tuesday, Doctor." The woman's eyes sparkled like polished silver when she smiled.

"And to you, Mrs. Adams."

"Come right in."

"Thank you." He closed the door behind them. She hung his coat and hat on brass hooks and led him into the parlor. Instead of crossing over to the sofa, she stopped beside the piano bench.

"I was just dusting this fine instrument of yours." She waved the cloth like a conductor might a baton.

Listening for any sound of the Sinclair sisters or Rosita, Morgan glanced over at the hallway and the staircase.

"Miss Kat Sinclair isn't here, Doctor."

"I came to check Rosita's ears," he said, but felt his cheeks burn.

"Of course you did." She winked. "Rosita's not here either. But thanks to your fine doctoring Sunday night, she's back to her delightful self today."

"That's good to know. Thank you."

"Does that mean you have a few minutes to spare?"

"Did you need something?"

"Well, yes. I could use some accompaniment." She patted the piano and smiled at him much the way Miss Taggart had. Only it worked for Miss Hattie. He slid across the bench.

"The piano must have special value for you to transport it all the way from the East," she said, sitting down beside him.

"It does." He opened the lid, letting out a flood of memories.

"Your childhood?"

"I was married." Morgan swallowed hard.

Why had he said that?

"She died like my George did, didn't she?" Hattie said.

He nodded and stared at the piano keys until he could find words.

"I saw it in your eyes the afternoon you rode up in your buggy with Miss Taggart."

He rested his fingers gently on the ivory keys. "Her name was Opal."

"You poor dear."

A comfortable silence gave him time to breathe again. "It was Opal's piano. A year after I married her, she was carrying our first child. At seven months, she hemorrhaged. She and my son both died."

Hattie patted his hand like a mother would. "I'm so sorry."

"I—"

"You'll love again." She smiled at him. "I'm sure of it."

"I...can't."

He appreciated that she didn't try to argue with him. Instead she sang. " 'This is my story. This is my song. Praising my Savior all the day long.' "

Morgan let the words sink in. Maybe they were right. His story was more than his loss. More than his struggle for independence. It was the story of God wanting to do something new in him.

Morgan positioned his hands and looked up into Hattie's kind eyes. Accompaniment might help Hattie at least remain in the same key. As he struck the first chord and she began to sing, a seed of hope began to sprout deep inside him. Perhaps he would find his way through the wilderness of loss and loneliness.

TWENTY

Tuesday had started especially early for Kat.

Sometime in the still hours before dawn her mind began to churn, awakening her to a quiet house and a host of noisy thoughts. She'd grabbed her wrap and slipped downstairs with her journal. While the moon and stars still filled the sky, she sat in the Queen Anne chair in front of the window in the parlor and wrote. The clock on the mantel ticked away the hours, and she penned paragraphs about a father moving to Paris and sisters still living in Maine. She wrote a story about a puzzling doctor and a motherless little girl with fever.

As the sky started to brighten, she'd stretched out on the sofa, and somewhere between brooding over a grandmother with no name and a mysterious home in the foothills, she'd drifted off to sleep. A couple of hours later, she awoke to the sweet sound of Hattie's humming and the rich aroma of fresh coffee.

After her preparations for the day and a hearty breakfast, she, Nell, and Rosita met Boney Hughes at the livery. Now the little girl sat atop Sal and bounced HopHop on her skirted knee. Hattie's earmuffs dwarfed her head, and Boney's mining equipment formed her saddle as they trudged up the road that rose above town. Kat and Nell followed on foot. They'd walked up First Street across Carr and Eaton, then turned right onto Golden Avenue. After a short jog, they turned left up Florissant Street.

The miner that led them spit onto the dirt, and Nell wrinkled her freckled nose. She cleared her throat, a frown shadowing her eyes.

"I hope you know what you're doing, Kat."

"Of course I do. I'm going to see Patrick's house…my house."

"I meant"—Nell crossed her arms and lowered her chin as if that would help her whisper not be overheard by their escort—"I hope you know what you're doing trusting that man." She bobbed her head toward Boney. "You barely know him, and he is a bit, well, uncouth."

"Looks, and manners, for that matter, can be deceiving." Kat sighed. She had enough to think about without having to defend the few decisions afforded her.

"So can letters," Nell said pointedly. "How do you know you can trust this man?"

"Rosita is not a trusting little girl. Yet she trusts *Mr. Boney.* You saw how much they adore each other." Her breathing labored from the higher elevation, Kat slowed her pace. "You can't force a child's trust. It's something you earn, and you either have it or you don't." The wind seemed to work harder up here too, and Kat tugged her hood up over her head.

"He showed me nothing but respect on Myers Avenue. He's trying to find Rosita's grandmother, and he knows where Patrick's place is. At this point, I don't have much choice but to trust him."

Kat's boot slid on the slushy roadbed, and Nell grabbed her arm, steadying her. "But I may need snowshoes to get to town in any kind of a hurry next winter."

"What are you talking about?"

"Getting down the hill from my new house."

Her eyes wide, Nell stopped and clenched her hands on her waist. "You can't mean you plan to live up here on your own."

"What would you have me do? Wait around for some man?"

Nell's eyelid took to jumping, and she pressed a finger to it. "Don't you go and spread your doom and gloom over me. Judson is coming back. This week, you'll see."

"I'm sure he will, and I'm happy for you, but I can't wait for a man. Besides, I'm not doing this on my own. You and Rosita are with me."

"Until I marry Judson, and Mr. Hughes finds Rosita's grandmother. Then what?"

"Then you won't live up here with me."

Only a few homes dotted the hillside this far up. Homes and the headframes of small mines, which meant she'd have mostly miners for neighbors. And if Patrick was as lax in his housekeeping as he'd been in caring for himself, her new home was bound to be a frightful sight.

Lord, help me. Maybe I don't know what I'm thinking.

Sal turned up a narrower street.

"This here's Pikes Peak Avenue, ladies," Boney said, gesturing at the snowcapped mountain in front of them. "And that's Paddy's place." Boney pointed at a building just ahead of him on the right.

She should've known it wouldn't amount to much. Patrick's house was a shanty with a crooked stovepipe and a closed flapboard window beside it. A coiled rope hung from a nail on the porch wall. Antlers jutted from a plank above the rough-hewn door.

Boney slid Rosita off Sal and nodded toward the back. "Even has its own outhouse."

She hadn't thought about not having plumbing or electricity. She looked at Nell. Her eyes wide, Nell tilted her head toward the shanty and walked with her to the stoop.

Boney pushed open a thin wooden door, and they followed him and Rosita inside. Glancing around her new home, Kat knew that Nell's faith would have to sustain them both. Hers had been swallowed up by spider webs that hung like drapes from the warped ceiling. She choked on the thick layers of dust, not to mention the stench of body odor and smoke. The place had obviously been closed up for a while.

Boney latched the door open, and then went to the flapboard window to the right of the potbellied stove. His tongue pinched between his sparse front teeth, he tugged the hook out of the eye. He pushed the wood flap out with the buttress stick, and then set the stick against the window frame, holding the window open. He crossed the room to the opposite wall and repeated the action on a second flapboard window.

He pulled a lantern off a peg and lit it. The glow didn't brighten the place any. Instead, it only pointed out the dust hanging in the air between the cobwebs.

"Miss Sunny has one like that." Rosita pointed her little finger at the lintel above the door, where two curved wrought iron nails formed a rack that held up a shotgun.

Kat decided that might come in handy, although she hadn't a clue how to use it.

"It could do with a woman's touch, that's sure enough." Boney righted one of two straight-back chairs.

"This sure is the sow's ear, Kat." Nell clomped across the uneven wood plank floor to a matching rough-hewn table. "Not sure what kind of purse it could be if we fixed it up. Make curtains. Add rugs." She stacked a dirty tin cup on a dirtier tin plate, then carried them to a stained wash basin.

"I can help." Rosita picked up a broom that lay helter-skelter among a pile of stuff—a small pick, a steel gold pan, a miner's tin helmet with a clip on it for a candle, dirty overalls. Long rubber boots caked with who knew what stood next to the door beneath a coat hook. A cast-iron skillet hung on a nail to one side of a potbellied stove. A ratty quilt lay crumpled on a bed made of rope tied around a wood frame.

Everything was dirty and smelled worse than that. The nine dollars the paymaster had given her wasn't going to get them very far cleaning this place up. Now it was Kat's eyelid that twitched.

"You have to see this view you have from your new home," Nell called.

"My new home?" Kat dug her heels into a warped seam in the boards and stopped short of the window, facing Nell. "I don't think so. You were right—an unmarried woman has no business living up here."

"Look." Nell cupped Kat's shoulders and pushed her toward the open window.

The snowcapped Sangre de Cristo Mountains glowed in the distance. Her breath caught. "It's so majestic."

"Remember the verse Hattie read from Psalms this morning?"

Kat nodded. "It talked about lifting your eyes to the hills."

"Where my help comes from. It comes from the Lord."

Kat and Nell both jerked toward the words spilling from the bearded man. What was he doing quoting Scripture? Nothing about Boney Hughes was predictable.

Kat stuck her head out the window and drew in a deep breath. With God's help, maybe she could make this place into a home. And this spot right here would be her favorite.

Please, God, help me be the woman You designed me to be. A woman of faith who places her prospects in Your hands.

TWENTY-ONE

*M*organ scooped another bite of mashed potatoes onto his fork and glanced around the austere dining room at the hospital. A crucifix hung on wall over the head of the long plank table, and a portrait of Pope Leo XIII hung at the other end. Pictures of various saints lined the walls on either side. Since he was taking a late lunch this afternoon, he had the room to himself. And while he wasn't Catholic, the symbols of faith provided a tranquil retreat from the stark and busy hallways.

He'd helped Dr. Hanson with a leg amputation this morning and welcomed a few minutes alone to think now. In Cripple Creek just a week, Morgan had already amputated two legs. What a difference from his work in Boston. But he knew that the miner from the fire-related explosion, Ethan Goeke, was lucky to have his life. Ethan was still rarely conscious because of the painkillers they were giving him, and Morgan felt that was some grace as the man had lost his leg and his cabin to the fire. He had asked Mrs. Adams and the Sinclair sisters to pray for Ethan, as he was still at high risk of infection, and for his mental state when he awoke.

It was Wednesday, and as he lifted his steaming coffee cup to his mouth, he couldn't help but wonder if Miss Kat Sinclair would actually show up to have her sutures removed.

The memories from Sunday night at the boardinghouse played across his mind. Rosita cradled in Kat's arms. The woman's timid agreement to tomorrow night's treat.

"Well, Dr. Cutshaw?"

Morgan almost choked on his last bite of leftover fried chicken. He had no idea how long Sister Coleman had been speaking to him. Unfortunately, the question that stretched across her face indicated that he'd missed at least a full sentence, and now she expected an answer.

Had he been looking at her and not even seen her there? This was bad. "I'm not sure what to say to that, Sister. What do you think?"

The reverend mother huffed and wagged her finger at him. "I think you didn't hear a word I said."

He pulled the napkin from his lap and wiped his mouth. "Not a word. Sorry, but I'm a bit distracted today."

Raising an eyebrow, she peered at him over wire-rimmed spectacles. "I'd say that's an understatement, Doctor."

It was all Miss Kat Sinclair's fault. He needed to clear his mind of the distraction.

"I apologize, Sister. I'm listening now. What is it you asked me?"

"The young woman from the birthing room is here to have her sutures removed," Sister Coleman said, enunciating each syllable. "But she seems reluctant to see you."

He felt his pulse rise. "Miss Kat Sinclair."

"Yes. Her sister worked tirelessly with us during the fire." She tucked a wisp of white hair under her headpiece. "The Miss Sinclair waiting in the hallway asked if Dr. Hanson could do it, but I can't find him, and I hate to make her wait when you're available."

Morgan nodded. "Just let me clean up here, and I'll be out to talk with her."

"I'll let her know. Thank you." While the reverend mother left the room, her black habit swaying with each step, Morgan stacked his plate in the tub on the side table.

When he stepped into the front hallway, Miss Kat Sinclair sat by herself, reading a copy of *Harper's Bazar*. That is, she might have been reading it if the magazine had been right side up.

"Miss Sinclair?"

"Dr. Cutshaw." She stood abruptly. The magazine slid to the floor.

"I'll get that." Morgan retrieved it and placed it on a stack on the small table between them. "Rosita is doing well?"

"Yes, thank you. Hattie said you came by to check on her yesterday."

"I was sorry I missed you…her." Morgan tugged on the stethoscope that hung at his white collar. "I wanted to make sure Rosita's fever had broken."

"It did."

"Sister Coleman said you came to have your sutures removed."

"Yes. But I told her—"

"Dr. Hanson isn't available this afternoon. Do you have a problem with my removing your sutures, Miss Sinclair?"

Her face tight, Kat shook her head. "The sooner, the better, Doctor."

"Then follow me, and we'll make short work of it."

Her boot heels tapped against the pine floor as she followed him down the hallway to an exam room. Sunday night they'd made progress toward getting along—at least he'd thought so. Now the exam room felt too small to contain the two of them. Miss Sinclair's wide brown eyes told him she felt the same way.

"You can hang your cape on the peg." While she did that, he pulled an instrument tray from a drawer in the cupboard and set it on a countertop near the exam table. "Please have a seat up there, if you will." He extended his hand to her. Her grip certain, she climbed the wooden step at one end of the table then perched herself on its edge. They both glanced at their joined hands and let go.

Morgan unbuttoned his cuffs and rolled his sleeves one turn. "Miss Sinclair, you're wearing your collar so high today that I can't even see the hint of a bandage. Which side are your sutures on?"

Her smooth cheeks turned cardinal red, and she glared at him. "Despite your early impressions, Doctor, I am a modest woman."

He couldn't seem to keep his foot out of his mouth around this woman.

"I didn't mean to—"

"You never do." She reached behind her neck with the grace of a ballerina and began unbuttoning her collar. "The cut over which entirely too much fuss has been made is on my left side, at my shoulder."

Studying the one-inch laceration near the scapula, Morgan reached for the forceps ready on the tray. "A cut this deep and in this location will have two layers of sutures. First, deeper ones that hold the muscle and soft tissue together." Trying to learn from the past mistake of saying too much, he kept the catgut part to himself. "All we have to concern ourselves with is the silk sutures at the skin. You might feel a sting. Just relax your muscles for a minute."

Breathing deep, Kat Sinclair lowered her shoulders. Morgan grasped the tied end of the first suture with the forceps.

"Ouch. That hurt."

"I'm sorry. This should go quickly." Morgan cut each suture with a scalpel in succession and gave them each a quick tug. "All finished." He set the silk sutures and the scalpel on the tray while she buttoned her collar. "It's a bit red along the healing laceration, but the scar will mature in a few weeks to a white, faint line. I won't even notice it."

"Excuse me?"

Morgan's jaw and ears burned, and he was sure the beets in his mother's garden wouldn't be as flush as his face felt. "Uh…when I check it again. I'd say four weeks would be good." She might be amenable to seeing him again by then. "Unless you'd rather have Dr. Hanson do it."

A throat clearing silenced them both. Neither of them had noticed the reverend mother standing just inside the closed door, and again, Morgan had no idea how long she'd been there. He needed to put a bell on the woman.

"I knocked. But you were…distracted, Doctor."

Was it permissible to glower at a nun?

"We just finished, Sister." Morgan returned the forceps to the metal tray.

The reverend mother offered Kat a hand and helped her down

from the table. "It looks like Dr. Cutshaw worked out okay for you after all."

Kat flushed. "Yes ma'am, although not without some pain."

Morgan kept his agreement to himself, maintaining the hope that he'd gain the woman's forbearance during tomorrow's outing.

TWENTY-TWO

ell grabbed the stack of newspapers from the table in Patrick Maloney's cabin and assessed their progress. She, Kat, Hattie, and Rosita had ridden up the hill to the house in Hattie's wagon this morning. Kat went to work in a flurry, scrubbing the floor with such intensity that Nell was sure her sister hoped to erase the boards and reveal perfectly tiled flooring underneath. Consequently, there hadn't been much conversation in that first hour. None of them dared to get in her way.

Kat had boxed up Patrick's things and placed them on the porch before she headed off to the hospital and the grocery. Hattie had scoured the shelves and the one glass window, and now an afternoon sunbeam shot through the sparkling glass, lighting the table where four-year-old Rosita folded a flour sack dishtowel.

"You're a good helper, Rosita."

"Mama said so." A smile lit Rosita's honey brown face. The child had been with them for a week now, and they were still waiting for word from Mr. Hughes concerning her grandmother. More than once Nell had considered her and Judson taking Rosita in as their own. But first, she needed to meet the man who would be her husband.

By the time she'd read Judson Archer's fifth letter, she had loved him. His heart had spilled out on every page and reached out to her. She couldn't help but love that about him. He had been derailing Nell's thoughts for some four months now, and she could only hope he was on a path that brought him back to Cripple Creek soon.

She never would have imagined that Wednesday would roll around and she still wouldn't have heard from her beloved. She'd rehashed a hundred times what the paymaster said. Judson wasn't at all like Paddy Maloney. He said Judson was as upstanding as the working day is long, and out of town until next week. Well, this was next week. Only the middle of it, but patience had never been one of her virtues. Father was fond of saying she was compassionate and caring as long as she could be about it in a timely fashion. She couldn't let impatience get the best of her now.

She and Kat stepped off the train eight days ago. She'd waited this long to lay her eyes on her intended; she could certainly wait another two or three days, because soon after that she'd be Mrs. Judson Archer. Then she'd have a lifetime with him.

Please help me be patient, Lord.

Hattie walked through the front door, swinging the empty wash bucket. "I saw my wagon bumping its way up First Street. That means Kat's done in town." She set the pail on the plank floor beside the pot-bellied stove.

Nell reached into the crate of pretties Hattie had donated to Kat's cause and pulled out a lace curtain. "Let's get these hung before she gets back. I'll do the climbing, if you'll do the threading."

"The good Lord only saw fit to give me brothers that never really got along." Hattie set an empty straight-back chair in front of the window. "Watching the two of you work together with Rosita and on this place sure makes me miss my George. Why, he would've been right in the middle of this. Building you girls a bookcase or a chest of drawers. Something, you can be sure of that."

Nell laid the curtain over Hattie's broad shoulder, then hiked her skirt. She took her friend's hand and stepped up onto the chair. "I don't know what we would've done without your help."

"Oh, fiddle-faddle." Hattie shook out the curtain. "You two are quite capable—made of strong stock, you and your sister. The other two like that?"

"I suppose so, but Viv's a bit more impetuous, and Ida's, well, she's bossy. She says it is mandated by being the oldest." Nell shrugged. "I do miss them. And Father, of course. We told you they're coming to Cripple Creek, right?"

"Your father too?"

"Just Ida and Viv, but not until Ida finishes her secretarial course and Viv finishes school." As Nell wrestled the simple wooden rod from hooks on the wall, she thought *strong stock* wasn't a way she would describe herself. The term best suited Kat. Since they'd boarded the train to head west, Kat seemed to be the backbone for both of them. Nell had no doubt that her sister would make a good life for herself in Cripple Creek despite Patrick Maloney's betrayal. He was gone now, and whether Kat believed it or not, there were better men around here for her.

Dr. Morgan Cutshaw topped Nell's list. It was true the man had put his wrong foot forward—on multiple occasions—where Kat was concerned, but it didn't take a scholar to see that he'd noticed her.

Now, if only Kat would pay attention.

∿◎∿

Kat drove Hattie's wagon up the hill and turned onto Pikes Peak Avenue. Nell and Hattie had continued cleaning while she went to town, but she was anxious to get back to work. The cabin wasn't much, with only one room and a few crude furnishings, but she would soon run out of rent money, and she needed a place to live.

As she parked the wagon and secured Hattie's horse to the juniper tree, Kat looked down at Cripple Creek. The town teemed with life and reconstruction. She was getting used to seeing burros and mules in the streets and hearing train whistles and the thud of the stamp mills, and that gave her hope that she could adapt to life in this cabin as well. She pulled the new washboard and kettle off the wagon seat and climbed the wood steps to the porch. The crate of Patrick's belongings sat to one side of the door. She'd finish dealing with them another time.

As soon as Kat opened the door, her eyes went wide and her jaw dropped. The chrome trim on the potbellied stove gleamed. Fresh newspaper lined the shelves above the cupboard and a lace curtain hung over the window. The place fairly sparkled. She set the washboard and kettle on the clean cupboard, and looked over at Nell. "It can't be the same place. It looks so homey."

"Good." Nell beamed, and a sprig of blond hair fell loose. She pushed it back behind her ear.

"It still needs a few finishing touches—a few knickknacks and pictures." Hattie returned the chair to the table, "I daresay you girls have done an amazing job."

Kat twisted to look into the woman's warm eyes. "Not without your elbow grease and your lace curtain."

Hattie waved the comment away. "So, did you see Doc Hanson, dear?"

"He wasn't available." Instead she'd just spent half a dollar to have Dr. Cutshaw confound her and remove her stitches.

Do you have a problem with my removing your sutures, Miss Sinclair?

Of course she had a problem with it. The man was kind. He treated women with respect and had a fatherly way with children—and he was maddening to no end.

"Dr. Cutshaw removed your stitches then." Nell's eyebrow shot up.

Nodding, Kat hung the washboard on a hook near the door. "And?"

"And I think he did a competent job of removing my stitches." Kat didn't bother to keep the sarcasm from her voice.

"That, my dear, is saying the least about our good Dr. Cutshaw." Miss Hattie patted her fleshy cheek. "Why, if I were a younger woman... I loved my George, don't get me wrong, but he'd understand me falling for a man like Morgan Cutshaw."

Kat refused to engage in such a conversation, and if Nell and

Hattie chose to play matchmaker, she wanted no part in it. Instead, she walked to the window and looked out at the hills.

She didn't need a husband. That was Nell's dream.

She was just recovering from the debacle with Patrick. Pursuing the "good doctor" wasn't something she cared to do.

In fact, it was absurd.

TWENTY-THREE

*Y*ou cheat!"

Lewis P. Whibley watched as the man across the table from him pulled a butcher knife out of his belt and slammed his fist into the faro table. Two sets of burly arms grabbed Lewis from behind and dragged him sideways through the Pullman coach. He heard the door open and then the sound of the wheels squealing against the rails. The room darkened as the train entered a tunnel, then as soon as it emerged, his captors hoisted him onto the landing and threw him out onto the gravel and dirt along the rail bed.

Tumbling, Lewis grabbed for whatever he could to slow his momentum. Pine limbs and scrub oak seemed eager to help punish him for his misdeeds in the rail car. Watching the train disappear into the distance, he could see first his valise, then his beloved faro table, being thrown to the elements.

Lewis quickly took an inventory of his body. There was considerable stinging and aching everywhere, but no serious bleeding, and nothing seemed broken. He pushed himself to his feet and stumbled over rocks for several hundred yards to recover his belongings. Only then did he look around to orient himself. There appeared to be a roadway a short distance down the hill, but nothing to indicate civilization anywhere close. It was late evening, and he knew he would need to find shelter soon. The train tunnel appeared to be his best hope for protection against weather and the natural inhabitants of these forests. There wouldn't be another train until morning, he hoped.

Darkness came quickly, with barely a sliver of a moon. Lewis shivered in the cold and drafty tunnel, even after donning every piece of clothing he had packed in the valise. The cold turned out to be merely an irritation compared to the recognizable *who-whooing* of owls and the unrecognizable growls coming from somewhere beyond the other end of the tunnel. At least, he told himself they were coming from beyond the tunnel.

Lewis looked up past the crescent moon. "If You're really up there, I could use a little help," he mumbled. "I believed in You when I was a boy, but got too busy to pay You much mind and kinda figured You don't care for drifters and gamblers. Well, anyway, if You are up there, and You have a mind to, I'd appreciate anything You can do. Amen, I guess."

Morning took way too long to arrive, but as soon as it did, Lewis shed his extra clothing and walked to the road he'd seen the night before. For several hours he sat on a rock and waited for someone to pass by. He had plenty of time to relive the events on the train. He'd have to be more careful to choose players who couldn't spot a well-practiced bluff. All in all, it was not the worst night of his career. At least this time he didn't have to start from scratch and buy a new table.

Lewis craned his neck and looked up the road, exhaustion weigh-

ing him down. He'd barely slept, afraid of being eaten alive by whatever owned that growl. Now, with no traffic on the road, he decided
that if he was to sleep in a bed tonight, he would have to start walking toward town. He set out. Within an hour, he heard the sounds
of a wagon behind him and set his table and bag on the ground. As it
approached, he could hear the man driving it ask him if he needed a
ride.

"Yes, yes! Thank you! I'm headed to Cripple Creek."

"Well, me and the missus are goin' to Victor, but we could give
you a ride as far as the Y in the road." The farmer had fewer teeth than
a one-year-old. "You plan on jumping off there, ya hear?"

Nodding, Lewis grabbed his valise and table.

The man's wife stared at the faro table. "Sir, we're not in favor of
gambling, and we don't regularly assist those that prey upon poor, mis-
guided souls. But seeing how the mister already promised, we'll give
you a ride."

Lewis found it hard to say whose mustache was thicker—the mister's or his wife's. "Much obliged, ma'am."

"At the back of the wagon."

"Ma'am, I—"

"Now or never, Slick."

Lewis fairly ran to the back of the wagon and jumped on as the
driver snapped the reins. It was only then that he saw the contents of
the wagon. Chickens. Hundreds of chickens in crates, covered by a
canvas tarp. The stench made his eyes water. Determined to be thankful for the ride, he leaned against the cages to get some rest. He was immediately set upon by the chickens, who pecked him through the
mesh.

Lewis jumped away. He nursed a few new wounds as he lay across the tailgate and, resting his head on his valise, soon closed his eyes. When the wagon finally stopped, his eyelids popped open and he grabbed his bag, ready to claim his cabin.

Lewis dropped to the ground, confused at the depot sign facing him. Why didn't the chicken folks wake him at the crossroads?

The big, black letters seemed to mock him. VICTOR. How could he have slept all that way? He cursed, dusted himself off, and headed to the first saloon he saw. The men on the train had taken what was on the table, but he had a few hidden dollars in his vest pocket. If he could set up for one night, maybe he could afford a bed after his take and get to Cripple Creek tomorrow. That's when his luck would change.

Tomorrow.

TWENTY-FOUR

❧

*M*organ parked the horse and carriage he'd rented from Jesse's Livery in front of the boardinghouse and tugged the pocket watch out of his vest: 3:50 p.m. He was ten minutes early, but he couldn't imagine how it had happened. Not after all the indecision. Women were supposed to be the ones concerned with fashion, fussing over their outfits like hummingbirds at a spring flower. Opal had done her share of it every time they went out. But he didn't understand his own fretting as this was simply a courtesy outing. He'd been rude to Miss Sinclair and he was trying to make it up to her. That was all. Drawing a deep breath of cool air, Morgan stepped out of the carriage and tied Jesse's black mare to the rail at the bottom of the steps.

As usual, music met him at the door. He'd grown accustomed to the greeting here and rather enjoyed it. The phonograph played tonight, accompanied by rhythmic footsteps. He removed his hat and knocked, wrestling with his errant thoughts, the ones that wondered what kind of music would come from Kat Sinclair's home.

Hattie opened the door, her cheeks pink. "You're here!" The words puffed out on shallow breaths. She must have been doing a dance more vigorous than a waltz. "Where did the time go?" She turned on her heel and motioned for him to follow her into the parlor. A frilled collar disguised her double chin, and she wore fine gloves and boots that looked freshly polished. He began to worry that the ladies expected an evening of fine dining.

Once Hattie quieted the phonograph, she looked him over, from the styling wax in his hair to his polished shoes. "If you don't look handsome, Doctor. I'm a widow wishing she were some years younger...maybe with auburn hair?"

Morgan felt the flush that tipped his ears. He did like reddish-brown hair, but did this woman have to be so blunt?

Hattie bent toward him and raised a crooked finger to her lips. "It'll be our little secret." She winked and led him to the sofa.

She settled at one end then he sat at the other. Both of them had a view of the staircase through the open parlor door. "You look lovely this evening, Mrs. Adams."

A blush pinked Hattie's fleshy cheeks. "Why, thank you, kind sir. But please, call me Miss Hattie."

"I've gone and scheduled this treat during mealtime, so I was wondering if it would be appropriate if I provided supper here at the boardinghouse afterwards." The doctor hoped she would agree, since he had already ordered the meal from the best restaurant still standing.

"Splendid! My George and I always enjoyed an evening at home with friends." Hattie's attention seemed to wander toward the hallway, and Morgan found himself glancing that way too. Quiet wasn't something he was accustomed to here, and the ticking of the mantel clock took over the room.

"Do you think it might snow again before spring?" he asked to break the silence.

She looked at him, tears pooling her silver blue eyes, and he wondered what he'd said wrong. "Well, it's been known to happen, and not too many years ago." She tapped her chin, her brows raised. "Maybe '93, can't remember exactly, but it was early May when we had us a whiteout that lasted three days. Flattened some tents, and people had to step out their high windows."

Footsteps on the wood staircase drew their attention to the doorway, and Morgan rose from the sofa. Nell Sinclair was the first of the three to make an entrance, holding Rosita's hand. Kat Sinclair followed them in, her skirts swishing in a swirl of forest green.

"Ladies, you look lovely." The compliment was true for them all, but it was Miss Kat who garnered his attention.

"Thank you, Dr. Cutshaw," Miss Sinclair said. "You look very well turned out yourself."

"Thank you. Shall we go, then?" Morgan wanted to get out the door before he said something characteristically rash. He set his derby on his head, hoping it would help hold in what good sense he had left.

Kat rode directly behind Dr. Morgan Cutshaw in the fancy rented carriage. Nell was at her side, and Hattie sat up front with him, Rosita, and HopHop. He guided the shiny black horse down Fourth Street to Bennett Avenue, and they rounded the corner past the depot, then climbed a steep hill. She tried to guess where he was taking them, but as far as Kat knew, even Hattie hadn't been able to wheedle tonight's itinerary out of the doctor.

It didn't really matter to her where they went. They'd all been working so hard on the cabin that it just felt good to be out for a ride that didn't involve a mine or housework.

Late afternoon sun gave Dr. Cutshaw's brown hair the sheen of the bark on a summer maple tree. She'd expect broad shoulders and a tanned neck on a miner or a cowboy, not a doctor, but then this city doctor had a flair for contradicting her expectations. His obvious enjoyment of the surrounding landscape also offered her occasion to view his profile. He had a strong chin, and a dimple on the right side of his face just above the shadow on his jaw.

"Did you always want to help people, Dr. Cutshaw?"

His shoulders sagged, and Kat watched him draw in a deep breath before he turned to speak.

"It was actually my father's choice. He's a surgeon, and on the board of Harvard Medical School. He pushed me toward medicine." Pausing, he faced the road ahead. "But, at the time, I suppose I needed a push."

Kat found it hard to believe that Dr. Cutshaw would need encouragement. He appeared so confident and focused.

"But you're so good at doctoring. It's hard to believe it wasn't your first choice." Nell gave Kat a raised eyebrow.

"That's kind of you to say, but as a boy I dreamed of seeing crowds of people come to hear me play the piano."

"I would have come." Hattie grinned at him, her wrinkles thinning. "I love your piano playing."

Kat smiled. She couldn't think of anything her landlady didn't love about the good doctor.

He looked at Hattie, his face reddening. The dimple in his cheek deepened with his boyish grin. "Sounds rather self-serving now."

"Poppycock! Wanting to spread joy through music is not self-indulgent. Music feeds the soul, don't you know." Hattie waved her gloved hand at him as if he were a musician and she were his conductor. "And we all have hungry souls, Doctor."

Kat sighed, wondering if her writing would ever be good enough to feed hungry souls. "And how do you feel about medicine now?"

"While I was in Boston, doctoring felt like an exercise that I did because it was good for me and for my patients."

"It's different for you here?" Even as Kat asked the question, she realized everything was different here. Terrain. Proprieties. There was more energy here than in the East. A sort of urgency to make the most of one's life. But she hadn't thought of the differences in terms of medicine and doctoring.

"There, I mostly treated patients with pneumonia, tuberculosis, and rheumatism." He'd glanced at Hattie's knotted fingers when he said it. "And I did so in my father's shadow. Here in Cripple Creek, I've treated burn victims and patched two men who each lost a leg."

"Don't forget the baby," Kat said. "You delivered at least one disinclined newborn without the assistance of a highly qualified midwife."

He chuckled, and Kat enjoyed its resonance. He pulled up on the reins, slowing the horse to a lazy *clip-clop*. "Before I came here, I'd never seen such a majestic panorama." He swept a welcoming hand toward the rolling hills and snowcapped mountains that enveloped them. "Since you two are new in town"—he gestured back at Nell and Kat—"I thought you might enjoy a little drive up to Tenderfoot Hill."

Clapping, Hattie looked at the sisters over her shoulder. "You girls are truly in for a treat. That was my George's favorite place."

"With the fire and all, Doctor, how have you already had the time to orient yourself?" Kat gazed at the sweeping vistas, wishing she'd thought to bring her journal.

"I drove my buggy here from Divide through Ute Pass." He pointed at the peak of the hill in front of them. "That, and a runaway wheel, gave me occasion to meet an old miner named Boney Hughes."

"You know Mr. Hughes?" Nell glanced at Kat.

"You know Boney?" Dr. Cutshaw said it over his shoulder.

"I met Mr. Hughes on my walk last Friday."

"Oh, that walk." The doctor grinned, and Kat had to laugh.

"Boney is the one who told me where I could find Miss Sunny." Boney was an unlikely friend at first sight, but then if her experience here was teaching her anything, it was that first sights couldn't always be trusted.

At the top of the incline, he pulled the carriage off the road into a wide area and stopped. "This is Tenderfoot Hill. Those snowy peaks are the Sangre de Cristo Mountains." He pointed off to the southwest.

"I thought we could step out for a better view."

Kat scooted forward on the seat. "We'd like that."

"You girls go ahead. Rosita's getting a little sleepy. I'll stay in the wagon with her." Hattie opened her arms to the little girl, who climbed onto her lap.

"I not sleepy." Rosita widened her eyes and bounced the bunny on her knees.

Kat nodded, and the doctor helped her out first, and then Nell. At this high elevation, a layer of snow blanketed the hilltop, and as soon as she moved away from the carriage, a hearty breeze tipped her hat and wagged the folds of her skirt. She held them down and followed the doctor to a level lookout.

"That mountain range to the west is the Rockies. Behind us is Pikes Peak—the easternmost fourteen-thousand-foot peak in the United States."

A display of light and shadow danced between the snowy tops and the mountain's dark base. "This is so incredible—sunbeams waltzing with the snow-clad mountaintops."

Morgan wasn't looking at the mountains anymore, but at her.

"Kat's a writer." Nell, standing behind them, said it with a confidence Kat didn't possess.

Kat liked to write. Had to, in fact, but was that enough to qualify her as a real writer?

"That explains your graceful way with words." Dr. Cutshaw didn't look startled by the fact, or disturbed that a woman would consider such a frivolity. "What do you write?"

"Mostly my journal, although I did write a couple of short pieces for the *Portland Press Herald* back home."

"You could do that out here. Write for newspapers, magazines. You may even have a book or two in you." His smile deepened the dimple.

Writing had been her dream, but could it be her livelihood? Without any possibility of marriage before her, she'd have to think on that.

He glanced back at the wagon. "Did you know Hattie before moving out here? Is that why you came to Cripple Creek?"

Kat looked toward the hills. "We didn't know anyone in town, except through letters."

"I came to marry Judson Archer," Nell volunteered, her voice dreamy. "We've been corresponding for several months. He's due to arrive back in town any day now."

"Then congratulations are in order." Dr. Cutshaw gazed at Kat, an eyebrow raised.

"My fiancé died."

His eyes widened in a stunned, awkward silence. "My condolences."

"I'm quite fine, Doctor," she said, turning away from the view of the mountains. "And thank you for the ride. It was lovely."

Nodding, he angled toward the carriage. "Perhaps we should head back into town. I've ordered a supper to take back to Hattie's."

Once they were all seated in the carriage, the doctor guided the horse back down the hill. He wove through the crowded streets and parked in front of the Third Street Café, then stepped out. "I'll only be a moment, ladies." He tipped his hat.

Kat watched as he took long, easy strides to the door. When he'd extended the invitation, she'd been anything but excited about the evening, but it had indeed turned out to be more enjoyable than she had expected. Dr. Morgan Cutshaw was proving that you could turn a first impression around.

He'd just closed the door behind him when a family walked up the boardwalk toward them. Kat didn't recognize the parents or the boy, but she remembered the young woman from Hattie's parlor. Darla Taggart.

The well-dressed woman saw them and smiled, and veered away from her family toward the carriage. "Good evening, Miss Hattie." She tilted her head at Nell. "Good evening. Nell, is it?"

"Yes, hello, Miss Taggart."

"Darla. Please call me Darla." She looked at Kat, a blank look on her face.

"It's Kat. Good evening." She dipped her chin. "Darla."

She glanced at Rosita asleep on Hattie's lap and then back at Kat. "Is this your daughter, Kat?"

"No. She lost her mother in the fire. We're caring for her until we can find her grandmother."

"How kind of you. Are you coming in for supper?" Darla glanced at the door where her family waited for her. When the door whooshed open, they all watched the doctor walk out carrying a shallow wooden box covered with a towel.

"Dr. Cutshaw?" Darla looked back at the sisters, her eyebrow raised and her jaw set.

Morgan greeted Darla's family and then walked to the carriage. "Good evening, Miss Taggart."

She stared at the box in his arms. "Seems it's the perfect evening for dining out."

"Yes. Our supper. I…we're having our supper at Miss Hattie's."

"What wonderful luck that I should see you here." Darla clasped her hands and stretched her arms down in front of her ruffled dress. "I wanted to thank you again for such a lovely evening last night."

Kat's pulse began to race. He'd been out with her last evening? Was taking women out for evening carriage rides a habit with this man?

"Uh, yes. It was." After he set the box on the floor in the back of the carriage, he stopped beside Kat and glanced back at the short, balding man by the door. "Miss Taggart and her father, the reverend, had a clinic for the wounded after prayer meeting last night."

"Oh, well. That explains it." Hattie shifted Rosita in her arms and shot Kat a glance. "Darla, dear, you'll have to excuse us, or supper will surely get cold."

"Yes, of course. I won't keep you. Doctor." She curtsied, a huge smile crossing her face. "Have a nice evening." Her enthusiasm faded as she addressed Hattie and the sisters. "And you, as well." Her gaze lingered on Kat a little longer than necessary, and she smiled.

"Good to see you again too," Kat said. It wasn't a lie, because Kat was glad for this meeting. It reminded her that she was better off without a man's attentions, especially since Miss Darla Taggart had designs on this particular man.

Morgan climbed up into the carriage and flicked the reins, driving up Bennett Avenue as the sun dipped to the west. They'd just crossed Bennett when a tall, lanky man spotted them and stepped into the road directly in their path, waving his hat.

The very sight of the familiar face caused Kat's stomach to churn.

Dr. Cutshaw pulled back on the reins. "Evening, Sheriff."

"Pardon me, Doctor. May I have a word with you?"

Dr. Cutshaw jumped down, and the sheriff gestured for him to step away from the carriage.

The sheriff kept his voice low, and Kat strained to hear his words. "Sister Coleman's wantin' you over at the hospital. A man's been robbed and beaten." The sheriff glanced at Nell, a shadow crossing his face, and Kat sucked in her breath.

A buggy passed by, and Kat couldn't hear the next part of the conversation, but after it passed, she leaned forward, trying to hear. She made out the word *Judson*. Nell must have heard too, because the color drained from her face.

"It's my Judson, isn't it?" Nell whispered. "Something horrible has happened to Judson."

TWENTY-FIVE

*A*t the hospital, Nell didn't wait for Morgan to help her out of the carriage. She scarcely waited for the carriage to roll to a stop before she sprang from it and rushed to the door. The sisters had insisted on coming to the hospital, even though Dr. Cutshaw had tried to get them to stay home when he dropped off Hattie and Rosita. As soon as they stepped into the entry hall, she felt Kat's hand capture hers. Nell felt a surge of strength steady her knees, but she still couldn't stop the tears that streamed down her cheeks. They'd read stories about the robberies in the West—beatings too—and now the man she loved had been attacked.

"I'm sure he'll be fine, Nell," Kat said.

Morgan rushed past them. "I'll find Judson. Wait here."

She was supposed to marry the man…was going to marry him, but she hadn't even heard his voice. "Please, God, let Judson be all right." Nell whispered the words, then silently recited, *God hath not given us the spirit of fear.*

Kat guided her to a chair. "Morgan has gone to see about him, and he'll send someone to get us." Kat's voice sounded as shaky as Nell's knees felt. "In the meantime, let's sit down."

Nell swiped at her wet cheeks. "He can't see me like this."

"No. You're as white as new dishtowels."

Nell pinched her cheeks, trying to add a little color to them. At least she had dressed well for the evening. "I'm sorry."

Kat sighed. "What do you have to be sorry about?"

"Your evening was ruined."

"It was our evening out, not mine, and it wasn't ruined. The carriage ride was wonderful."

Nell had seen how much Kat was enjoying the ride and Dr. Cutshaw's attention. She reached for Kat's hand. "You're right, it was, but—"

"And next time Judson will be with us, and the evening will be perfect." Kat looked like she wanted to believe what she said. Nell did too.

"But a robbery is violent. He could be badly—" Before Nell could finish, Sister Coleman stepped out of a door at the end of the hallway and walked toward them, her headpiece flopping forward with each step. Nell and Kat both stood and rushed to meet her.

"Have you seen Judson Archer, my intended? Is he…?"

"Dr. Cutshaw is tending to his needs."

There was something strange in the sister's demeanor. She didn't look Nell in the eye like she had last week. Was it pity she saw there?

"What are his needs, Sister?" Kat stood behind Nell. "The sheriff said Judson was robbed. Can you tell us what happened?"

"Let's sit down, shall we?" The white-haired woman offered a thin smile as they all perched on the few chairs that lined the hall.

"I need to see Judson," Nell said, her voice insistent.

"As I understood it, Mr. Archer was on his way back to Cripple Creek," the nun said calmly, "when two men spooked his horse and robbed him."

"But he was strong enough to make it to the hospital." Kat squeezed Nell's hand, infusing more strength.

Kat was right, Nell decided. Judson couldn't be too bad off if he'd made it to town.

"Yes, well, a miner brought him in on the back of his mule."

"He didn't ride his own horse?" Nell heard her own voice climbing the suffocating wall of fear.

Sister Coleman looked up at the stamped tin ceiling. Judson had to be worse off than they were saying for the sister to pause for prayer in the middle of their conversation.

For God hath not given us the spirit of fear.

Nell pinched the skin on her wrist, bringing some solidity back to her thoughts. Judson needed her. She would take care of him, and he would recover. She'd be strong and sensible like Kat.

"We are going to be married. I need to see him. He needs to know I'm here."

"Not yet, dear." Sister Coleman patted her hand. "Mr. Archer knows you're here. Dr. Cutshaw told him."

"Good." Nell rose from the chair. "I'm ready to see him now."

Kat and the sister both stood, and the nun laid her hand on Nell's shoulder, her eyes dark. "I'm sorry, dear, but he doesn't want to see you now."

Nell's heart pounded. She looked to Kat for support, but Kat only stared at her in the same disbelief. "That can't be true! He loves me. I have his letters. Kat, tell her!"

"Dr. Cutshaw is seeing to Mr. Archer's wounds." The sister looked over at Kat. "He suggested you take Nell back to the boardinghouse."

"You must have misunderstood. I can't leave Judson!"

Kat rested her hand at Nell's back. "He needs to rest too. Dr. Cutshaw will take good care of him. You know he will."

"But I—"

"We can come back in the morning when he's feeling better." Kat's eyes radiated compassion and she smiled encouragement—the face of a loving older sister, caring for one of her own.

Nell swept her hair from her face and looked at the nun. "I have to know that he's going to be all right. How badly is he hurt?"

Sister Coleman placed her hands on Nell's shoulders and looked into her eyes, her own full of compassion. "He's going to be fine, dear. He only needs to be tended to, and then a good rest."

It made sense that Judson didn't want her to see him banged up and bruised, but how would she wait another twelve hours to see for herself that he would be all right? "You'll send someone for me if he changes his mind, or gets any worse?" Her voice cracked on the last word.

"We will. You need your rest, and like your sister said, Dr. Cutshaw will take good care of him."

"Tell him I'll be here early." Nell willed her chin to stop quivering. "Tell him I love him."

"I will, dear. This will all work out, you'll see."

She nodded. Judson loved her, and he wasn't like Kat's Patrick Maloney. He wasn't going to leave her alone.

Moments later, Nell and Kat walked hand in hand down the steps of the hospital. They'd only walked a few yards when Nell spotted a mule and a man rounding the corner. Sister Coleman had said a miner brought Judson in on his mule. She'd seen a lot of old men with mules around town, but only one as lean and woolly as Boney Hughes.

"Mr. Hughes!" Nell waved.

The bearded man led his mule over and peered at her and Kat. "Well, if it isn't the Miss Sinclairs! Whatever are you little ladies doing out at this hour?"

"Was it you, Mr. Boney, who brought in the man who was robbed?"

His whiskered face lengthened, and he removed his hat. "I did, but what does—"

"Judson Archer is my intended."

"Sakes alive. I done forgot you'd said somethin' about that at the livery." He spit, and Nell turned away. "Sorry, ma'am. Some habits are hard to break even in the presence of refined women."

"Was he badly beaten?"

"Not too bad as beatin's go."

"Was he bleeding?" Just the thought of blood turned her stomach, but she had to know.

"I wouldn't really know, ma'am."

"How did you find him?"

With a dirty hand, Boney covered his face to hide what looked to Nell like a smirk. What was wrong with him? The man had helped Kat find the cabin. He adored Rosita. So why would he laugh at her? At Judson? He couldn't. Her anxiety had to be getting to her. She'd nearly convinced herself of it when Boney turned away and bent in the middle, laughing.

Nell crossed her arms, her head beginning to throb. "You're laughing? How can you laugh when Judson is lying in a hospital bed, beaten?"

"Sorry, ma'am, but I can't help myself." He could hardly get the words out around a snort. "I really am sorry. Truly."

"You're sorry about Judson, or you're sorry for laughing in my face?"

"Both." He'd practically coughed the word out from behind his hand.

"Then you best tell me what you find so funny about this. I could use a good laugh after being told that my intended was robbed and beaten, and doesn't want to see me."

"I would, ma'am, but it's just too personal." He waved his hat like a fan, laughing harder.

A man getting beat up and robbed was not a laughing matter. Something else was going on here. She'd find out what it was, and she'd do it right now.

Nell spun toward the hospital door. Kat grabbed for her arm.

"Nell, don't—"

Nell looked back at Kat. "You can stay or go, but you can't stop me."

"I wouldn't go in there if I was you." Mr. Hughes stepped in front of her.

"Well, you're not me." Nell stomped out around him and off toward the building. Her sister would either follow her in or not. It didn't matter. Judson was her man, and no one could stop her from seeing him tonight. She had waited long enough.

Nell burst through the front door, then stormed down the hallway. Judson needed her, and they couldn't keep her from him. When she heard a man's yelps coming from a nearby room, she twisted the knob and flung the door open.

Judson lay on the table on his stomach, facing her. She froze mid-step and closed her eyes. But she had already seen Morgan sitting on a stool behind his patient, holding a tool of some sort over Judson's red, bare backside.

"You? Get out." Judson's cry echoed off the walls. "I don't want you—"

"I'm…I'm sorry," she stammered. She would have fled if her feet hadn't grown roots. She felt arms snake around her waist from the back and pull her out of the room. Silently, Kat led her back down the hallway and out the door.

"Oh, my gracious, Kat! Did you see? It was Judson. I wanted to look away, and he told me to go away—but oh, my gracious. I just couldn't stop staring. His backside—oh!" She grew solemn and whispered, "I think it might have been…cactus."

Kat's eyes widened, and she put her hand to her cheek. "Well, Boney did say it was personal."

Nell couldn't hold it in any longer. She started to giggle, but as soon as Kat joined her, they both were laughing so hard, tears dripped off their chins.

Poor Judson.

TWENTY-SIX

With Miss Sinclair out of the room, Morgan continued the task of removing the cactus spines from Judson Archer's derrière. He couldn't imagine being any more thankful that he wasn't this unfortunate fellow. The pain of the cactus ordeal would be torture enough without the horrified look on his intended's face. She never should have seen him in this delicate condition. But she had, and that probably explained his patient's sudden silence. Mr. Archer hadn't uttered as much as a groan since Nell Sinclair's intrusion and his subsequent outburst.

Morgan certainly couldn't fault the man for being upset with her. The extrication, as uncomfortable as it had to be, would appear anemic in comparison to the stab of humiliation. Morgan wouldn't want Kat to see him like this.

Kat.

He'd thought of Kat first. Not Opal. And surprisingly, he didn't feel the pangs of guilt over it he would have a week ago.

Morgan continued to extract inch-long spears from Mr. Archer and drop them into a tin bowl.

Morgan had much to be thankful for, especially here in this post-fire community. He had a place to live, even if it was just a basement for now. His doctoring job in this gold mining district was an exciting and unpredictable one, to say the least. In addition, he had the memory of standing atop Tenderfoot Hill beside Miss Kat Sinclair. He had witnessed the awe on her face—an intoxicating mix of joy and wonder.

"Wasn't she beautiful?"

Yes. Morgan knew, of course, that Mr. Archer wasn't talking about Kat. He was glad to see that the man had feelings for his intended beyond mortification.

This is so incredible. Sunbeams waltzing with snow-clad mountaintops. Kat had said it from the top of Tenderfoot Hill. Yes, she was easy to look at, but there was more. Her fiancé had died. She knew what it was like to lose someone, and yet she was strong and supportive of Nell and Rosita. Best of all, she didn't apologize for her knowing her mind.

"Those eyes." Judson Archer sounded like he'd drifted off course too.

"Mr. Archer, I'd say we both learned a valuable lesson tonight. You don't say no to a Sinclair sister and get away with it." Morgan stilled his hand while he laughed, and his patient joined him.

"Call me Judson. Sounds like you know the Sinclair sisters. Was that Nell's sister who grabbed her?"

"Yes, that was Miss Kat Sinclair." Morgan paused, the forceps midair. "I met her first, here at the hospital, in a similarly awkward situation."

Judson glanced at his backside. "You can top this?"

Morgan shook his head. "No, not this, I can't."

"Nell wrote me about her—all three of her sisters—in her letters. She told me Kat was the writer, but it was Nell's words that got to me. Did they tell you their father lost his job in Maine and moved to Paris without them?"

"No" Morgan pulled out another spine and laid it on the table. "Only that you are Nell's intended and that Kat's fiancé had died."

"That's terrible. I hadn't heard about Kat. The poor girl. In her last letter Nell said one of her sisters had also received a promise of marriage and was coming out with her on the train, but they weren't due to arrive until June."

Morgan put the forceps around another spine, and Judson tensed.

"The sheriff said you were robbed," Morgan said to distract him.

"Two cowboys showed up out of nowhere," Judson said. "Spooked my horse, then took my coat. I'd gone home to Manitou Springs to tend to my mother in her last days. I'd sold her house and was bringing my inheritance back to fix up my place here with electricity and a claw-foot tub before the wedding." He let out a breath as Morgan pulled a spine free. "Should have trusted the bank. Now I don't have any of it. And who knows where my horse is. Good thing Boney Hughes came along when he did."

That old miner again. He'd come to Morgan's rescue too, and now Morgan couldn't help but wonder if there was more to the codger.

Morgan adjusted the monocle that helped him spot the spines. "Where'd you find this nasty stuff, anyway? I thought cactus was Arizona Territory's reputation."

"You won't find any up here in the higher elevations, but I was headed home from down in the flatlands. And as you can see, my horse didn't have any trouble finding plenty of them before bucking me off." Judson scrubbed his face with his hands. "The first time I see Nell, and I yell at her. My first spoken words to her, and I told her to get away from me."

"You heard what Sister Coleman said after she talked to Nell. Nell wanted you to know that she loved you."

Judson groaned. "That was before she saw me like this. We were supposed to marry soon."

"Don't worry. Once you two recover from this, I'm sure you'll marry." And Morgan knew just the place for it. if they didn't mind an outdoor wedding.

❧

When Kat opened the boardinghouse door, Nell shrugged out of her mantle. Kat took it from her and hung their wraps and bonnets on brass hooks near Hattie's front door. Her sister hadn't uttered a sound since their outburst outside the hospital.

Kat couldn't remember when a laugh felt so real, but it had been at Mr. Archer's expense and Nell was probably feeling guilty for it, as well as smarting from her intrusion into his hospital room.

"Let's go to the kitchen. Some chamomile tea will do us both some good." Kat took Nell's hand and led her down the hallway.

"Tea won't fix this, Kat."

Kat couldn't argue. "No, but it can't hurt."

"Whatever possessed me to do that?"

"The man was robbed and you were worried about him. No one would tell you anything. I understand completely."

Nell sank into a chair at the kitchen table. "Yes, but you're not the one who rushed headlong into the room. Judson will never forgive me."

"He will. I just know he will." He had to. Kat crossed the room to the cupboard and pulled the teapot off the shelf. At the stove she twisted the spigot on the hot water tank and filled the pot. Then she measured tea into the steaming pot.

Hattie swept into the kitchen wearing her white nightdress and a purple and orange sweater. "I thought I heard you down here. I've been up in my room reading the Psalms for our Mr. Archer, practically beside myself waiting to hear about him."

"He's never going to speak to me again." Nell buried her face in her hands.

Scooting a chair beside Nell, Hattie looked over at Kat with questions pinching her brow. "Things can't be as bad as all that."

Kat nodded, setting out teacups while the tea steeped.

Hattie rubbed Nell's back. "How about you girls tell me what happened, and we'll figure all this out."

"I don't see how we can." Nell's face was pressed in her hands so her words were muffled. "The first time I hear his voice and his only words to me were 'Get out. I don't want you!' "

"That's men for you, dear. My George was a terrible patient."

"But it's not Judson's fault. He didn't want to see me, and I saw him. So much of him." She began sobbing.

Kat knew she couldn't giggle again. Not when Nell was so worked up. She focused on explaining what she knew to Hattie while she poured tea into their cups. "Mr. Archer's horse bucked him off, and he...uh, we're pretty sure he landed in cactus." She sat down beside her sister and patted her arm.

Hattie fanned herself with her hand. "Oh, that's dreadful."

"Yes." Kat nodded. "Backside first."

"Oh my. You're telling me Mr. Archer has cactus in his…" Hattie's face turned all shades of red, and she fanned faster. Kat watched her lips twitch against a smile. "And, Nell, you said you saw him?"

"I didn't know."

"Of course you didn't. How did you say you ended up…uh, see-ing him?"

Nell blew her nose and sniffled. "Judson refused to see me. Boney Hughes was laughing, and I—"

"Mr. Hughes was there?" Hattie's lips twitched again.

"Not in the room." Kat lifted her cup to her lips. "He's the one who found Judson."

"I just couldn't stand not to see him, so I opened the door."

"I walked up behind her and pulled her out, my eyes closed," Kat added.

"What a wild evening." Hattie jumped up from the table, bump-ing it and rocking the teacups in their saucers. "I know just what we need to do to make things better."

"You do?" Nell peered up at Hattie, her face blotchy.

"Absolutely." Hattie dug in her pantry and pulled out a sack of flour. "We need to bake cookies. It always worked for me and George."

Nodding, Nell stood and wiped her face.

Kat wasn't sure she agreed that baking cookies could fix such a humiliating incident, but she pulled a mixing bowl off the shelf any-way. It was better than any idea she had.

TWENTY-SEVEN

❧

Kat sat on the bed with Rosita and plaited the little girl's midnight black hair. They'd all gotten a slow start to their morning, so they hadn't tended to her hair before breakfast. Now the two of them were alone in the bedroom. Nell was downstairs fussing in the kitchen, and Hattie was in town for her meeting of the Women for the Betterment of Cripple Creek. Certainly, Nell's situation with Mr. Archer occupied Kat's mind, but it was competing heavily with thoughts concerning the little girl's future. Three days had passed since Boney wired the sheriff in Santa Fe about Rosita's grandmother, and Kat couldn't help but wonder if the woman was even alive.

Kat was ten when her own mother died of pneumonia. She'd been much older than Rosita, but still she couldn't imagine what she'd have done if her father and her sisters hadn't been there with her. If this poor child had any family of her own, Kat had to find them. Neither Kat nor Nell could offer her what blood family could, and neither could the Sisters of Mercy.

She spoke a quiet prayer and then sat down on the bed beside Rosita. "Did you like the carriage ride last night?"

Rosita nodded. She wasn't one to spend many words. In fact, the only times Kat had seen any real emotion from the girl were when she'd first spotted the child near the fire looking for her mama, and when Rosita heard Boney Hughes's voice in the livery.

"What color ribbon do you want in your hair today?"

The little girl peered into the box on the bed beside her and pulled out an orange striped ribbon and a yellow gingham one. Not the colors Kat would've chosen to go with the red muslin dress Hattie had made for the child, but she was working on letting others make their own choices—big ones and small ones.

After Kat tied off the first braid, she picked up the hand mirror her mother had given her and gave it to Rosita. While Rosita angled it left and right and up and down, Kat tied the yellow ribbon onto the tip of the second braid. As she did, she saw the little girl's eyes in the hand mirror. Rosita had angled it and was studying Kat.

"You don't look like Mama."

"No, I'm sure I don't. What did your mama look like?"

"Like a angel. That's what one called her."

One? Was Rosita referring to one of her mother's…patrons? Kat felt her cheeks flush. This little girl had seen and heard too much. Kat's heart ached for her, and for the child's mama. She thought about the pain and need that must have driven her to that life. The lengths she had gone to provide for her girl. With Rosita sitting beside her, it wasn't hard for Kat to imagine what the woman looked like. "Did your mama have shiny black hair?"

Another nod. "With flowers."

"I'm sure you miss her. I miss my mother too."

"She's with the angels."

"Yes. So is my mother." But at least she had a father who loved her, and within a year or so, she and Nell would be reunited with Ida and Vivian. Kat took the mirror from Rosita, and the little girl headed straight for the chest of drawers and pointed to the bottle of lilac perfume.

"Please."

"A little bit." While she rubbed a scant drop on Rosita's neck, Kat heard the front door slam.

"Yoo-hoo. Girls, are you here?" Hattie was home from her meeting and business in town. "I'm home." The announcement came from the foot of the stairs.

"In here, Hattie." The monotone statement came from Nell in the kitchen.

Kat hurried to the landing at the top of the stairs. "Rosita and I are up here." She looked down at Hattie, who balanced boxes and sacks in her arms.

The woman glanced up at her, setting her hat askew. "Well, dear, I dare say you'll want to fuss yourself right down these stairs. I have a letter."

That news brought Nell from the kitchen. "From Portland? Or Paris?" Nell was wiping her hands on her skirt when Kat followed Rosita down the stairs.

"It's from Maine." Hattie handed the letter to Nell.

"It's Ida's handwriting." Nell led them all into the parlor. Hattie settled on one end of the sofa while Nell perched on a wing-backed chair. Kat sat in the Queen Anne chair, opposite her, and pulled Rosita onto her lap. She breathed in the slight scent of lilac before giving Nell her full attention.

Dearest sisters,
    At the time of this writing, we have not yet heard from you.
    We are trusting God that you arrived safely, but please write at your first opportunity.

Nell glanced at Kat and shrugged.
"She'd probably just mailed it when we wired Aunt Alma."

    No doubt you are wed by now.
    I pray that you are happy in your marriages.

Nell's eyes narrowed in a frown. "We have to tell them about Judson and Patrick, and about our move to the cabin tomorrow."
"Soon we'll have good news to share. We'll tell them then."
Nell nodded.

    My courses are going well and keeping me busy.
    Still, I miss you both.
    Kat, I long to hear one of your poems.
    Last week brought six inches of fresh snow, and I tried to imagine what you might write about it.
    Viv begged me to go back to my numbers.

Kat giggled, imagining what clumsy rhyme Ida might have dreamed up, and she made a mental note to write her older sister a poem about six inches of snow.

Nell, I've been practicing my checkers moves with Aunt Alma, and I'm just about ready to take my title of Checkers Champion back from you.

Pausing, Nell looked over at Kat, her chin quivering and a tear spilling from her blue eyes. "I wish they were here."

"I do too, but it's probably best that we have a few months before Ida arrives. We'll be more settled by then." Kat motioned for Nell to resume the reading.

Viv is well, and plans to pen a letter tomorrow after church.

She sends her love, and so does Aunt Alma.

I'm sure she'd say her cat does too, although it would be in the form of yellow fur all over your clothes.

We haven't heard from Father yet.

Aunt Alma says letters take at least a month coming from Europe.

We long to hear your news. Please write soon and often.

Sunday afternoons aren't the same without you.

I miss you terribly!

All my love,

Ida Mae

Kat blinked back her tears. "Thank you for picking up the letter, Hattie."

Nell slipped the paper into the envelope and then swiped at the dampness on her cheeks.

Hattie reached across the gap between them and patted Nell's knee. "Happy to do it. Besides, the post office is where I heard the other news."

"About Judson?"

"No, dear, I'm afraid not. It was news from our friend, Mr. Boney Hughes."

"Oh." Her posture as terse as her response, Nell crossed her arms. "Was he laughing while he spoke with you?"

Hattie giggled. "No, and he said he felt mighty bad about that." Hattie glanced at the child on Kat's lap. "He heard from the sheriff in Santa Fe."

"He did?" Kat tried not to shout.

"They found Rosita's grandmother."

"Is she on her way here, then?" Nell's eyes were wide.

"Tomorrow. Her son is traveling with her, and they'll leave Santa Fe tomorrow. This is Friday." Hattie counted the days on her fingers. "Saturday. Sunday. That means they should be here Monday."

Kat sighed. At least one of them needed a happy ending. On Monday the child bouncing the bunny in her lap would be reunited with her family.

Hattie suddenly directed her attention out the window. "That man has the good timing of a cool breeze in July." She stood and Kat joined her, curious to see whom the woman was referring to.

Dr. Cutshaw waved as he walked toward the house. Kat waved

back, enjoying the coolness of this particular breeze. Then she remembered the good doctor's self-appointed shadow—Miss Darla Taggart—and, knowing that sometimes breezes warned of storms ahead, she stepped away from the window.

TWENTY-EIGHT

⁓⦚⦚⁓

Kat Sinclair stood beside Hattie Adams in the open doorway, leaving no doubt in Morgan's mind that this was the right place to be.

"Dr. Cutshaw, do you have news of Judson?" It was Kat, not Hattie, who greeted him first.

"Good afternoon, Miss Sinclair, Rosita, Miss Hattie." Morgan tipped his hat as he greeted each one. Nell Sinclair wasn't in the welcoming committee, and he couldn't help but wonder how she was faring after last night's incident. "I can give you some information about Mr. Archer's condition. Is your sister home?" He looked past the women to see if she was in the hallway. "What is that heavenly aroma?"

"I daresay you smell the shortbread cookies we baked last night, Doctor. Come right in, and I'll fetch tea and a plate of cookies for our visit."

Morgan hung his hat and coat on a brass hook, then pulled the latest copy of *Harper's Bazar* out of his coat and tucked it under his arm.

Nell met them at the parlor door, her gait hesitant. "Doctor, is it

Judson? How is he?" She blushed, no doubt recalling their first meeting. "Is he all right?"

Hattie perched on the sofa while the sisters sat in the chairs across
from it, and Rosita settled on the floor in front of a bookcase with the
stuffed rabbit on her lap. "Yes, how is our Mr. Archer today?"

Physically or emotionally? Morgan knew he needed to tread lightly
here, teetering between decency and respect for Judson's privacy. Morgan could tell from Nell's slumped shoulders that she had suffered
greatly, so he wanted to put her at ease. But how?

"He is, well, he's…" Sore? Was that too personal? She'd seen the
cactus spines in Judson's backside, and the man's yelps and bellows
were no doubt what drew her into the hospital room, but Morgan
thought better of sharing too much. "As can be expected, Judson is
uncomfortable but recovering."

"I hope you know how sorry I am for my intrusion last night. I
didn't know." Nell rose from her chair, her brows creased and her lips
quivering. Morgan stood as well. "Judson has to know how sorry I
am. I never would have gone against his wishes had I known."

"You didn't know the nature of the injuries," Morgan said. "When
Judson found out you were in town, he insisted that you not be told
the specifics. It wasn't your fault."

"I only hope Judson will be as gracious as you are. But then, you
were the one with the forceps, not the one…in a compromised position." Nell swiped at a tear at the corner of her eye. "I'm afraid I've ruined everything."

"A robbery. Of all things." Hattie jumped in before Morgan could
come up with something reassuring. "What's the matter with people
that they can't keep their hands on their own purse strings?"

Morgan shared the woman's sentiment but also understood the power of wanting more than you have. It had nearly caused him to accept the job in Boston even though he would've had to marry the boss's daughter, and that was the last thing he'd wanted to do.

"Did they take much money from him?" Kat asked.

Morgan couldn't say. It was up to Judson to tell his bride how much he'd lost. But looking at Nell's heartbroken face, Morgan was sure she didn't care about a claw-foot tub or electricity or wallpaper as much as she cared for him.

"Is he still in the hospital?" Nell's blue eyes were filled with tears. "I need to tell him how sorry I am."

"I expect to send him home soon." He couldn't tell Nell he was still concerned about the possibility of infection. "I'd give him some time. I'm sure you'll hear from him when he's feeling better."

"Of course." The frown on her face deepened. "I'll do my best." Nell stood and tugged the sleeves of her shirtwaist straight. "In the meantime, we have a lot of food left from the café last night. Can you join us for lunch, Doctor?"

"What a splendid idea." Hattie jumped to her feet, and Kat rose from her chair. "But Kat, dear, you needn't join us yet." Before Morgan could answer, the woman shuffled to the parlor door with Rosita, holding the stuffed rabbit, at her heels. "After lunch we can have the cookies I promised you."

Nell pinned Kat with a gaze Morgan recognized as a directive. "It'll take us a few minutes to finish the preparations. We'll let you two know when it's time to eat." Nell brushed Kat's hand on her way by and followed Hattie and Rosita out into the hallway, leaving Morgan alone with Kat.

Why hadn't he seen it earlier? The way she'd talked about Kat during the carriage ride, extolling her sister's virtues and her writing. The way Nell lagged behind them on the hill last night. It was easy to see now that Nell and Hattie were playing matchmaker, and he suddenly realized he rather liked It. Truth be told, he could use all the help he could get. He hadn't exactly proven himself charming where the complex Kat Sinclair was concerned.

"Can we sit down?" He motioned toward the sofa. A meal wasn't the only reason he'd stayed. She needed to know that, and why he'd come here in the first place.

"Perhaps I should go help prepare the table for our meal, Doctor," she said, but her feet didn't move.

"Morgan. Please call me Morgan, and I wish you wouldn't go. I wanted to speak with you."

"Very well, then. Morgan it is," she said, and sat in a wing-back chair while he sat on the sofa across from her. He laid the latest copy of *Harper's Bazar* beside him.

"Our evening was cut short, and I wanted you to know how much I enjoyed it."

Pink tinged her cheeks, and she studied her fingernails. "Thank you. I did too."

Morgan savored the image of Kat looking out at the mountains and over the town, and her poetic descriptions of God's magnificent creation. She had expressed what Morgan himself was unable to put into words, yet she managed it so well. And it was high time he learned to express himself better.

"We didn't get off to a good start."

Kat nodded and giggled. "That's a bit of an understatement, Doctor."

He smiled. "Yes, but I think we've moved beyond that, am I right?"

"Yes, of course. I consider you a friend now."

Was that it? Morgan chided himself for thinking she might consider anything more. How could she? She'd just lost her fiancé, and she was caring for an orphaned child. Even though Morgan couldn't say it yet, he knew what it was like to be headed in one direction with someone, and then have that person and that life taken from you.

"Miss Sinclair?"

"Kat. Call me Kat."

"Kat, did your fiancé die here in Cripple Creek?"

Her eyes widened, showing obvious surprise at his frankness.

"I apologize if I—"

"His name was Patrick Maloney. Folks here called him Paddy. We'd corresponded. He sent me train fare for my trip to Cripple Creek, and then he died in the fire last week."

Morgan picked up the magazine and set it on his lap. Mr. Maloney had been one of the statistics he'd read in the newspaper. "I'm sorry. I know how painful it is to lose someone you love." As he heard the word spoken, Morgan wondered if she had indeed loved the man. He wouldn't have thought it possible to fall in love with someone through a few letters, but then he met Nell and Judson.

"Thank you, but Patrick's death wasn't cause for great sorrow on my part. The man turned out to be a drunken scoundrel that I never really knew, and I'm better off without him."

The clock above the mantel struck noon, and when it started chiming, Kat rose from the wingback chair, and Morgan stood. With each *dong*, she took another step toward him. If she came much closer he'd be taken in by the lilac perfume he'd caught a whiff of on the hill last night. Kat stopped in front of the magazine he'd left on the sofa. "Is that the latest issue?"

He picked it up and began fumbling through it as he sat down. He'd thought the notice was only a page or two past the full-page ad for Pears soap. "Have you been writing since you've been in Cripple Creek?"

"I've written some in my journal, but not as much as I'd like to." A shadow crossed her face. He'd seen that same look on Opal's face when she'd not taken the time to play her piano.

He found the page he was looking for and bent forward. When she leaned in, he held the magazine out to her. "I found something I thought would suit you perfectly," he said, pointing to the two-inch advertisement for a contributing writer.

As she read, light replaced the shadow in her eyes. "They're advertising for a female writer." The tenor of her voice rose as exhilaration rode her words, and her full-faced smile melted his heart.

Morgan returned her smile. "And not just any female, but a woman who would serve as a stringer out here in the West."

"Morgan, this is unbelievable."

"As soon as I saw it, I thought of you."

She stared at him, tears pooling in her eyes. "You surprise me."

"Is that a good thing this time?"

"Yes, this time it is." She laughed. "Thank you."

"My thanks will be seeing your first article printed in *Harper's*

Bazar." He couldn't wait to read the part about the handsome doctor who mistook her for a midwife. Good thing the chap was wising up.

"Time to eat," Rosita called. They both twisted toward the parlor door where the little girl rocked heel to toe.

"Thank you, Rosita. Please tell Miss Hattie we're on our way."

Before Morgan gave it any thought, he offered Kat his arm. She laid her hand on his sleeve, sending a quiver up and down his spine, and he knew friendship wasn't going to be enough for him. Pausing at the edge of the hallway, he studied her brown eyes. "May I call on you Sunday afternoon?"

She hesitated and then nodded. "That'd be fine."

When they strolled into the dining room, Morgan noticed the smug smile on Kat's sister's face. Hattie and Nell stood behind their chairs, looking pleased with themselves. Hattie had left two place servings available on the table, one at the end opposite her. And although the chair sat empty next to Hattie, so did the spot on the table in front of it. They'd set the fifth plate directly to Morgan's left. Taking the cue, he pulled the chair out for Kat and then sat down at the end beside her.

"Dr. Cutshaw," Hattie said, extending one hand to Nell and the other across the emptiness to Kat, "it is indeed good to have a man in the house for a meal. Would you do us the honor of asking the blessing?"

Morgan nodded, and following Hattie's lead, he reached for Kat's other hand. A knowing smile warmed her soft face. They'd been set up again, and as Kat slipped her hand into his and he bowed his head, he had no complaints.

They were halfway through a pleasant lunch when Hattie set her fork down, clanging it against her plate. "Doctor." She dabbed at the corners of her mouth with her napkin. "I almost forgot that the women wanted me to talk to you."

Morgan glanced first at Kat, who shook her head, and then at Nell, who shrugged. Looking back at the landlady at the other end of the table, he raised a questioning eyebrow.

"Oh, me. Not the Sinclair sisters." Hattie giggled. "The Women for the Betterment of Cripple Creek."

She declared the title as if it would serve as sufficient clarification. He scooped up a forkful of potato salad and waited for her to continue.

Hattie spoke in a rush of words. "We have weekly meetings on Fridays and a special guest once a month during a Wednesday luncheon. Mr. Tanner was coming this month to talk about his rock collection." Hattie lifted the bowl of potato salad from the table and motioned for the sisters to pass it to Morgan, certainly with the idea that he would replenish his rapidly disappearing serving. "His mother took sick in Kansas, and he left on the train to go see her."

"I'm sorry to hear that." He spooned another helping of salad onto his plate.

"Yes, well, we all were…but then I got to thinking about you."

"Me? Kansas is too far away for a house call, Miss Hattie," he teased.

Her smile reached all the way up to her silver eyes and gave them a sparkle. "That'd be just plain silly sending you that far away when we need you here, Doctor." She lifted her teacup to her lips and said, peering over the rim, "You'd be the perfect guest for our luncheon Wednesday after next."

Morgan refolded his napkin in his lap, buying time to think about her request. He'd done his fair share of presentations in Boston for various academic groups and charity events. It would do him some good to get out and meet more people in the community, although a women's luncheon wouldn't be his first choice. But Hattie had been especially kind to him, and his belongings still took up space in her parlor and attic. "I'd be happy to be the guest for this month's meeting."

"That's wonderful!" Hattie clapped. "Thank you, Doctor. Our members will be so thrilled."

Morgan reached for his coffee cup. "What did you want me to speak about? I have three or four different topics related to health and medicine I could address."

"Oh, we don't want to hear you talk." The woman tittered. "We want to hear you play."

Morgan was caught off guard for a moment, but he grinned and nodded. He should have seen it coming. "Next Wednesday, you said?"

"Yes. Wednesday at ten in the morning."

Morgan made a mental note to add the concert to his calendar, and then realized he'd forgotten to set a time for Sunday's visit. He leaned toward Kat. "Is five o'clock on Sunday afternoon acceptable? Perhaps we could go for another carriage ride." He'd said it in a quiet tone, but that didn't matter. Matchmakers have hypersensitive hearing. Spoons and feet and teacups quieted.

Kat nodded, and her sister pinned her with a furtive glance. "Kat, does he know not to call for you here?"

"Where will you be?" Morgan suddenly feared they may be leaving town.

Kat laid down her spoon. "We're moving out of the boarding-house tomorrow."

"Sad, sad news for me, to be sure." Hattie shook her head, and her extra chin wobbled. "Having these girls here has been like having family you like come to stay awhile."

"You have a house full of boarders arriving tomorrow, and with all the rebuilding going on this spring and summer, you'll have plenty of company." Kat turned back toward him. "We're moving into a place off of Florissant, on Pikes Peak Avenue."

Morgan was relieved they were staying in Cripple Creek, but he remembered that he'd been up in that area and he hadn't seen many homes suitable for a woman, especially not one like Kat. "Up where the miners' shanties are?"

"I didn't have much choice in the location, as it was Patrick Maloney's place."

"You said the man was a scoundrel." Morgan's fingers curled around his knife.

"Be that as it may, he was my intended. He promised me a home. He is dead, and the cabin is mine."

"Please tell me you're not really planning to move into an abandoned shanty out where proper women would never live."

Kat scooted her chair back, scraping wood against wood. "You still think I'm not able to be a proper woman?"

Morgan wanted to muzzle his mouth about now, but he couldn't, not when her safety was in question. "It is unthinkable that you would intentionally place you, your sister, and Rosita in harm's way."

"This from a man with plenty of money to do as he well pleases. I'm sorry, sir, but I do not have that luxury." Kat stood abruptly, and her chair would've fallen over if he hadn't stood as well and set it straight. "You, Dr. Cutshaw, are still a very maddening man."

And you are an exasperating woman. "I'm sorry you feel that way."

He directed his attention toward Nell and Hattie. "I'd best go. I'm working this afternoon. Thank you for the lunch, Miss Hattie, Nell." He patted Rosita's head before turning back toward Kat. "Good day."

Hattie followed him out of the dining room. "I hope we can do it again soon. Come by anytime." She made his parting sound as if they'd just had a perfectly pleasant luncheon, Where had the woman been the past few minutes?

Nodding, he grabbed his derby from the coat hook near the front door. Nell followed him with a plate of shortbread cookies. "These are for Judson. Will you see that he gets them after you've had a couple?"

"I will."

Nell laid a tea towel over the plate. "Thank you, and don't worry about Kat."

"I'm only concerned for her—"

"I know." Nell's smile told him that she knew his interest in her sister wasn't purely professional.

Why did women have to be so complicated?

TWENTY-NINE

❧

*K*at and Nell helped Hattie clean up the dining room and kitchen while Rosita sang a song about rabbits.

"Rosita has the right idea, girls." Hattie passed Kat the last clean plate and dried her hands on her apron. "We have the use of a fine piano, and Nell plays, so I say we should have us a sing-along."

Kat added the dry plate to the stack on the shelf. "I'm sorry, Hattie, but I'm really not of a mind to sing right now."

"Of course you aren't, dear, but sometimes the want-to only shows up after the fact."

Sighing, Kat hung her apron on the hook and reminded herself that the woman rarely took no for an answer.

"It'd probably help us get our minds off them." Nell shot her a sly smile from the doorway, and Kat stuck her tongue out at her. Childish to be sure, but Nell deserved it. Good riddance to Dr. Cutshaw and to Nell's absurd matchmaking. The man was way off center as far as she was concerned. One minute he supported her independent spirit, encouraging her to write, and the next, he was treating her as if she'd deliberately set out to threaten his manhood.

"Come along, dear." Hattie tugged her arm. "We need you to sing alto."

Kat doubted if anything could improve her disposition, but she followed Hattie into the parlor anyway.

Rosita sat on the piano bench beside Nell with HopHop in her lap. Kat stood on one side and Hattie on the other.

Sweet hour of prayer! Sweet hour of prayer!
That calls me from a world of care…

Hattie warbled on the rhymed words—*care* and *prayer*. Kat wouldn't consider their landlady's voice that of a songbird, but then she had no grounds to disparage another's singing. According to all three of her sisters, Kat had the pitch of a crow. Her heart definitely wasn't into singing right now. Despite Hattie's attempts to distract her, all Kat could think about was the aggravating man who owned the piano Nell played.

At least Hattie, Nell, and Rosita sang. She tried. If only she could keep her mind from whirring like a train wheel on a wet track.

Suddenly, something sounded terribly wrong, and the singing stopped. "What happened?" said Kat.

"We'd switched songs." Nell giggled behind her hand.

A wave of warm embarrassment swept all the way to Kat's scalp. Rosita's gleeful giggles proved contagious, and laughter echoed off the wallpaper. Soon all four of them cackled and crowed.

When the amusement subsided, Kat looked up into the wet face of the woman who housed them. "I'm sorry, Miss Hattie. I've gone and ruined your solemn, sweet time with the Lord."

"Don't be sorry, dear. Laughter is a natural sweetener, and the Lord says it is good medicine for the soul." She pulled her apron hem to her face and swiped at the happy tears that had formed rivulets in the wrinkles there.

Hattie possessed an ability to sing and dance in the face of sorrow, disappointment, or frustration, and Kat envied her for it.

Morgan stomped up the street toward the hospital. He slipped another cookie out from under the tea towel. Of all the imprudent things a good woman could do, moving into a miner's cabin had to top the list. And in the midst of men who rarely see women by sunlight. Morgan bristled and bit down hard on the cookie.

Kat Sinclair wasn't playing fair. But then she hadn't from the moment he met her. He'd started off at a disadvantage not knowing she was a patient instead of a midwife, and she'd had him off kilter ever since. One minute she was shy and demure, such as when Hattie and Nell left them in the room alone. The next, she was moving into a shack thinking she could conquer the Wild West.

Morgan had taken the long way to work. When he rounded the corner at Eaton, he took the steps to the hospital door two at a time, then yanked it open. He'd see Judson Archer before he started his rounds.

When Morgan knocked on the door and let himself into Judson's room, he saw that the man had changed out of the hospital gown into denim breeches and was buttoning a broadcloth shirt.

Judson looked at him as if he'd expected to see a bear, his eyebrows raised and his eyes wide. "It *is* you. I was beginning to think I'd have to spring myself from this place." He studied the plate Morgan held. "But since you brought me dinner."

"Cookies from Nell." Morgan set the plate on the bed and Judson lifted the tea towel.

"She sent only two on this big plate?"

"I need to do a follow-up exam before I can sign you out." Morgan closed the door and went to the washbowl to clean his hands.

"I figured as much." Judson pulled the back of his breeches down and bent over the bed. "You want to tell me what's wrong, Doc?"

Morgan studied the puncture wounds. "The irritation is beginning to clear. I don't see any sign of infection. I don't see anything wrong, but you'll be sore for a few days. I'll sign you out, and then you're free to go home."

"That's good news." Judson pulled up his pants and buckled his belt. "But I was wondering what was wrong with you. You usually knock, not pound the door, and something happened to your bedside manner. Not to mention my shortbread cookies." He grabbed both cookies off the plate and bit into one. "Mmm-mmm."

The man had been robbed and tossed into a patch of cactus, and he'd picked up on Morgan's foul mood that quick? Morgan pulled a small jar of petroleum jelly from a drawer near the sink.

"You look like you just lost your best friend and you're mad about it. Given my own recent experience, my guess would be woman trouble." Judson finished off the first cookie.

Did he dare talk to Nell's intended about her sister? "It's complicated."

"Yep, definitely sounds like a woman." Judson propped his elbow on the back of a straight chair. "Happy to listen. As long as I don't have to sit down to do it." His laughter reminded Morgan of a foghorn on a steamer in Boston Harbor.

"You won't want to do much of that for a few more days." Morgan handed Judson the jar. "You'll want to apply this at least once a day for a week."

"So you've seen Nell?"

"Just came from the boardinghouse."

"She never wants to see me again, right?"

"Wrong. She sent you cookies, didn't she?"

"But you saw the look of revulsion on her face last night. She pities me."

"What I saw was out-and-out surprise and then embarrassment. She was told you'd been robbed, and that's all she'd been told. Then she walked in and saw you with your pants down, and looking like a pincushion, how would you expect her to react?"

Judson laughed. "Good point." He shook his head. "But we're supposed to be solving your woman trouble."

"Good luck with that." Morgan heaved a sigh. "I apparently hadn't learned my lesson. I just said no to a Sinclair sister."

Judson gasped in a melodramatic manner, his blue eyes wide and his chest puffed out. "Let me guess—you didn't get away with it either."

"Not in the least. Kat thinks moving into a dead miner's cabin up in the hills is a good idea, and I don't."

"A dead miner?"

"She came out here to marry a fellow named Maloney."

"Paddy?"

"Yeah, that's him. He died in the fire last week. You knew him?"

"We worked for the same mine." He shook his head. "If Nell had told me who was writing to her sister, I would've warned her."

"Yes, well, now that he's gone, she's moving into his cabin. Tomorrow."

"And taking Nell with her?" He downed the last cookie.

Morgan blew out a long breath. "As far as I know, and the little girl she's caring for. Why would she go and do such a foolhardy thing?"

Judson's finger shot up into the air. "I think I know."

"You do?"

"Simple, really. The same set of endearing traits that sent her sister dashing into my room last night."

"Pray tell." Morgan sat down on a wooden chair.

"The Sinclair sisters are determined."

"Stubborn."

Judson chuckled. "Steadfast."

"Bullheaded."

"Strong."

It was Morgan's turn again when a knock on the door interrupted their list. He was about to add *irresistible*. It was good that he didn't. That would have no doubt taken the conversation in a different direction.

"Dr. Cutshaw?" It was the reverend mother's voice.

"Excuse me." When Judson gave him a nod, Morgan opened the door and stepped out into the hallway. "Sister Coleman, is there an emergency?"

"No, Doctor. Pardon my intrusion, but Mr. Goeke and his sister stopped by. He said it was important that you have this." She handed Morgan an envelope. "I wanted to attend to it before I got distracted."

"Thank you." Morgan glanced back at Judson, who was setting a cowboy hat on his head. "Sister, Judson Archer is going home today. Could you find the paperwork I need to sign for him?"

"I will, and I'll bring it right in." She walked away, and Morgan stepped back into Judson's room.

"I heard her mention Goeke."

Morgan nodded.

"I talked to him this morning. Lost his leg in an explosion. His cabin burned too."

"I'm the one who did the surgery. The reverend mother and I, that is. Ethan's sister came out from Philadelphia to help him get home. They're leaving on the four o'clock train." Morgan tucked the envelope into his jacket pocket. It was probably a thank-you letter.

"That's horrible. My sufferings seem so small compared to what he's been through. What so many here have been through the past couple of weeks." The compassion in Judson's eyes showed an impressive depth to the man. "My vantage point on the back of Boney's mule yesterday wasn't the best, but I saw enough to know that a lot of people around here are homeless. That some lost loved ones. I've heard some staggering stories in here this morning."

"The little girl Kat is taking care of lost her mother because of the fire on the twenty-ninth," Morgan said. "That's just one of many stories of hardship and grace. It makes me want to make the most of every day."

"What does that mean, Doc?" The sly smile on Judson's face said he knew exactly what it meant.

THIRTY

~∽∾~

It wasn't a ray of sunlight that woke Nell Saturday morning. Rosita's whimpers stirred her long before the sun would rise behind a veil of gray clouds. She went to the pallet on the floor and pulled the thrashing child onto her lap, easing her out of another bad dream. Even after she had calmed the little girl and Rosita crawled into the bed and drifted off to sleep, Nell lay awake thinking and praying, and whimpering some herself.

According to the news from Boney, Rosita's grandmother and uncle would board the train in Santa Fe this morning. Day after tomorrow, the little one would no longer need her or Kat. She'd be reunited with her blood family. It's what they'd prayed for. But lying there, listening to Rosita's soft snores and breathing in the light scent of lilac, Nell mourned losing the child and the comfort she'd brought into her life.

As her tears dampened the pillow, she prayed for Judson—for his healing and for his love. She still hadn't heard from him, and this was moving day. She, Kat, and Rosita would leave the comforts of Hattie's home for what Dr. Cutshaw had referred to as an abandoned shanty out where proper women would never live.

She stayed in bed until the sun started to stain the clouds with a palette of gray-blues, and then Nell rose and moved through her morning routine. She fought the urge to tell Kat they should stay with Hattie. But when she remembered her sister's indignation over the doctor's concerns, Nell decided to save her breath.

Rosita woke and went downstairs to Hattie, and Nell and Kat slogged through packing and cleaning their room in silence.

Nell pulled a set of clean bed linens from the cupboard at the end of the hallway. Music from the phonograph drifted up the stairs, along with the sounds of shuffling feet, and she guessed Hattie and Rosita were doing a little dancing before breakfast. Carrying the sheets back down the hallway to the bedchamber, Nell wondered if perhaps she and Kat shouldn't stop their work and join them. Hattie had told Dr. Cutshaw that music feeds the soul, and hers was surely feeling hunger pangs this morning.

Kat was bundling the sheets they'd taken off the bed when she walked in. "Once we finish with the bed, we're done with our cleaning." she said. Leaving their quarters clean was the least they could do for the woman who had so graciously and generously given them reduced room and board for their household assistance.

Nodding, Nell laid the fresh linens on the chair atop the quilt. She could hear the sound of hammers at work close by. This town was beginning to bulge at the seams as construction workers poured in to help rebuild, and reporters came from all over to report on the much improved brick-and-stone face of Cripple Creek. Most of the men had been sharing tents, but Nell knew of three who had sent for their wives and let Hattie's vacant rooms. Those couples would reunite at the depot today and move into the boardinghouse in time for lunch.

Kat set the bundle of soiled linens near the door and peered out. "I may miss Hattie's parlor and the phonograph, but I'm sure I won't miss hearing those same three songs over and over. I heard them in my sleep last night." A hint of a smile widened her face.

"But the piano." Nell carried a sheet to the bed. "I'll miss the piano."

"I'm sure the doctor will soon move into a proper house and take his fancy grand with him." Sarcasm dripped from Kat's every word.

Nell flipped the sheet toward Kat's side of the mattress, ignoring her sharp comment. "And the bed. I'll miss the bed."

"I'm going to miss this place too," Kat said, sliding the sheet over a corner of the mattress.

"I don't know what we would've done without Hattie. She's been so good to us." Nell tugged on another corner. "I'll miss our sing-alongs and her chitchat."

"Believe me." Kat regarded her with a creased brow. "I wish the cabin was a house, and that it wasn't, well, where it is." She reached for the last edge of the sheet. "I know it would be easier to stay here with Hattie."

"Why can't you do the easy thing just this once?"

"And what?" Kat jerked the sheet over the corner of the bed. "I'm not like you, Nell."

"I know." Her eyelid twitching, Nell straightened. "I know…you wouldn't wait around, pining over a man."

"I came here for a man, remember? That's not gone so well, has it?" Kat grabbed the quilt off the rocker and plopped it onto the bed.

"I remember." Nell sighed, reaching for an edge of the quilt. There was little chance that she or anyone else would soon forget that Patrick Maloney had wronged Kat.

"But now I'm on my own and I don't need rescuing." Kat tugged the quilt out of Nell's hand. "I'm not going to hide away in Hattie's comfortable boardinghouse. I'm not helpless."

"And you're saying I am?"

"You've certainly been acting like it. Judson will either come to his senses or he won't. But it's not the end of the world if he doesn't."

"There's a difference between waiting around doing nothing and having a little patience." And as Nell drew in a deep breath, trying to calm herself, she knew she could use a big helping of it about now. "I care deeply about Judson, and he cares for me. We're going to be married."

Please, Lord, let it be so.

"I know you're going through your own trial, Kat, and I might be a little too accommodating to suit you, but it's as if you've set out to prove to God and everyone else that you don't need anyone."

Kat huffed and jerked the top of the quilt straight.

With both hands on the quilt Nell tugged her side smooth. "Not every man is Patrick Maloney, Kat."

"I didn't say Judson is like Paddy."

"I'm not talking about Judson."

Kat stilled, not looking up. "I don't want to talk about him, either." She slid a pillow into an embroidered case. "I'm not keen on the idea of trading an electric light for a lantern or an indoor lavatory for an outhouse either, but I have to do this."

"I know you do."

"You don't have to go with me." When Kat lifted her head, the firestorm had faded from her eyes. "You can stay here."

Nell shimmied the second pillow into a case, knowing full well that she wasn't about to let her sister move up the hillside alone. No doubt there would be plenty to get used to up there, but they'd do it together. Straightening her posture and squaring her shoulders, she spoke in falsetto. "Whither thou goest, I will go."

Kat giggled, which only encouraged her.

"Thy people shall be my people." Nell barely got the words out before she and Kat were cackling hard and dropping onto the bed.

Once they'd both exhausted their laughter and returned to their feet, Kat pulled the quilt straight again. "Nell, I'm serious. You don't have to move with me. You're not Ruth, and I'm not Naomi."

"But we did journey together to a foreign land, and if you're moving into the cabin, I am too."

"Thank you." Kat glanced at the two trunks that sat under the window. "Those are next, then."

Nell thought better of mentioning that men had carried them up. When Kat grabbed a handle on the first trunk, nearest the door, Nell gripped the handle at the other end.

On the count of three, they lifted the trunk. Kat shuffled backward through the doorway then out into the hallway. "We'll stop at the top of the stairs," she said, each word a grunt.

If I make it to the top of the stairs. With each heavy step, Nell wondered about Ruth and Naomi. When Naomi decided to move, the inside of her home in Moab was probably one level, and she wasn't headed for the side of a mountain or someplace as shoddy as Paddy's place. It had to be easier to start a new life with a daughter-in-law than it was with a sister. And if Nell could catch her breath, she would tell Kat so. She couldn't help but wonder if the main reason God made men was for heavy lifting. Moving trunks and wooing women.

"Let's set it down on the count of three."

On three, they both set their ends down. Their toes were safe, but the thud rattled the staircase and the phonograph suddenly ceased to play. Hattie stepped out of the parlor and looked to the top of the staircase, her eyes the size of buttermilk biscuits. "How did that trunk get there?"

"We moved it." Kat said it in a confident tone, as though the act was effortless.

"Well, don't do it again." Huffing, Hattie wiped her brow as if she'd been the one doing the lifting. "I have two men coming over from the depot at 9:00 a.m. to help us with such things. In the meantime, let's stir up some breakfast." Hattie shook her head, ambling off, still talking. "Strength and wisdom are *not* the same thing. A wise woman knows her limits."

That was music to Nell's ears. From the moment she stepped off the train and didn't see Judson there, she was sure she wasn't strong enough to make it here in Cripple Creek. But Hattie was right. It wasn't strength she needed the most. While others in this camp dug for gold, she would mine wisdom.

❧

Morgan carried his meal tray into the hospital dining room. Five nuns huddled at one end of the table, including the reverend mother, Sister Coleman. The sisters were deep in conversation, leaning toward one another, heads down, which suited him just fine. He needed time to himself to think, so he took his breakfast to the empty end of the long, narrow table. For the most part, the basement afforded him privacy, but the drab walls, the stored medical equipment, and the rattling pipes hardly allowed for relaxed reflections.

He took a healthy gulp of coffee, enjoying its savory warmth on his tongue, and as it slid down his dry throat, he gazed up at the crucifix on the wall. He knew the image was supposed to remind him of Christ victoriously conquering death, but this morning, he could more easily envision Jesus the Good Shepherd, His scarred hand outstretched to Morgan, leading him through a wilderness He'd already passed through.

Thank You, Lord. Now, if You'd just help me see my way through it.

When he'd accepted the job here, he'd planned to devote his life to medicine—to his work. He didn't expect to find a woman in this wilderness who would challenge his resolve to avoid romantic entanglements. The only good thing was that he wouldn't have to worry about that now. He'd probably already scared Kat away for good.

Morgan took another sip of coffee and stared down at his fried egg. The egg was runny, not fully cooked. He poked at the filmy white with his fork.

Naturally, she hadn't taken his ultimatum well. He hadn't earned the right to offer counsel, let alone impose his opinions. He didn't know what possessed him to be so bold as to tell her what she could and couldn't do, but he knew why he had reacted so strongly: fear. Fear for Kat's safety. Fear that she'd be too far off for him to protect her. The hospital was only a couple of blocks away from Hattie's, and he liked it that way.

But his worst fear of all was that he'd lose Kat. He'd already lost Opal, and he couldn't suffer that kind of loss ever again.

Morgan slathered orange marmalade on his slice of honey wheat toast, but it didn't help. The bread was still dry and hard to choke down, and so was Kat's move and the fact she was too stubborn to hear his concerns. He needed to tell her about his past…about Opal. She needed to know why he'd reacted the way he had. He knew that she also needed time to recover from her own ordeal.

"Like another cupful, Dr. Cutshaw?" Morgan rose from his chair. The reverend mother stood beside him, holding an empty coffee mug in one hand and the blue enamel percolator in the other.

"Good morning, Sister." He nodded, and she poured coffee into both mugs. "Thank you."

She returned the coffeepot to a sideboard and glanced at the empty spot across from him. "Mind if I join you?"

"Please." He pulled the chair out for her and then sat back down, watching steam rise from his cup.

"You're doing fine work, Doctor, and we consider ourselves truly blessed to have you working in our hospital." Her headpiece sat squarely atop her head, wisps of white hair framing her work-worn face.

"Thank you. That means a lot coming from you. You're a most capable and gracious assistant." Following the fire, they'd worked together to save dozens of lives. Eleven days ago, they'd spent the better part of three hours together saving Mr. Goeke after he'd lost his leg in an explosion. "Folks around here really know how to make a doctor feel needed."

"You are needed here." She held her cup to her lips and took a sip. "And I'd say the Lord made you for this kind of doctoring."

Morgan glanced up at the crucifix. "I think I'm beginning to realize that."

"Beginning to?" She set her mug down on the scarred table and wrapped her hands around it. "That's not what you were expecting when you came to Cripple Creek?"

"No ma'am." Morgan stared down into the rich, dark coffee in his cup. "My aspirations would've had me locked away in a research lab."

"What happened to change that?"

He hadn't intended to say so much, but something about this gracious woman made him want to answer her. There was curiosity etched in her warm brown eyes, but more importantly, compassion.

"A woman." He shook his head. "Penelope Covington and I practically grew up together in Boston." He imagined Penelope's gloved hand waving to him over the fedoras, bowlers, and mushroom-style hats at his parents' last soiree. "Our fathers are both surgeons. Both serve on the board of trustees of the Medical Research Institute in Boston."

The sister sipped her coffee, her gaze still fixed on him, and he took another bracing gulp before continuing his story.

"When Penelope turned sixteen, I became her bull's-eye. She wanted a husband. But she and I were never more than friends as far as I was concerned, and I married Opal."

"You're married?" Sister Coleman asked, gently touching his hand.

"I was. Opal died nearly three years ago."

"I'm so sorry," she whispered, her voice full of maternal compassion.

"When my wife died, Penelope's father took up Penelope's cause, as did mine. Though I still felt spoken for, in their eyes I was again an eligible bachelor."

"Some women don't know when to give up, do they?"

"No, and Dr. Covington didn't know when to tell his daughter no. The man offered me a job as a research scientist at the Institute, but the position came with a wife."

"No!" She set her coffee cup on the table with the same force he remembered feeling when he'd finally used the word on the two doctors trying to control his life.

"He said, and I quote, 'You'll have a top-notch lab and be able to provide well for my daughter.'"

"Of all things." Her face hardened for a brief moment. "Well, all the better for us, I say. Like I said, the Lord made you for doctoring in this kind of place."

It felt good to have her as an advocate.

"If my father and the Covingtons had their way, I'd be living the life they thought I needed, in their shadow." He took a sip of coffee.

Here in the company of the reverend mother, Morgan believed he really could live a new life and make a difference. And as he drained his coffee cup, he found himself hoping that new life included Kat Sinclair.

THIRTY-ONE

*C*louds in various shades of gray and white had escorted Kat, Nell, and Rosita all the way up the hill to the cabin Saturday morning. Now, as the three of them sat at the kitchen table, a steady stream of raindrops tap-danced on the tin roof—a fitting punctuation for their first evening in her new home. Kat looked up from her stack of pages and glanced over at the open flapboard window on the back wall and breathed in the aromatic scent of the spring rains.

Her mother's quilt covered the rope bed, and the two trunks formed a wide V in the corner. A scrap of yellow cloth graced the center of the table, and the lantern sitting on it cast a golden glow over the homey room. It certainly didn't boast the comforts of Hattie's place, but it was hers. Patrick was most certainly a scalawag, but he had provided this house for her, and for that she was thankful.

"I make Mama. See?" Rosita pushed her drawing across the table and slid it on top of the pages Kat had written for *Harper's Bazar.*

Kat studied the sweeping lines, dots, and swirls, and then looked up into the child's eager face. "Your mama was very pretty, like you, Rosita."

The little girl nodded, her eyes shining like polished black pearls.

Nell closed her Bible and leaned forward, gazing down the length of the table at the drawing. Rosita rose to her knees and slid the artwork over to her. Nell scanned the page with her finger.

"Miss Kat is right, Rosita." Nell looked up, her blue eyes wet. "We're going to miss you when you go with your grandmother Monday."

Rosita patted Nell's hand, and then grabbed her drawing and flipped the page over to the blank side. "I make Abuela now."

The cast-iron kettle on the potbellied stove began to hiss. Kat rose and took the few steps to the cupboard, glancing back at Nell, who was wiping away tears with a handkerchief. "It won't be a true tea party without teacups and saucers," Kat said, pulling three tin mugs from nails above the wood plank countertop. "We'll have to use our imaginations some, since we don't have much in the way of fancy here in Kat's Kitchen."

Nell giggled and laid the hanky on top of her Bible. "Kat's Kitchen. I like it."

"May not have much, but I do have the teas I brought from Maine." She pulled two small canning jars from the shelf. "Chamomile or peppermint?"

"Peppermint sounds good to me, but you need to finish your writing. Let me get that." Nell started to stand, but Kat waved her back down.

"Thank you, but this is my thinking time. It's an important part of the writing process." At least that's what Kat hoped, and she also hoped that something printable came out of it. She'd written a couple of pages last evening before turning out the light, and a couple more this evening after supper. Now she needed to think before she wrote the ending and recopied the story in her finest penmanship.

While Kat steeped the tea, filling the one-room cabin with a pungent fragrance, she saw Nell pick up the copy of the magazine from the table. It had been tucked under Morgan's arm yesterday. Applying for the job of "woman out West correspondent" for the magazine had been his idea. It was a kind gesture that Kat had greatly appreciated— at least, until he felt the need to offer his opinion about her cabin. Her cheeks burned. From there, things had sped downhill faster than a runaway train.

As she poured the tea into the mugs and the steam rose, so did her indignation. She and Morgan hardly knew each other. She had to make certain decisions at the depot when Patrick and Judson did not meet their train. She tracked down Patrick Maloney at the saloon to discover the truth. She wasn't mindless, and Morgan had no right to tell her what she could and couldn't do. Kat huffed and set the cups on the table harder than she meant to, then returned to her chair.

Nell looked up at her with a pinched brow, then glanced at the pages Kat had written. "Your writing seems to be going well. What did you decide to write about?"

"It's a story about women finding strength and gaining wisdom in the Wild West."

"Hmm." Nell's blue eyes shimmered in the lantern light. "That ought to be good."

"Thank you, Nell. I appreciate your support." Her sister hadn't been happy about her decision to move into the cabin, but Kat's feelings were different. Morgan wasn't family and it was inappropriate for him

to weigh in on Kat's decisions where Nell might. They weren't courting, so it wasn't his place to comment on her limited choices. While
Rosita scribbled and Nell sipped her tea, flipping through the pages of
the magazine, Kat dipped her pen in ink and began writing the con-
clusion to the story.

She'd just added the period to the last sentence when a gunshot
startled her and sent her pen streaking across the page. Nell sat in
stunned silence, her eyes wide, while Rosita scrambled under the table.

Kat had heard about gunfights in town, but she hadn't expected
any up here, at least not so soon. When male shouts rang out and pots
and pans rattled, she darted to the open flapboard window beside the
stovepipe. Pulling the prop stick out of the window frame, she pulled
the board shut and quickly latched the hook and eye. The commotion
behind her told her that Nell was doing the same thing with the flapboard on the back wall.

"What's going on? What do we do?" Nell's chin quivered in the
way it always did when fear was about to claim the best of her.

Someone pounded on the door. Kat put her finger to her mouth.
She wasn't sure what good being quiet would do at this point, but she
didn't know what else to do. The three of them were here alone. No
one but Hattie and Morgan knew they were here, and neither of them
would come calling at dusk.

Following Nell's gaze, Kat looked up at the two long bent nails
over the door and the shotgun they cradled. She'd never touched a
gun before, but then, they'd never been women alone in a miner's
cabin either. Nell stood and carried her chair toward the door, and
then set it down. She hiked her skirt and stepped up onto the chair.

An even louder knock startled them. Nell jerked and lost her balance, letting out a shriek. Kat caught her sister's arm and steadied her, keeping Nell from falling on top of her. She held her finger up to her lips, but it was too late. Whoever was out there knew they were inside.

"You Sinclair sisters all right in there?" The man's voice was gruff but familiar.

Her heart still racing, Kat opened the door. Boney Hughes stood on the stoop, chewing tobacco, water dripping from his tattered hat.

"Mr. Hughes?" Nell pushed a fallen curl from her pallid face.

Rosita ran toward the man, her arms open wide, and he stepped inside to embrace her. "I heard you ladies moved in today." He looked down at the wet floor, then up at Kat. "Sorry for the mess, ma'am."

"Was that you shooting out there?" Kat glanced past him and out at the road. She didn't see anyone else.

"Yep, that was me. That's what I came to talk to ya about. Just scared me off a big black bear."

Kat and Nell both gasped.

"A bear? Where?" Kat refused to look into the falling darkness and quickly closed the door behind their fusty guardian angel. She made a mental note to avoid the outhouse anytime after sunset and before full sunlight.

"More paper, Miss Kat?" Rosita tugged on Kat's skirt. "I make Mr. Boney."

Kat moved to oblige Rosita, pulling a clean sheet of paper from her stack. She set it in front of the girl, who set to work.

"I was headed up to my claim for the night and saw the light on in here. That's when I heard that old bear grunting around that cabin down across the road from ya. I'd done forgot all about warnin' you about the critters up here." The miner's bushy brows ran together, and he grew serious. "You still got Paddy's shotgun? They come in mighty handy for scarin' off the four-legged kind, and most of the two-legged ones." He angled his head toward the weapon over the door.

"Neither one of us has ever touched a gun before." Her voice quaky, Nell crept backward, away from the door.

"Never you pay any mind to that." Boney climbed onto the chair and lifted the shotgun off the nails. "I'm here to show you how to use it."

Kat gave Nell a quick glance. Nell's taut face mirrored Kat's own trepidation.

"You shouldn't need it none...ya know, for people. Had me a talk with the fellas up here"—Boney gestured vaguely behind him—"and they'll look out for ya. Every last one of 'em knows there's only two men allowed at this place."

"Two men?" Kat narrowed her eyes.

"Unless you holler for more, ma'am." A smile lit his eyes. "Me, of course, 'cause I'll be needin' to check in on you. And that doctor gentleman friend of yours."

"Morgan Cutshaw." Kat heard the wistfulness in her own voice and turned away from them. Was that what Morgan was—her gentleman friend? At the moment she wondered if he wasn't a thorn in her side.

THIRTY-TWO

ewis P. Whibley cut himself a big bite of steak. He almost
had his fork to his mouth when the silver-haired crone at
the head of the table regarded him with a frown and shook her head.

"Mr. Whibley," she droned, "you've forgotten about giving thanks
again."

This time he didn't bother to act surprised or repentant. He just
gazed at the piece of meat on his fork and reluctantly set the utensil on
his plate. Soon enough he'd bid the Sylvanite Inn and the town of Victor adieu and settle into his own place in Cripple Creek. There, he'd
do as he well pleased. In the meantime, he nodded and closed his eyes.

"Would you do the honors this suppertime, sir?"

His eyes closed and his head bowed, Lewis waited for the short
man across the table to squeak out another long prayer. He waited in
the silence and wondered if he could manage to sneak that bite up to
his mouth without being caught. When he peeked out to check on the
possibility, the other folks at the table were staring at him.

"You, Mr. Whibley. I meant you."

"Me? You want me to say grace?"

She nodded, her lips tight and her hair bobbing like a quail pecking at seeds.

"Ma'am, I would, but my throat's feeling tinder-dry this evening."

"Seemed right fine when you were taking my money last night, Whibley," the short man said.

Short and whiny. Lewis made a mental note never to board in the same house with his prey again, but he knew the man was right. He was perfectly fine while taking money from him and all the others.

Giving thanks had been the last thing on his mind when his eyes had popped open on the back of that wagon and he found himself in Victor. Why, he was still finding chicken feathers in his bag even today, and he'd used up most of an expensive bottle of toilet water trying to get rid of that awful stink. But thanks to all the patsies here, his luck had shifted. Another night of the same, and he'd have a healthy stake for setting up in Cripple Creek. Even enough for a visit to his favorite redhead. And Cripple Creek was bound to be just as lucrative—even more so with all construction workers he'd been hearing about.

The proprietor at the head of the table cleared her throat.

Two prayers in one week seemed a bit much after so many years of not speaking to God, but he'd try it. If God didn't strike him dead for being so familiar with Him, he might even make it a habit, since the last one seemed to work.

"Very well, then. Shall we pray?" He cleared his throat. His mother had asked that question before every meal. One time, he'd answered no. He was picking himself up off the floor before he'd even seen the back of her hand. He'd taken women and their prayers seriously from then on, but until now he hadn't had to do so with a juicy steak turn-ing cold on his plate.

"Dear Lord, we like to eat, so we thank You for Miss Mabel's fine grub. Amen." The *amen* didn't echo off the china plates like it usually did, but he was already too busy shoveling steak into his mouth to pay the others any mind.

His room here was nice enough, but being smack-dab in the cen-ter of town had its disadvantages. Street noise made it nigh impossi-ble to get any rest during the day, making his Cripple Creek cabin all the more attractive. As he recalled, the fellas up in those foothills kept to themselves. They liked their privacy as much as he did.

"You got another piece of that meat, ma'am?"

"I don't."

Lewis scooped another spoonful of mashed potatoes onto his plate and buttered a third biscuit. Steaks would taste better cooked in his cabin anyway.

THIRTY-THREE

On Sundays, Morgan liked to treat himself to a breakfast out, away from the hospital. He clicked his tongue and flicked the reins, guiding his horse down Hayden Street. If he hadn't planned a day of zigzagging across town, he would've been on foot this Sunday morning. Instead his coupé shimmied across the uneven roadbed at Bennett Avenue, and he parked in front of the Third Street Café. After he wrapped the reins around the hitching rail, he stepped into the well-appointed restaurant.

He had only been to one other eatery spared by the fire, but this one's polished walnut tables and door frames offered warmth, and it had quickly become his favorite.

A waitress approached him, carrying a coffeepot and an empty cup. "Have the perfect table for you this morning, Doc."

Morgan looked around the room. Only two of the tables were occupied.

"I know how you're partial to that one over there." She tipped her head toward the empty table against the wall, and the feather that stuck up out of her single white braid bobbed.

"Yes, thank you."

She beat him to the table, and as soon as he sat down, she set a full cup of aromatic coffee in front of him. "You need a menu today, Doc?"

"No, thanks."

"A man who knows what he wants, that's what I like." She pulled the pencil from behind her ear and tapped her forehead with the eraser. "What'll you have my mister stir up for you today?"

"Buckwheat waffle with syrup. Two eggs over hard. Three slices of bacon and hash brown potatoes."

"You've got it." Her smile revealed gaps in her lower teeth. "We'll have that right out for you," she added, and turned toward the kitchen.

Morgan set his hat on the empty chair beside him and smoothed his hair into place. He looked around at the paintings that dotted the walls—all landscapes. The watercolor above his table featured the same view of Pikes Peak that he'd shown Kat from atop Tenderfoot Hill. Remembering the quiver that crept up his spine that day as she stood beside him and took in the view, he wondered if he might see her at church this morning. He hoped so. They hadn't spoken since their heated discussion Friday about the cabin. Although he still disapproved of the move, he hated that things were strained between them.

"Hey, Doc." Judson Archer lumbered toward his table. "Mind if I join you?"

Morgan reached out for a handshake. "Good morning, Judson." He pointed at the empty chair across from him. "Please, have a seat."

"Thanks." Judson carefully lowered himself in the chair. "Saw your buggy out front and I hoped you might have a minute."

"A couple of minutes. Maybe even three or four for you." Morgan chuckled, but when Judson's facial expression didn't change, he quieted and lowered his voice. "You're healing all right?"

Judson shifted in his seat. "Yeah, I'm all right as long as I don't sit for too long."

Morgan lifted his cup. "You want some breakfast?"

"Nah, but the coffee smells good. Might have a cup."

Morgan could see the waitress already on her way to the table with his plate and a jug of syrup in one hand and a coffee mug in the other. She set the plate down in front of Morgan and the full cup in front of Judson.

"Thank you. Just what I needed."

She studied him and raised a brow. "Ain't you the one that got thrown off his horse?"

Judson nodded, reaching for the bowl of sugar.

Clucking her tongue, she shook her head. "You sure you don't want something to eat, darlin'?"

"No, thanks, ma'am." When she nodded and walked away, Judson wrapped his hand around the cup and looked up at Morgan as if he wanted to say something, but he didn't speak.

Morgan offered God silent thanks for his meal and then lifted a fork full of potatoes to his mouth. "Hope you don't mind if I eat while we talk."

Judson shook his head, seemed to study the table, and cleared his throat. "I've had a lot of time to think while I've been cooped up the last couple of days."

Morgan stabbed a bit of fried egg. "Knowing our recent history, I'd say this has something to do with a Sinclair sister. Nell?"

"I'm afraid I've ruined everything." Judson set his elbows on the table and rested his chin on his folded hands. "I sent for her, but then all the money I had for our future was taken. I thought it was important, that I could only marry her if I could give her what she was used to. You know, the tub, electricity, frippery, and such."

Morgan chased the last of his egg down with a big gulp of coffee. "And now?"

A shadow darkened Judson's blue eyes. "I want to marry Nell. I know God will provide for us. She cared for me before, Doc, but do you think she still does?"

Morgan understood the hope in Judson's voice. He recalled the joy of talking to Kat about her writing and sitting beside her at the lunch table Friday—before her move came up in their conversation.

"I'm certain she does." Morgan set his fork on his plate. "Remember, I told you Friday she asked me about your welfare. And she did send you the cookies."

"That's just good upbringing, Doc." Judson sighed. "She's all I think about. I have to make it right!"

Morgan raised an eyebrow and asked, "Have you given any thought to how you might approach her? Find out for yourself how she feels about you?"

"Yeah, but...no good thoughts. You have any idea of the best way?"

"I suggest we ask her confidante."

Judson shifted in his seat. "Her what?"

"Hattie Adams."

"The one that owns the boardinghouse?"

Morgan tapped the table with his index finger. "The very one.

The sisters were staying with her, and Hattie's become a good friend to us all."

"Just tell me when and where, Doc."

"Hattie's place, up on Golden Avenue. Two o'clock this afternoon."

"I'll be there." Judson jumped up from his chair. "Thanks."

As Morgan returned the man's wave, he made a note to ask Miss Hattie about his own need for ideas.

⟳

Hattie sat comfortably in the seat in front of Kat, driving her wagon with complete control. Her Sunday hat, a regal burgundy that matched her outfit, dipped its brim with each rut in the road.

Kat glanced back at the crate that rattled around in the bed of the wagon. A miner's hat. A lunch bucket. A pick. Overalls. Mucker's boots. Patrick Maloney's life had been reduced to a wooden box. Ever since the fires, the local churches had served as collection and distribution sites. The more fortunate brought extras for those who had lost all they had to the flames. She'd heard of many miners among those devastated by the destruction. Surely someone could benefit from Patrick's belongings.

Horse hooves slapped the slushy road, and the wheels on Hattie's wagon groaned against the rocks. If it weren't for the weight of Patrick's things, she, Nell, and Rosita would have walked to church this Sunday morning and met Hattie there, but Hattie had insisted on picking them up at the cabin.

The Lord had given them a perfect day. Last night's storm had passed, and now pockets of white clouds floated in an azure blue sky. The sun warmed Kat's back—a sweet sampling of summer. Her wool cape had remained on the hook inside the cabin, and she wore her crocheted shawl and bonnet this morning. Kat had endured her fill of bracing cold, and now the warmer weather gave her hope that this latest season in their lives would soon give way to a brighter one.

They'd spent their first night in a place Kat could call her own. She'd finished her application and writing sample for *Harper's Bazar*, and she'd send them out in tomorrow's mail. Rosita's grandmother had been notified, and they expected Rosa Santos Lopez to arrive on the 11:00 a.m. train tomorrow. Everything seemed to be changing.

"It feels good to be going to church." Nell's smile lit her eyes, which rivaled the sky's stunning blue.

Nodding, Kat took Nell's hand in hers. She missed Ida and Viv, but having Nell here with her in this endeavor was a gift. And as long as she was counting gifts, she had to consider the opportunity to write for the prestigious magazine, although she didn't want to think any more on the man who had brought it to her attention. Best to change the subject. She shifted on the seat to face Nell. "Do you think Judson will be at church this morning?"

"I was just wondering the same thing about Dr. Cutshaw." Nell's mouth turned up in a sly smile.

"Now that I think about it," Kat said, "it's probably still too soon for Judson to sit so long on a hard surface."

Pink tinged Nell's cheeks.

A chiming bell drew Kat's attention to the white steeple atop a red brick building. Hattie pulled back on the reins, slowing the horse and changing the rhythm of his hooves to a slow *clip-clop*. The First Congregational Church stood on a neatly manicured corner ahead of them. Men, women, and children poured out of wagons and carts and buggies, while others tied mules, burros, and horses to the hitching rail at the side of the building. Hattie parked off to the side of the road opposite the church.

As the sisters climbed out of the wagon, Nell tapped Kat's shoulder. "There's the answer to my question."

Kat followed Nell's gaze to the parking area at the church building, where Morgan stood beside his buggy. "He's not alone." Miss Darla Taggart stood beside Morgan, and they were deep in conversation.

"That woman definitely has her sights set on him." Nell regarded Kat with a raised eyebrow, which didn't help to dispel a startling twinge of jealousy.

"Dr. Cutshaw helped Miss Taggart and her father with a clinic for those wounded in the fire," Kat said quietly.

"I don't doubt his intentions." Nell touched her arm gently.

And Kat didn't doubt Darla's either, but she couldn't concern herself with that. She had no right to feel proprietary toward the man. Right now, she didn't even like him much.

Nell lifted Rosita out of the wagon and twirled her twice, which brought on a round of giggles. Nell set her on the ground and looked at Kat, her chin lowered and an eyebrow raised. "He's probably setting Miss Taggart straight as we speak."

Kat stole another look at him to gauge his progress. Morgan saw her and waved, and Kat, caught off guard, returned his greeting. He gave her a bright summer day smile, and Darla Taggart scowled. It didn't matter. Kat had no interest in challenging Miss Taggart. If Morgan chose to be friends with her and to help the young woman with her humanitarian efforts, that was his business.

She had other business to tend to. As Kat glanced again at the wooden box, Hattie patted her cheek like a mother would. "You have no need to worry yourself about Miss Taggart. She's a bee seeking honey, that one. She'll move on." Holding her hat on with one hand, she stood on her tiptoes and peered over the edge of the wagon at Patrick's things.

"Hattie, what would I worry about? The doctor and I haven't spoken a word to each other since his outburst Friday."

"Dear, have you even seen each other since Friday?"

Kat shook her head. Hattie did make a good point, and now that she had seen him, Kat had no idea what she'd say to the infuriating man. His wave would indicate that he had forgotten about his frustration over her moving plans.

"Miss Hattie. Ladies." The sound of the familiar baritone voice made them all turn. Dr. Morgan Cutshaw sauntered toward them, looking quite dapper in a brown suit and starched white shirt, but it was the smile that lit his grass green eyes that Kat found difficult to resist.

"Dr. Cutshaw." Nell dipped her head in greeting.

"Good morning." Morgan looked at each of them in turn. He smiled at Kat last, and his look lingered. She felt a flush rise into her cheeks. "The way you were studying the back of the wagon, I figured you might need a little help."

"I've said it before, Doctor, but your timing is splendid." Hattie gave Kat a squinty-eyed look, prompting her to speak next.

Kat straightened. "We're fine. Thank you."

"The three of us will go inside and find seats," Nell said, glaring at Kat and motioning to Hattie, Rosita, and herself.

When they headed toward the church steps, Morgan looked over the edge of the wagon at Patrick's belongings. His smile disappeared.

"Hattie said the church is collecting things for those in need. I brought Mr. Maloney's things." She cleared her throat. "They were in his cabin."

"I wanted to talk to you about that. I don't—"

"We moved into the cabin yesterday." She raised her chin and crossed her arms over her chest. "And I don't choose to discuss it any further."

He removed his derby, a frown darkening his features like an afternoon storm. "Kat, I care what happens to you. That's why I said what I did Friday."

Kat didn't answer, but she could see in his eyes that he was telling the truth and had strong feelings about her well-being.

"I had no right to be so adamant," he continued. "You're not a foolish woman. You didn't make the decision lightly."

"I didn't." She let her arms fall at her sides.

"I'm sorry for reacting the way I did." Morgan touched his hand to her arm.

She lifted her chin a little higher. "Dr. Cutshaw, you were never asked to watch out for us…for me. I am quite cap—"

"Kat, I apologize for the sarcastic way in which I expressed my opinion," Morgan interrupted, "but I won't apologize for caring. And I know you are more than capable. I'm sorry if my words caused you to feel otherwise."

Kat nodded, humbled by his tender honesty, and whispered, "I'm sorry too."

"Apology accepted. Will you let me help you?" His smile had returned, and so had his dimple.

"Yes…thank you." She gave him a slight smile.

Morgan lifted the crate out of the wagon as if it was as light as a hatbox, and turned toward the church. Inside the vestibule, he set the crate under a table by the door. As he did, the short, balding man Kat recognized from outside the café walked toward them with spectacles set low on a crooked nose.

"Welcome, Morgan. Ma'am." After shaking Morgan's hand, the man faced Kat and scooted his spectacles back up his nose. "I saw you in the carriage Thursday evening speaking with my Darla, but we didn't meet. I'm Reverend Harold Taggart."

Morgan removed his hat. "Pardon me, Reverend. This is Miss Kat Sinclair."

"Welcome." He extended his hand to her, and Kat shook it. "That was your sister I met, then, with Hattie Adams and the little girl." He glanced at the box Morgan placed under the table.

"Those are things Miss Sinclair brought to contribute to those in need."

Kat sighed, thankful Morgan had spared her the explanation.

"Much obliged, ma'am." Reverend Taggart dipped his head. "After the service, I'll make sure it all gets distributed."

"I'd appreciate that, Reverend. Thank you."

A piano played an introduction to "All the Way My Saviour Leads Me," and then voices rang out from bass to soprano.

Morgan's hand cradled her elbow and guided her into the sanctuary. She scooted into the pew next to Nell, who had left enough space on the end for both Kat and Morgan.

A tiny woman with big sleeves held a hymnal and led the singing while Miss Taggart played the piano. Kat would rather hear Morgan play it, but hearing his baritone singing voice was joy enough right now.

> All the way my Saviour leads me;
> What have I to ask beside?
> Can I doubt His tender mercy,
> Who through life has been my Guide?

Kat felt her shoulders relax. Her Lord was leading her in His tender mercy. He was her Guide, and she could trust Him completely. If only she could do so without wavering.

Despite the distractions of Morgan sitting beside her and Miss Taggart looking out at them from the piano, Kat thoroughly enjoyed the service. When the minister closed the service with a prayer and they all stepped out into the aisle, Hattie clutched Kat's forearm. "Are you and Nell still planning on coming for lunch tomorrow?"

"You can count on it. There isn't much in my kitchen yet." They would join Hattie at the boardinghouse after they met Rosita's grandmother at the depot.

"Very good. We'll all need a little cheering up about then." Hattie bent down and kissed Rosita's cheek, and quickly wiped a falling tear from her own cheek. "I'll miss you, little one."

When Kat looked up again, Morgan's eyes met her own. "So… may I pick you up at five o'clock today? As we talked about on Friday?"

She nodded.

"How do I get to your place? I know it's on Pikes Peak off from Florissant, but which place?"

Kat laughed. "I suppose that is an important detail."

After she gave him directions, he placed his hat back on his head, tipped the brim toward her, and said, "I'm looking forward to it."

"Me too." She found herself caught by surprise at how she hoped the afternoon hours would pass quickly.

Hattie and Morgan said their good-byes and left. The minister greeted Kat, Nell, and Rosita again, and they headed down the steps. As they reached the edge of the building, Darla Taggart rounded the corner, turning toward them with her eyes narrowed and her lips pinched tight.

"Miss Taggart, I hope you enjoyed your supper the other night," Kat said.

"Miss Sinclair." She fairly hissed the greeting, then glared down at Rosita, ignoring Nell. "She doesn't belong here."

Kat knew she was referring to Rosita's Mexican heritage, and that didn't improve her opinion of the young woman. "She belongs here as much as I do."

"That's my other point." Darla Taggart pursed her lips in a childish pout.

Looking out at the parking area, Kat watched Hattie wave at Morgan as he drove away from her in his coupé. Apparently, whatever he'd said to Miss Taggart hadn't set well.

"Did your Dr. Cutshaw…"

He wasn't *her* Dr. Cutshaw, but Kat was beginning to like the sound of it.

"…tell you he's married?"

"What?" She took a step back.

"I believe you heard me." Darla crossed her arms over her chest.

The acidic woman couldn't be talking about Morgan. "Dr. Cutshaw married?"

"Just as I suspected." Darla lifted her nose and looked down at Kat. "The man didn't bother to tell you about his wife."

He wasn't. He couldn't be married. He was different. He wasn't like Patrick Maloney.

"Don't listen to her." Nell clasped Kat's hand and tugged at her.

Kat moistened her lips, but her mouth had dried out, and she couldn't manage any answer.

Just as well, since she felt herself wavering again and had no idea what to think, let alone what to say.

THIRTY-FOUR

ewis P. Whibley pulled out the shiny pocket watch he'd won last night. Why were watches such a popular wager and so much easier to win in a poker game than coin? Tipping the watch rim away from the sun glaring in through the window, he studied its porcelain face. Half past ten. The ride from Victor to Cripple Creek on the Midland Terminal Railroad had already been longer than the eternity his mother was always talking about, and the train had only left the depot seven minutes earlier.

Wham!

Squaring his shoulders, he glared at the kid sitting across from him. If the boy kicked his faro table one more time, Lewis would own a new pair of miniature cowboy boots and the runt would have sore ankles to go with his tender feet. He had never gotten away with such bad manners if his folks were anywhere around. You spare the rod, you spoil the child. His daddy had quoted it like it was Scripture. Could be, for all Lewis knew, and it'd do this boy's father well to learn it.

"Mister, if you don't want my son kickin' that thing, stick it in the baggage car where it belongs." The boy's stocky father sounded and looked like a bulldog. He sat in a seat diagonal to Lewis and peered at him over the top of a newspaper.

"Or you could teach your son to keep his feet to himself."

The bulldog dropped the newspaper, and Lewis reached for the shield across from the boy's feet. "Just who do you think you are—"

"Now, now." The woman sitting next to the boy set her knitting on her lap and patted the leg of the man across the aisle from her. "Cool your smokestack, Boris, the man is right. I should've been payin' Timmy more mind." She turned to the brat with a stern crease in her brow. "Timmy, what do you say to the man?"

Grunting, the bulldog returned to his own world behind the newspaper.

"Timmy?"

"Sorry, mister." He'd spit it off his tongue.

Lewis reached into his valise and pulled out a piece of the stationery his mother had given him. He had far better things to do with his time than to listen to men growl, women sigh, and children cry. He'd only had three hours' sleep, and the clacking locomotive wheels and the stench of burning coal was more than enough to unravel his nerves. Each serpentine mile peeled another raw nerve back and split it, leaving him nauseated and travel weary, but he wasn't about to let himself doze off and end up God only knows where. He'd learned that lesson well. Writing his mother was sure to keep him awake.

Lewis had just signed the letter when the whistle blew and the train pulled into the depot in Cripple Creek.

As Lewis stepped onto the platform, trying to make his way through the family reunions, he wondered if having a woman with a welcoming voice might help mend his frayed nerves faster. The smack of bricks being stacked onto wagons and the screech of bucksaws overpowered the footfalls on the wood platform and the shouts and chatter of people greeting one another. Construction workers scurried everywhere.

Good, fresh blood in town to get into a game.

Lewis carried his valise in one hand and the folded faro table in the other. He trusted no one with the object of his livelihood. He walked out around the depot and along Bennett Avenue. Eight or nine months had passed since he took his leave, and the town definitely had a new face. Tent businesses sat in the street in front of brick and sandstone buildings in various stages of completion. From this angle, it looked like very few businesses had survived the fires.

He angled toward the hill, thinking how his life was like this town. *It has been beaten and bruised, but it was coming back, stronger than ever.* In the past few weeks, he'd seen it all: mousy landladies with burly brothers, sore losers in train cars, pecking chickens, surly men in saloons. He'd had his fill. He'd endured more than his share of muscle aches and hungry nights. But things were about to change.

Paddy's death made way for a new beginning, and Lewis wasn't about to apologize for being happy about that. The man was a no-good drunk with a foul mouth and a caustic tableside manner. The past couple of years Lewis had been chewed up and spit out by everyone on his path, but now he was starting fresh. This opportunity had been a long time coming.

Now that his house was just round the corner, Lewis felt the nausea and the pain in his neck from the long trip subside. He picked up his pace on First Street and walked quickly all the way up to Golden and over to Florissant. When he saw the charred remains of some places and new construction in others, his heartbeat raced. The paymaster said Paddy died in a saloon, not at home. Surely his cabin hadn't burned, although it'd be just like Lewis's luck to draw such a lousy hand.

He turned up Pikes Peak Avenue and walked past the first and second cabins, both still standing. He breathed a deep sigh of relief when he caught sight of the third one. As soon as he saw the outhouse out behind the plank board cabin, his pulse eased and his steps slowed as he surveyed the place. He'd never actually lived here, but he'd seen it, just after he lost it. The antlers and ropes that hung out front were gone, and a lace curtain draped the one glass window. It was not something a drunken miner would hang.

But a woman would.

Paddy had either lost the place to a man with a woman, or he'd taken a wife. If a man was involved, he'd just have to walk away and make other living arrangements. No sense getting shot over a cabin. But if there was a widow, the house could be his before she knew what happened.

Lewis set his bag and folded faro table on the stoop and straightened his suit jacket before knocking on the door. The only sound he heard was the stove pipe rattling in the breeze. He'd knocked plenty loud enough for a one-room cabin, but he knocked again. When no one answered, he lifted the metal peg from the latch and opened the door to a clean and orderly household. Thinking better of leaving his things outside, he brought them in and set them near the door. He saw plenty of dresses and hats, and not one pair of overalls or trousers.

This definitely wasn't the home of a miner. Not a live one, anyway.

Lewis ran his fingers over the cheery tablecloth. A stack of clean dish-towels sat on freshly papered shelves. He spied two trunks in the corner, and after a quick glance out the window, he lifted the lid on the first one. Underthings. A couple of books. Stationery. And a dishtowel wrapped around something heavy at the back of the trunk. Lewis gripped the towel, and his pulse began to race as he unwrapped the package. His lucky flask. A bit charred, but it had been salvaged. After sliding it into a pocket and closing the lid on the trunk, he crossed the room to the rope bed.

Lifting a corner of the clean quilt to his face, he breathed in the scent of woman. This might just work out even better than he'd thought. Paddy hadn't lost the place to a man or sold it, and no woman who wore hats and dresses like these would set out to live here alone. Paddy had obviously found himself a wife, and the Widow Maloney was a refined woman.

So where was she?

It's Sunday, Whibley. He might have taken to praying of late, but church was a whole other matter. Not so for a cultured woman. She was no doubt at church this morning and would soon be on her way home. It wouldn't set well for her to come home and find him inside.

Fortunately, he'd come on a sunny day. He'd just make himself at home on the stoop and wait for her. There'd be plenty of time to enjoy the trimmings of the indoors once she'd succumbed to his charms.

THIRTY-FIVE

K at stood outside the basement door of the hospital with Nell and Rosita at her side. She would've preferred to speak to Morgan in person, but he hadn't returned from church. He'd told Sister Coleman he planned to be out all afternoon, and she'd been kind enough to give Kat a piece of stationery to leave the man a note. If there was any chance that Morgan was married, he had to understand that she would not compromise her principles. She'd written down her concerns, and now all she had to do was slip the message under the door.

Nell stayed Kat's arm. "He was talking to Darla when we arrived at the church, and left her to help you. You saw the way she batted her eyelashes at him in Hattie's parlor. The way she cooed at him outside the café. I think she's the kind of woman who might say or do anything to get what she wants."

"And Morgan, what kind of man is he, really? You don't believe he is married now"—Kat waved the sheet of paper—"but that doesn't change anything for me. If he ever has been married, he should have told me before he began showering me with attention."

"Don't leave the note. Wait until this evening." Nell tugged on her arm. "Talk to him about it then. You don't know that it's true."

Holding her ground, Kat looked up into Nell's face. Her sister shared Hattie's hopeless romantic ideals, but things weren't always what they seemed. And they were certainly not always what one desired them to be. If anyone knew that, Kat did.

"I don't know that Darla was lying." She shook her head. She wanted to believe Morgan wasn't married, and she wanted to believe that if he had been, he would have told her so, but something about the set of Darla's face told her she believed what she was saying. "And I won't make another mistake."

He hadn't told her much of anything about his past. Instead, he'd given her every indication that he wanted more than a friendship. The invitation for a carriage ride alone with her this evening was proof of that, and she'd accepted, not knowing any more about the man than that he'd come from a wealthy family in Boston and he played the piano. She may have chosen to live in a simple cabin in a community of miners, but she was a proper woman. Kat freed her arm from Nell's hold and slipped the envelope under the door.

Kat held Rosita's hand and clomped up the stairs, all the way out into the sunshine. As the three of them made their way up the hill to Florissant, Kat tugged her bonnet back from her forehead and tilted her face toward the warmth. This morning the pleasant change in the weather had her believing she'd entered a new season in her life. Morgan Cutshaw had played a central role in that speculation.

Now, she could only see him as a man who didn't trust her enough to tell her the truth. Thankfully, her sister knew her well enough to change the subject. It's Sunday. "I want to play checkers this afternoon." Nell sounded too cheery.

"We left the set with Ida and Viv."

"You have paper, and we have red beans and lima beans. We can make do."

"I was going to write to Viv and Father before Morgan came to call, but now that I've canceled those plans, I suppose I'll have plenty of time for both."

As they rounded the corner of Pikes Peak Avenue, Nell pointed toward the cabin. "Who is that?"

Kat had never seen the man who was sitting on the steps. He wore black breeches, a vest, and a top hat, and he was looking at something he held in his hands. He didn't look at all like a miner. He looked more like a hawker, and she noticed a case of some sort propped against the stoop. "He probably wants to sell us the latest elixir for gout or some such thing."

He looked toward them and shoved whatever he'd been studying into his vest. He stood, and a quizzical expression creased his chin as he descended the two steps to their level. "Ladies. Miss." He looked down at Rosita, who peeked at him from behind Nell, and then back up at Kat. "I heard about Mr. Maloney's unfortunate passing, and I've come to pay my respects, ma'am." He removed his hat and held it to his chest. "I'm Lewis P. Whibley, at your service."

The formal name didn't improve the man's image any. She didn't see a wagon of potions or wares nearby, but that didn't mean he wasn't peddling something. Her mind churning, Kat straightened to her full height. This man wasn't just a salesman passing through. He knew of

Patrick's death and he knew where Patrick lived, but who was he and why was he on her stoop? It was entirely possible Patrick had family that no one in town knew about.

"Are you relation to Patrick, sir?"

"No ma'am, I lived here In Cripple Creek until eight or nine months ago." He stared off toward the juniper before continuing. "Me and Paddy were business partners."

Ollie had already collected Patrick's horse for payment at his saloon. Could he have owed money to this man too?

"Business partners," Kat repeated. "Patrick was a mucker, a drinker, and a carouser, Mr. Whibley. In which of those three enterprises were the two of you involved?"

He chuckled.

"You're finding this entertaining?"

"Ma'am, I didn't mean to offend you, but I do find your witty directness a bit amusing and refreshing."

"You've shared your sympathies," Kat said, brushing past him. "And now I'd appreciate it if you'd step aside."

"I do need to speak with you about the cabin, ma'am."

A headache began to form at the base of her neck.

"You asked about my business with him. Well, you might say Paddy and I were co-owners in this house. And now that he's gone, I've come to take possession."

Now the ache climbed the back of her head. "I have papers to prove this is my home." She knew any papers she had could be contested in a court of law, but she'd learned from Patrick that a good bluff could go a long way. "You may as well just leave, sir, as I have no intention of sharing ownership of my house with any man."

He looked around, as if he was not accustomed to doing any business in the open. "I'm sure we can reach an amicable agreement. I have the deepest respect and sympathy for widows, and I'd like to help you out any way I can."

"Then kindly step aside."

He frowned, but stepped aside, his hand motioning her toward the door.

Watching his every move, Kat climbed the steps with Rosita and Nell right behind her. The stench of his cheap toilet water burned her eyes as they passed him. Once Nell and Rosita were inside the cabin, Kat stood in the doorway and faced the man.

"This aloofness is so unnecessary, Mrs. Maloney." He waved his hand at the distance between them. "I can see you worked hard to make this a fine home for you and Paddy, and I'm sure we could come to an agreement that could benefit us both."

He would only have known she'd made it a fine home if he'd been inside. Kat's blood began to boil. "You went inside?"

"I told you I'm here to claim ownership."

"That hardly gives you the right to enter my home as you please."

"But it does, ma'am." His tone had suddenly changed from sugary sweet to business professional. "This is my cabin."

"This was Patrick Maloney's home, Mr. Whibley. And now it's mine. I'm not sure what your business together was, but you should consider the partnership officially dissolved."

"Ma'am, of course you're distraught. This has to be surprising news, and so soon after your loss."

The man either didn't know Paddy or he was patronizing her, hoping she'd think of him as some sort of gentleman. Either way he was lying. Kat glanced at the hillsides. Where were the miners Boney Hughes said were looking out for them?

Never mind that. She would take care of this herself.

"Mrs. Maloney, you're alone in this rough town here without a man, and I'm simply offering you a solution to your problem. I'm willing to compensate you for Patrick's ten percent stake in the cabin. You surely don't want to remain here among these uncivilized miners, vulnerable and defenseless. "

As soon as he made that last statement, a solution came to Kat's mind. She twisted to look at Nell. When she had her sister's attention, Kat gazed toward the top of the door, hoping Nell would understand. Nell hesitated, then hurried to the table and retrieved a chair.

"Like I said, ma'am, there's a simple answer for all of this. If it would help, I could prove the cabin belongs to me."

He couldn't. He had to be lying.

When he reached into his pocket, Kat flinched. She hadn't considered the man might carry a pistol. As soon as he pulled out a charred silver flask, she bristled. It was the same one the sheriff brought to the boardinghouse the day after the fire.

"You took that from my trunk."

Grinning, he flipped it over and held it out to her. "Look at the inscription on the back near the bottom of it."

Kat snatched it from his hand and studied it. *L.P.W.*

"Stands for Lewis P. Whibley. My father gave it to me."

Those were this man's initials, not Patrick Maloney's. She shook her head. Well, maybe the flask was his, but that didn't mean the cabin belonged to him.

"How did Patrick get your flask?"

"Well, ma'am, let's just say he was having a remarkably lucky night—the kind of luck a fella has when an ace is hidden in his trouser pocket."

Gambling. That explained the whole situation. This may have been Whibley's cabin at one time, but he'd lost it to Paddy, along with his flask. And since Paddy was gone, the scoundrel thought he could waltz in and reclaim it.

The thud of Nell's shoes returning to the floor was music to Kat's ears. From behind the door, Nell held the shotgun out to her. Kat took it, and cradling it with both hands, she cocked the hammers. Then she positioned her finger across both triggers.

"Whoa. You could hurt yourself with that thing." Lewis P. Whibley flew backward off the porch. "No need to get your petticoat in a tangle."

"Mr. Whibley, I don't believe in luck. But if I did, I can promise you that I am more fortunate than Paddy Maloney. Willing to chance a lucky shot? It's time for you to leave my home and never come back."

Three burly miners were headed up the hill toward them. "This weasel giving you some trouble, ma'am?" The one who spoke had a pick resting on his shoulder.

Kat couldn't believe it. As she watched, more men joined them, forming a half circle off to the side.

Kat stepped to the edge of the porch, directing the business end of the shotgun toward Lewis's feet. "It seems Mr. Whibley is confused. He apparently thinks this is his cabin."

"You need some help convincin' him otherwise?"

Kat held the intruder's gaze. "I think Mr. Whibley understands now. Thank you."

"We'd be happy to escort him to the edge of town, if you'd like." The pick still resting against his shoulder, the man advanced toward Mr. Whibley.

Whibley regarded her with a smirk. "I can find my way back to town, gentlemen. I must have misread the contract with Mr. Maloney." He raised his hands in surrender and then looked back at Kat. "Sorry to have bothered you, ma'am." Grabbing his valise and case, he studied her. "Perhaps we could discuss this further at a more appropriate time. Maybe we can have a meal, talk about books and journal keeping?"

Kat arched an eyebrow and nearly growled, "You step foot on my property again, and the sheriff will become involved."

When Whibley turned to leave, the men waved at her and she waved back before stepping into the house. As soon as she did, Nell took the shotgun from her. Then Kat sank to the floor.

THIRTY-SIX

After Morgan's brief talk with Hattie out in the church parking area, he drove his coupé up to Mount Pisgah. In his short time in Cripple Creek, the spot had become one of his favorite places to go to think. He'd set aside a good hour and half after the service to do just that. He didn't know too many people who considered a burying ground a good place to sort things out, but he appreciated the sense of earthly time passing in that quiet place. It wasn't where Opal was laid to rest, but after walking among the stones for a while, he believed that she'd be happy that he came to Cripple Creek, that he was moving forward with his life. That Kat Sinclair might be part of his future.

Just before two o'clock, he reined his horse at the hitching rail in front of Hattie's place. Judson waved to him from a group of men seated in rocking chairs on the porch. By the time Morgan met the builders and claimed an empty chair, Hattie and three other women had stepped outside, each carrying generous servings of berry pie.

Once the pie was gone, Morgan, Hattie, and Judson left the group and stepped into the parlor.

Hattie and Judson had discussed Miss Nell Sinclair's feelings for him prior to Morgan's arrival, leaving the three to concoct a plan for Judson to express himself properly to Nell. Then Hattie helped Morgan select music for the Women for the Betterment of Cripple Creek concert.

After nearly three hours at Hattie's, Morgan stepped off the woman's porch with a picnic basket and a quilt. He'd planned to stop by the hospital to change clothes before driving to Kat's cabin, but she expected him at five o'clock and he only had fifteen minutes to spare. He guessed that she probably cared more about promptness than she did about his being overdressed for a picnic.

It felt good to have the misunderstanding behind them. He still didn't like the fact that she was living in a miner's cabin with no one to protect her.

First, though, he had to earn the right to protect her. He needed to tell her about Opal and about his son. He needed to explain why he'd reacted the way he had in the birthing room, and why he'd reacted to her move the way he had.

Yes, they were becoming friends, but his feelings for her ran deeper. And he believed he'd seen more than friendship in Kat's eyes Friday in the parlor and this morning at church. Or was it just wishful thinking? Morgan understood that Kat was striking out on her own in part because Patrick Maloney had deceived her and hurt her, but it didn't make it any easier to watch.

Please, Lord, protect Kat.

He and Kat would get to know each other better, and today was a wonderful day for a picnic. To the east, sunbeams lit the snowy heights of Pikes Peak. Mount Pisgah glowed to the west, its thinning snow top giving way to patches of green carpeting. Kat had him thinking like a poet, and he rather liked it.

Following Kat's directions, Morgan guided his horse across Golden Avenue and up Florissant Street. Small homes, cabins, and shanties dotted the hillsides. He shifted the reins to turn east onto Pikes Peak Avenue and stopped in front of the third cabin off to the right.

Lace curtains framed the window, and he suddenly wanted a house with lace curtains. He wanted a home warmed by someone who would walk through life beside him. And the woman who peered out at him was the one he had in mind. But Kat's look wasn't welcoming. Instead, her mouth dropped open, and she jumped back from the window.

He said five o'clock, he was sure of it. So why did she look surprised to see him?

At the sight of Morgan Cutshaw, Kat froze, her eyes widening. He smiled at her from his buggy, and she stepped away from the window. "It's Morgan. Why is he here?"

Nell looked up at her from the rocker, stilling her knitting needles. "You have to ask?"

Huffing, Kat peeled off her apron. She'd made her stand quite clear in her note. She'd canceled their plans and told him not to come. He shouldn't have, but now that he was here, she'd make sure he understood. He needed to know the two of them could only be acquaintances as long as he was married. And as such, they would not be going out alone for carriage rides or sitting in church together.

Morgan Cutshaw's wistful glance at her through the window wouldn't make this any easier. With Patrick, she could read back through his letters and talk to the people he'd worked with and see signs that pointed to his bankrupt character. Nothing in her interactions with Morgan so much as hinted at such a deception.

He rapped on the door. Nell made no move to get up. Instead, she hitched her brows, narrowing her forehead in a telltale sign that she had no intention of intervening.

Fine.

Kat had traveled thousands of miles. She'd moved into a shanty in the midst of coarse men. She'd chased off the slick gambler. She could see to the doctor. Squaring her shoulders, Kat opened the door, just wide enough to see him.

The doctor wore the same dressy clothes he'd worn to church, minus the jacket. A watch chain looped out of a pocket in his vest. He didn't wear a wedding ring. Nothing about him shouted that he was hiding a misleading past or that he was otherwise spoken for. But Kat knew that looks could be deceiving, and she refused to be deceived. Not again.

Studying her, Morgan removed his hat. "Is there something wrong, Kat?"

"You know there is, Dr. Cutshaw."

His eyes widened, and he shook his head.

"It was in the note I left for you."

"You left me a note? Where?" He ran his hand through his dark hair, smoothing it down.

"Under the basement door at the hospital directly after church."

"I didn't go back to the hospital." He stepped forward. "I went for a drive and then to Miss Hattie's to pick out the songs I'll play at her ladies' meeting Wednesday next."

"Oh, yes…the Betterment of Cripple Creek meeting. How ironic." She'd practically spit out the words.

"Pardon me?" Morgan cocked a brow. "I don't understand, Kat. I didn't see any note. I came straight here from Hattie's house."

Hattie adored the doctor. She would never believe that he would intentionally deceive or hurt anyone. In the end, however, it didn't matter what Hattie did or didn't think about the man. Kat couldn't afford to be taken in by him, or anyone else.

"Is Nell here?" Morgan asked, peering through the narrow opening.

"I'm here, Doctor," Nell called. "And so is Rosita. She's napping."

If Nell had meant the announcement as a reminder, Kat caught the hint and drew in a deep breath, trying to calm herself.

"Nell, I have word from Judson."

"You do?" Nell rushed to the door and pulled it wider, looking out at him. "What did he say?"

"He's starting to feel almost like himself again, and expects to call on you soon."

Nell exhaled in relief and leaned into the door frame. "Oh, thank you, Doctor. That's comforting."

Morgan returned his attention to Kat. "Kat, I thought we'd resolved our misunderstanding this morning."

"We did. That one."

"That one?"

Kat offered him a slight nod.

"All right, then. I didn't get your note telling me what this is about, so what did it say?"

Nell stepped closer to her sister, offering welcome support.

"I learned that you have a wife," Kat said, crossing her arms over her chest.

His jaw tightened and his dimple disappeared. "Who told you that?"

A cold shaft of a breeze stung her cheeks. He hadn't denied it.

"It doesn't matter whom I heard it from."

"It matters to me." He spun his hat around by the brim in front of him. "It matters because it's not true, and I need to know who's spreading falsehoods so I can set it straight."

"You're saying you don't have a wife?" Kat tilted her head, trying to read his face.

"I did have a wife, Kat, but I don't anymore." He stopped toying with his hat and looked at her, his mouth a grim line. "And I'm sorry I didn't tell you myself. I planned to do so during our visit this afternoon."

Even while her mind remained stuck on the fact that he hadn't told her himself, her heart rejoiced that he wasn't currently married.

Nell pulled the door wider. "Come in, Doctor."

Morgan looked at Kat, his brow raised. She stepped aside, allowing him to enter.

"You two sit down at the table." Nell stared at Kat, her eyes permitting no argument. "I'll brew some coffee." She didn't wait for an answer before busying herself with a tin of coffee grounds and Patrick's old percolator.

Morgan pulled out a chair for her and then sat across the table, his hands clasped in front of him. "I should've told you Friday before I invited you for the carriage ride today." He looked down at his hands. "You'd been hurt so badly, and so recently, that I didn't feel it was wise to share such information yet."

"And yet you chose to tell Darla Taggart about your wife?"

"I didn't…" His voice faltered. "She was prying…and it just came out."

"So is that how it works?"

He stared at her, a vein on his forehead jumping. "She asked if the piano was mine, and I told her it had belonged to my wife. When she kept questioning me, I blurted out that I couldn't fathom ever being married again. My involvement with her is—"

"I know, professional and humanitarian." She met his gaze. "This isn't about Darla. After church this morning, she asked me if you'd told me about your wife." The last word came out louder than she'd intended. When Rosita stirred and turned over, Kat continued in a whisper. "This is about your not telling me you'd been married."

"And, naturally, you thought…"

"What was I supposed to think? I don't know you very well." She tugged the gingham cloth in the center of the table straight, her thoughts bubbling right along with the coffeepot.

"Perhaps that I was a man who knows what it's like to lose someone you love. Who knows what it's like to move across the country in a new beginning and have it turn out far differently than you'd expected."

That's what she wished she'd thought, but he was right. She'd thought the worst of him.

"I didn't love him," she said quietly.

Morgan nodded. "Opal died in childbirth nearly three years ago now. So did our son, William Morgan."

Tears stung Kat's eyes and she pressed her fingers against her welling eyelids. "I'm so sorry," she said, and gazed up at him. This man who sat across from her, blinking back his own tears, truly knew what it meant to love and lose. In her haste to protect herself from more pain, she never even considered the possibility that Morgan might have suffered losses of his own. Kat's tears began to spill over her face. "I'm so sorry about Opal and William."

Morgan pushed the empty lantern and gingham cloth from between them, and held his handkerchief out to her. When she reached for his handkerchief, the backs of their hands touched and his lingered, and she looked up into moist green eyes brimming with understanding and compassion.

"You're not like Patrick Maloney."

"No ma'am." He dipped his chin. "I'm surely not."

"I shouldn't have doubted you. I'm sorry."

"Apology accepted. Am I forgiven for not telling you myself... sooner?"

"You're forgiven." Kat felt the corners of her lips turn up a little. "But you have to promise me that you'll tear up the ugly note waiting for you in the basement. Before you read it."

"You've got a deal." He released the handkerchief and stood. "I brought a picnic supper, but the wind is picking up a bit and the shadows are lengthening. The spot I had in mind will soon be shaded and, thus, too chilly. How do you ladies feel about a picnic supper inside tonight?" He looked from Kat to Nell and back to Kat.

"That sounds wonderful," Kat said.

As he took long strides out the door, Nell sniffled and Kat stood up from the table and went to the window. Dabbing at her tears, she watched Morgan reach into the back of his buggy and pull out a picnic basket. He was a good man. A man she could trust.

A man who couldn't fathom ever being married again.

THIRTY-SEVEN

*M*onday morning, Kat could hardly keep up with Rosita and HopHop.

"Choo-choo! I see Abuela today!" The little girl sang as she skipped ahead of Kat and Nell on the way down the hill. Last evening they'd been setting out Morgan's picnic supper when Rosita woke up. After they'd all eaten their fill, she and Nell crafted a makeshift checkerboard complete with beans for checkers. It wasn't the same without Ida and Vivian, but they'd still laughed a lot. It was a different family she had here in Cripple Creek, but it was a kind of family nonetheless, and Kat was dreading saying good-bye to its smallest member.

They turned onto Bennett Avenue. They'd only been here two weeks, but Cripple Creek wasn't the same town she and Nell had seen when they stepped off the train. When the false-fronted wood buildings had been reduced to ashes, the whole community had pitched in to haul off the rubble and rebuild the town. Men were hard at work with hammers and trowels, raising fire-resistant brick and sandstone buildings in their stead. With the new buildings came a new direction, and a new sense of purpose.

God had been doing the same for Kat. She now had a home and a focus for her writing. She had new friends, including her gentleman friend. He brought her unexpected joy, even if she still had questions about what was to come. Kat couldn't help but wonder if Morgan would ever change his mind about marrying again, and Nell was concerned about seeing Judson when he came to call, wondering what direction their relationship would go.

"Now I see Abuela? *Tio* Ray?" Rosita tugged on Kat's skirt. Her small knapsack of belongings hung over her shoulder.

"First, we have to go to the post office so I can mail my story." Kat patted Rosita's silky black hair. "Then we'll go to the depot. We'll find Mr. Boney and wait for the train." Thankfully, the miner would be there to translate. Saturday night after Boney's shotgun lesson, he'd given Kat the telegram from the sheriff in New Mexico. Rosita's grandfather was gravely ill, so the little one's grandmother and her uncle would need to get right back on the train with her to return to Santa Fe. She and Nell had hoped to be able to spend some time with Rosita's family, partly to extend the time with her, and partly so they would know that Rosita would have a good life with them in Santa Fe. However, judging by the child's excitement this morning, Kat doubted she and Nell had reason to worry.

At the sound of the faint whistle when the train came out of the mountain pass, Rosita's eyes widened. "Choo-choo," she whispered. "Choo-choo. I go on the train."

"Yes. Very soon," Kat said, shaking her head as the three of them crossed the boardwalk and made their way into the post office.

Kat recognized the couple at the counter immediately. They were unmistakable. A familiar shock of red curls spilled down the woman's back—clothed this time—and a baby fussed, his head sticking out from the cradle of her arms. The man at her side wore black breeches and a top hat, and the room smelled like cheap toilet water.

Kat grabbed Nell's arm to turn them all around, but it was too late. The couple turned to leave, and the woman grinned in recognition.

"I was wonderin' if I'd see you around here sometime. Thought maybe I'd scared you off with that mess." The woman beamed at Kat. "Didn't even get your name. Mine's Iris." She turned toward the man who escorted her, dragging her red curls across the baby's face. "This is the woman I was tellin' you about. The one the new doc thought was a midwife."

Kat squared her shoulders and offered him a half nod. "Mr. Whibley."

"You know him?"

"Mrs. Maloney." Removing his hat, the slick gambler tightened his jaw in a frown.

"You know her?" Iris jerked back toward Kat, her eyes wide. "You were married to Paddy?"

"No, we were never married."

"You aren't Paddy's widow?" Whibley shoved his hat back on his head.

"I didn't say I was married to Mr. Maloney, sir. You did."

"But you pointed a shotgun at me like you were his widow."

"I pointed a shotgun at you because you wouldn't leave my property."

"You want to tell me why this woman had to pull a shotgun on you?" Iris glared at him, a hand on one hip and a baby on the other.

"A misunderstanding is all the lovely lady and I have between us," Lewis said, holding up his hands. "Paddy's cabin was mine."

"*Was.* Before you lost it to him, Mr. Whibley."

"Yes." Whibley nodded. "And I woulda won it back from him fair and square, but since he's dead—"

"You thought you could move into Paddy's cabin and call it your own?" Iris shifted the baby to her shoulder.

"I didn't know there was a woman living there."

Iris shook her head and looked at Kat, her brows arched. "Sounds like my Lewis, all right."

"Your Lewis?" That question came from Nell, and earned a slanted stare from Iris.

Kat saw green in the woman's brown eyes and cleared her throat. "This is my sister, Nell."

Lewis nodded.

"Yes, my Lewis." Iris stepped closer to the gambler. "We got close the last time he was in town." She grinned at the newborn in her arms. "Real close."

Kat remembered him saying he'd been here in Cripple Creek about eight or nine months ago gambling with Patrick and no doubt behaving in the same indecent manner. Was this scoundrel the baby's father? Kat needed to remember to pray for the little one who wiggled and whimpered in his mother's arms.

"We've had us some real good work last night and Lewis is takin' us to California. Sending a letter right now to warn my brother that we're coming. That is, if Lewis can behave himself long enough." Iris laughed and elbowed the man. Lewis continued to glare at Kat. "Thank you again for helping me and my son." She stroked her son's cheek.

"I wish I could have done more."

She nodded. "God bless you all."

"And you." The couple turned to go, and Kat tried not to look at the man wearing the top hat and carrying his gambling table. When they walked out, Kat turned her envelope over to the postmaster. Then she led Nell and Rosita down the new boardwalk and over to the Midland Terminal Railroad depot where Boney Hughes stood beside his mule that was tied to the hitching rail. True to form, the man spit a stream of brown into the dirt as they approached.

"Ladies." He removed his hat and bent to the little girl's level. "Rosita," he said, his open arms accepting the little girl's hug.

"I see Abuela and Tio Ray today."

Boney nodded and looked up at the sisters. Kat was sure she saw tears pool the man's eyes before he turned away.

Rosita pulled Boney toward the platform, and the sisters followed. Kat reached for Nell's hand and squeezed it as the train puffed into the station. Rosita squealed with excitement, singing a new song about her grandmother.

Nell's hand started to quiver, signaling tears coming on, and Kat squeezed a little tighter. "I know, Kat. I just…" Nell's voice cracked as tears spilled down her face.

As the train came to a stop, a stream of people disembarked and milled around on the platform. Finally, an older Mexican woman wearing a long dress made of cotton, with bright flowers stitched into the yoke and the hem, stepped out of the car with a younger man.

The man, Kat guessed, was Rosita's Tio Ray, and he stayed by the door of the Pullman.

"Abuela!" HopHop dangled from Rosita's open arms as she ran toward the stocky woman. Even from here, Kat could see how much the woman's face mirrored Rosita's.

"*Mija*!" She rushed toward her granddaughter, her long, full dress swooshing with every step. Rosita all but leaped into her arms. Rosita's legs wrapped around her grandmother's middle and their foreheads touched.

Both Rosita and her grandmother looked at Kat and Nell, their dark eyes shimmering with joyful tears. They chattered in a language Kat might not understand, but she knew enough to know it translated into love.

The grandmother's gray hair hung in two braids, interwoven with bright strips of cloth, and suddenly Kat saw why Rosita always insisted on having her hair plaited with cloth ribbons.

She said something in Spanish and looked at Boney.

"She thanks God for you," Boney said. "You have cared for Rosita, and she will be grateful for as long as God gives her breath."

The woman stroked Rosita's hair. She was taking Rosita with her. It was an answer to Kat's prayers. So why did it hurt so much?

Nell seemed unable to move or speak. Drawing in a deep breath, Kat held tight to her sister.

The woman set Rosita on the ground, and she ran back to Kat and Nell.

"I go home with Abuela."

Kat nodded, unable to get any words out. Nell embraced Rosita. "I will miss you, little one," Nell said, tears brimming in her eyes.

Kat knelt down on the platform and hugged Rosita good-bye. When Kat stood, Rosita held HopHop out to her, her bottom lip extended. "He's yours now," Kat whispered. "HopHop will go wherever you go."

Rosita's smile lit her eyes as she squeezed the bunny tight.

The grandmother spoke again, raising her hands and placing them on her chest. *"Salud, pesetas, y amor. Y tiempo para gustar."*

Kat smiled at the woman and then looked to Boney for the translation.

"She wishes you health, wealth, and love, and time to enjoy them all."

Kat watched Rosita tug on her grandmother's colorful skirt as she spoke. "Please tell her thank you. That we pray for God to bless her, Rosita, and their family."

As soon as Boney finished translating, he patted Rosita on the head. "I'll miss you, little one."

Rosita slipped her little hand into her grandmother's, and the two of them turned to join Tio Ray at the train for the loop through the rest of the Cripple Creek mining district and back to Colorado Springs.

Kat's knees went weak, and she laid her hand over her heart.

THIRTY-EIGHT

***

ell and Kat watched Rosita skip toward the train, hand in hand with her grandmother. Nell knew the girl was where she belonged, but it still hurt to see her go.

After the sisters bade their good-byes to Boney, they walked away from the depot in silence and down Bennett Avenue toward Hattie's. It wasn't Nell's own tears and sadness that surprised her, but Kat's. Of course her sister was fond of the little girl she'd taken in. She'd seen to it that Rosita had clothing, and braided her hair. But if anyone had asked Nell how Kat would react in this moment, she would have answered with quick certainty: her sister would maintain her stoic exterior.

But by the time they reached the corner at Hayden Avenue and stepped off the boardwalk onto the hard-packed dirt, sobs shook Kat's body. Nell stopped and pulled her into an embrace. She knew she'd miss Rosita, and her heart ached to know what Judson considered to be the future of their relationship, but seeing her sister so sad hurt worst of all. Nell pulled a handkerchief from her pocket and slid it into Kat's hand.

Kat cried into the handkerchief until her tears finally subsided. Sniffling, she stepped back from Nell, her cheeks blotchy and her eyes red. Her bonnet sat askew atop her head, her auburn hair poking out of it at angles. "You're all right?" she asked, blotting her face with the hanky.

"Compared to you, I am." Nell smoothed her sister's hair back from her face and tugged her hat straight.

"I'm going to miss those shy smiles that we would tease out of Rosita." Kat sniffled. "And I'll never forget that focused expression on her face when she tried to put the broom to good use in the cabin."

"I know. You need purpose, and caring for Rosita and finding her family had given you that." As Nell took the first step forward, she prayed for wisdom. "Let's get to Hattie's. She always makes us feel better."

Nodding, Kat wiped her face again and took heavy steps up the street, passed by a burro pulling a cart full of groceries.

"You'll have plenty to keep you busy soon." As Nell slowed her steps to match Kat's, she wanted to mention Morgan but decided against it. "You'll have your writing and your own home to take care of."

Kat huffed. "A home without a real cookstove. Where we have to use a chamber pot, or traipse out to an outhouse. Where it's drafty, and we can expect all manner of vermin and creepy-crawly things."

"The cabin's not all that bad. You've forgotten about the lace curtain and the shotgun."

A smile played on Kat's lips. "That shotgun did come in handy, didn't it?" She laughed. "That wasn't the behavior of a city girl."

"No ma'am, it surely wasn't. Annie Oakley would be proud of you. I know I was."

Kat's smile faded, and her eyes clouded over again. "I didn't even want to be married. I was doing it to help Father, and to help all of us get settled here."

"I know."

"So why did he have to do this to me?"

Nell slid her hand into Kat's. "Father or Patrick?"

"Morgan Cutshaw."

Nell bit her lip to stay a flood of words, and nodded instead.

"I was doing fine. And then he had to take us for that carriage ride and bring me that magazine."

"And that's bad?"

"Yes, it's bad. You heard him last night at the cabin." Kat pulled her wrap tighter against the spring breeze. "He said he told Darla he couldn't fathom ever being married again."

"That's what this is all about?"

"It's crazy, I know," Kat said, staring off toward Tenderfoot Hill. "I didn't expect to feel this way about any man."

Nell laughed. "It's about time you acknowledged how you felt."

"I know." Kat's smile didn't quite reach her eyes. "You trusted him. And I thought the worst of him."

"The man who brought you here deceived and betrayed you. It's no wonder you're having trouble trusting again." As they turned onto Hattie's street and the yellow house came into view, Nell prayed the woman would have the ability to make them both feel better.

"He not only told Darla he couldn't fathom being married again, but then repeated it to me as if he wanted to make sure I knew it too." Kat paused. "I thought I wanted to be alone."

"You know people say things they don't mean." Nell fluttered her hand, watching a sparrow that perched on a feeder that hung off a cottage porch. "Or they say things and later change their minds." She was sure the latter applied to Morgan. Whether the doctor knew it or not, she knew he'd fallen for her sister.

Kat wiped her eyes. "At least I have my writing. I can always do that, no matter what happens."

At the yellow house with the white trim, Nell led Kat up the walkway to the front door and grabbed the knocker.

The door whooshed open, and Nell felt as if her heart had raced right into her throat. The man standing in the doorway had written her twelve wonderful letters. She would've spoken his name, but her mouth had gone dry.

"Nell." His voice sounded like spring, and he had eyes bluer than a jay. "I thought you'd never get here."

As far as she could tell, he was feeling much better.

"I have a surprise for you," he said, his face widening into a grin.

"Judson, just seeing you is a wonderful surprise. There's more?"

Nodding, his eyes full of promise, Judson Archer reached for her hand and led her into the parlor. She hardly dared to look down at their joined hands. She was afraid she was imagining the whole thing.

Hattie sat in the wing-back chair, waving a handkerchief, and Morgan smiled at her from behind the piano. Kat went to sit on the sofa while Judson escorted Nell to the Queen Anne chair that sat empty by the window.

"Maestro." Judson motioned to Morgan. As soon as the first chord sounded, Judson began to sing.

Low to our hearts love sung an old sweet song.

Judson's tenor voice sounded like the wind whispering through the pines, and Nell thought she might faint. But she willed herself not to allow it, for she intended to remember this moment forever.

She had to be dreaming.

Lord, please let this be real.

Still to us at twilight comes love's old song…

It wasn't a dream. Judson hitched his breeches and bent to one knee. As he knelt in front of her, his voice tender, she felt his warm breath on her face. And tears fell in this, her old sweet song—their song.

When he'd finished the song and the piano stilled, Judson cupped her face. Her skin tingled, alive and warm under his touch. She could live like this forever.

"Judson, I'm so sorry you were robbed and hurt. And I'm sorry I didn't respect your wishes and barged in on you at the hospital." Her words were a mere whisper.

"I'm sorry for yelling at you. Those weren't words I ever wanted to speak to you, and certainly not the first ones."

"I forgive you." Another whisper. She couldn't take her eyes off his smile. "You're, uh, well now?"

"I go back to work tomorrow, but I'll be doing most of my office work standing up."

A giggle escaped before Nell could catch it, but she covered her mouth anyway.

"I love that."

"What?"

"Your laughter. I love your laughter."

And she loved him.

"Miss Nell Sinclair, I have loved you from the time I read the signature on your first letter. 'In God's hands, Miss Nell Sinclair.' Will you marry me Saturday next?"

"I've waited this long." Nell's eyes brimmed with tears. "I suppose I can wait another twelve days. Yes, Judson. My answer is yes. Oh, yes." A grin lit his irresistible face, and Nell bent down and kissed his lips.

Thank You, Lord. He was so worth waiting for.

Kat sighed, remembering how Morgan's fingers moved across the piano keys as if God made them to play. God had indeed blessed the man with many gifts—doctoring, music, and a romantic spirit, to name a few.

She hadn't seen her sister so happy in a long while. Nell's patience had paid off. And now Kat couldn't help but hope Nell was right about Morgan too. That he would change his mind about never marrying again.

"That's one of the songs Dr. Cutshaw will play at my luncheon next Wednesday. You girls simply must come." Hattie dabbed at her eyes with a pink hanky.

To hear Morgan play again, Kat would go anywhere. She'd be there, front and center.

"And Judson, dear, you must sing it for the Women for the Betterment of Cripple Creek. They'll adore you for it." Hattie rose and strolled over to Morgan and patted his cheek as if he were her own son. "You boys are so gallant. Just like my George. Why, you two could fill an opera house. How I wish we had a proper one here in Cripple Creek. Heard plenty talk about it, but nothing's come of it yet."

"Let's get through next Wednesday's concert first," Morgan patted Judson on the back. "And I think that's a right fine idea, your singing in the program. I could use the moral support."

"If Nell's going, I'll be there with my pipes tuned and ready." Judson laced his fingers with Nell's.

Hattie sniffed. "It smells like love is in the air," she said, although to Kat it smelled more like fresh-baked bread. "Are you all about ready for lunch?"

Morgan held his arm out for Kat. She laid her hand on it, feeling a zing of warmth shoot to her toes and back up into her face. He stood tall and strong, and she suddenly felt grateful for his strength. Perhaps she didn't need to be quite so independent.

"Are you busy this Saturday?"

Kat glanced at his arm while she considered the question and the possible inference. "Why?"

"I thought if you're not too busy helping Nell with her wedding plans, we could finally have our outdoor picnic."

"I'd like that."

Morgan nodded and escorted her to the dining table.

It wasn't a marriage proposal. But it was something.

Thirty-Nine

Dear Ida,

Nell and I were so excited to receive your letter last Friday.
I can't believe another week has already passed.
We received a second letter today. Thank you!
Nell and I have had nary a dull moment since we arrived
in Cripple Creek.

To say the least.

Kat tried to concentrate on her letter, but the anticipation of
tomorrow's picnic with Morgan Cutshaw kept distracting her. She laid
her pen down next to her letter and sat back in the chair. Warmth em-
anated from the potbellied stove, adding to the cabin's cozy feel. A pot
of columbines topped Nell's trunk under the window. A canning jar
full of daises rested on the countertop next to a set of canisters Hattie

had given her. A milk bottle brimmed with posies in the center of the table. All gifts from Judson Archer.

Kat breathed in the earthy scent of fresh flowers.

Her sister had floated out of the dress shop this afternoon, talking about the most beautiful dress in the world. Nell sat in the rocker now, stitching a sampler to hang in her new home. Kat turned back to her letter. Their oldest sister would finish her secretarial schooling in Maine at the end of summer. She planned to arrive in Cripple Creek shortly thereafter. Good news to be sure, especially since Vivian would follow her a few months later, and the four of them would be reunited.

But come next Saturday, one week from tomorrow, Nell would marry Judson and make a home with him.

Leaving Kat alone.

Kat had thought that was what she wanted—that self-sufficiency would be her only remaining option in Colorado. But now that she had gotten to know Morgan Cutshaw better, the idea of being alone seemed a burden rather than a blessing. A lonely reality rather than a noble quest.

Kat gave up on the letter and walked to the bucket full of dirty dishes. She'd just stuck her hand in the soapy water when she heard the sound of wheels churning rocks out front.

"Someone's here." Nell rose from the rocker and left her stitching hanging on the arm of the chair.

Kat nodded. "It's not Boney this time, unless he traded his mule for a wagon." She dried her hands on her apron while Nell pulled a corner of the curtain back and peeked outside.

"Oh." A smile lit her sister's blue eyes as she unlatched the door and pulled it open.

Kat expected to see Judson standing there, but it was Morgan who stood on the small porch. He held a single yellow rose—its vibrancy surpassed only by the brightness of his smile.

"Morgan?"

"Good evening, Kat. Nell. I must get back to work, but I thought you might need this." He held the flower out to her.

As Kat reached for it, the little finger on her left hand brushed his thumb, sending a blissful shiver down her spine.

"Thank you." She leaned forward and sniffed the rose. "But what's the occasion?"

"I'm looking forward to our picnic." His dimple deepened with his smile.

"I am too," she said. She wished she had a plate of fresh-baked cookies to give him in return, but she supposed she'd have plenty of other opportunities.

"Have a good night, and I'll see you tomorrow, picnic basket in hand."

"Good night." She closed the door and looked around the room. None of the other flowers spoke to her soul as this one yellow rose did. And Kat desperately desired a future with the man who delivered it.

A private picnic that he was looking forward to was a promising start.

FORTY

Kat woke early Saturday morning and looked out the window. The early morning sun was just peeking up over the mountains. The sky was clear, and the air was already starting to warm. It was perfect picnic weather.

"Do you think I look all right?" Kat twirled, and her long skirt swished around her feet.

Nell stilled the broom in front of the stove and studied her. "You look beautiful. And I think that green cotton is his favorite of your dresses. I don't think he noticed anything else in Hattie's parlor the last time you wore it."

That's why she'd chosen it. Kat lifted the jelly jar containing Morgan's rose from the top of her trunk and breathed in the sweet fragrance of the bud.

"If the man doesn't get here soon, you're going to wear out your sniffer." Nell crinkled her nose.

Kat giggled. "One rose, and I'm a goner."

"Don't be silly. You were a goner long before he arrived with that rose."

"It probably started the night he came to the boardinghouse to take care of Rosita and had her put the scope in HopHop's ear."

Nell nodded. "That was a tender moment." She bent and swept her pile of dirt and lint into a dustpan. "He was so good with her. He'd be a good father."

"That is, if he still wants children. He didn't just lose his wife, but a son too."

"People heal, Kat." Nell emptied the dustpan into a trash bucket and looked at Kat. A look of admiration lit her eyes. "Just look at you—you've made this place a home. And you're well on your way to becoming a famous writer."

"Famous, huh? I may be the writer, but you're the dreamer."

"Famous or not, you're a living example of a person who is healing from hurt."

The sound of a horse's hooves grating against rocks drew their attention to the window. Morgan's buggy bumped its way up the road, and Kat pulled her cream-colored shawl from a hook by the door.

Please, Father. I want Morgan to be a living example of a person who is healing too.

Five minutes later, Morgan offered her his hand and helped Kat into the buggy. As she climbed in, she spied the picnic basket nestled on a quilt under her seat.

Morgan eased in beside her and took the reins. "Do you and Nell have everything ready for the wedding next weekend?"

"I think so. We should—it's about all we've discussed." That, and a certain man and a yellow rose. A man with moral conviction and spiritual devotion whose smile caused palpitations.

Morgan guided his horse down to Eaton Avenue and turned left as if he were going to the hospital.

"Where are we going? Do you have a patient to see before we head to Tenderfoot Hill?"

Morgan stared at her. It seemed he was studying her lips, but it may just have been wishful thinking on her part.

"I thought we'd save that spot for another day." Pulling up on the reins, he stopped in front of a vacant lot with sticks and twine stretched out across it. "I have something I want to show you." After he helped her out of his buggy, he reached for the basket.

Kat looked down at her dress, then at the sticks. They were going to picnic on dirt?

Morgan handed her the basket and pulled the quilt from his buggy. "We're celebrating new beginnings today."

"We are?" Kat followed him to the edge of the strange pattern of sticks and twine. She was curious to find out what he was talking about, but no doubt it had something to do with Judson and Nell.

Morgan unfolded the quilt and laid it on a smooth piece of ground inside the perimeter of sticks. Then he took the basket and set it on a corner. "Kat, take a good look around you, because you're looking at my property."

Kat gazed around the empty lot.

"Remember hearing about the man who lost his leg in one of the explosions last month—Ethan Goeke?"

"We prayed for him. He'd lost his house and his job."

He pulled a piece of paper from his pocket. "This was his land."

"You bought it?" Kat leaned forward, trying to make out the writing on the paper.

"He tucked the deed into a thank-you letter and gave it to me. Actually, he'd given it to Sister Coleman and she delivered it to me."

Kat studied the panorama. Located on The Hill on Carr at Fourth Street, Morgan's property overlooked Cripple Creek, with clear views of Mount Pisgah to the northwest and Tenderfoot Hill to the northeast. A ribbon of afternoon sunlight showcased the frosted Rocky Mountains to the west. Taking in a deep breath, she fought the urge to picture herself here with Morgan, enjoying the views for the rest of her life.

She turned back toward him and saw that his attention was fixed on her, not on the vistas. He captured her hand, and her breath right along with it. "I'm building a house here, Kat."

She moistened her lips. "It's a perfect location. Close to the heart of town, but not smack dab in the middle of it. Only a few blocks from the hospital."

"I really like it here, but I could use your help."

She laughed. "What, you need someone to hold a shotgun on the builders?"

He rewarded her wit with a baritone chuckle. Laughter deepened his dimple.

"That's not exactly what I had in mind. Not at all what I had in mind, in fact. I was hoping you could help me with the design." He let go of her hand and opened the sheet of paper. "This is a rough sketch."

"The big cookstove will go in here." He pointed to a square on one edge of the drawing. "The house will have indoor plumbing and electric lights, of course."

"That sounds wonderful."

"And a porch with a railing and spindles."

"I like it." *Just one thing missing—me.*

Smiling, Morgan supported her elbow and led her over the twine to the quilt. He seated her first, and then sat down and removed his shoes. "We're having our picnic in the parlor."

Ah, that's what the sticks and twine was all about—Morgan had laid out a floor plan.

Looking around, Kat tapped her chin. "The room could use a couple of walls, and maybe a sofa and a piano."

His tender gaze made her glad she was sitting down. She feared her legs wouldn't hold her up right now if she did try to stand.

"A big window would be nice on this wall for the view of the mountains."

"There'll be a nice big one in the dining room too." Morgan pointed to a roped-off space directly across from them. But as he turned back around, his countenance became serious. "Do you mind if I ask you a personal question?"

She shook her head, suddenly unable to form words.

Morgan leaned forward and took her hands in his. "I was wondering if you would be willing to consider our relationship something other than a friendship. A courtship, perhaps?"

"I think that'd be a fine idea, now that we're getting along." She winked at him.

Her prayers had been answered. Morgan had changed his mind, at least about the possibility of marriage. She knew that meant he was on the road to recovery from the grief of losing his wife and son. And as she thought about it, she realized that her acceptance of the offer meant she was well on her way to her own recovery from hurt and loss.

FORTY-ONE

❧

at tapped her toes to the music while Hattie stood in front of the phonograph, reading the telegram. A boy about Vivian's age had delivered it to the cabin just moments before she and Nell left this morning.

"Oh, this is such wonderful news, dear." Holding the telegram high in the air, Hattie wrapped Kat in a warm embrace. And for a moment, Kat pretended it was her own mother sharing in her joy.

"It is finally official. My sister is a real writer." Nell beamed with pride, and Kat soaked it in.

"And *Harper's Bazar*." Soft wrinkles framed Hattie's smile. "Oh, won't Morgan be so pleased."

Kat knew he would, and she couldn't wait to tell him.

Hattie glanced up at the clock. "I know we need to go soon, but with all the talk about weddings and courtship, I wanted to show you girls the dress I wore when my George and I wed." Her gray eyes glistened. "I'll only be a minute." Before Kat could suggest a later time, their dear friend scuttled up the stairs.

"We were so excited about the telegram that I forgot to tell her about my dress." Concern creased Nell's forehead. "I hope she won't be too disappointed that I won't be wearing hers on Saturday."

"Now that she knows Morgan is courting me, she's probably hoping I'll wear it someday." Kat lifted the needle off the phonograph, and she and Nell met Hattie at the bottom of the stairs.

Nell took the lovely two-piece dress from her and displayed it over her arm.

"It's silk mull." Hattie drew her bent fingers across the full skirt. "My mother made it for me. George's chin nearly flopped to the floor when he looked up and saw me in it."

"It's beautiful." Kat liked its simple yet elegant style. The shirt-waist was trimmed with a lace insertion and pintucking, and had three-quarter sleeves.

"As you can see, I've added some padding over the years." Hattie laughed, and gazed at the dress. "I didn't think it would suit you, Nell. I suspect you chose something with a bit more frill and pill."

Kat smiled. "That describes her choice to the letter."

"But I thought you might wear it, Kat. That is, if you'd want to."

"I do." As soon as the words left Kat's mouth, she burst into laughter. Clearly, trying to hide her affection for Morgan was a futile exercise. She'd failed miserably.

Hopefully, the doctor was as astute as her two companions.

⌒♥⌒

Every time someone walked into the small meeting room at the Elks Lodge, Morgan glanced at the door, expecting to see Kat.

"Relax, Doc. They'll be here." Judson stood at the piano while Morgan checked the order of his songs. "You know how long winded Miss Hattie can be."

Morgan nodded. The woman's affinity for gab was the reason he was here in the midst of all these women in the first place.

He hadn't seen Kat since Sunday. Nearly three days—far too long. If he had his way, he'd see her every day—morning and night. He'd swing with her out on the porch every summer evening while they sipped lemonade. And they'd picnic every Saturday—inside or out.

"There they are." Judson nudged him with his foot.

All three women—Hattie, Nell, and Kat—sauntered into the room, and Morgan stood. They all looked lovely, but it was Kat's smile that sent pure bliss straight to his core. He and Judson met them at the front row, where they'd reserved five seats.

"Hello, Morgan." Kat held a telegram out to him. "I received a telegram from *Harper's Bazar*."

"You're the new female western correspondent for the magazine, aren't you?"

"I am." She affected a mock swagger in her shoulders, her smile lighting the gold flecks in her deep brown eyes.

"I knew you could do it, and they're smart editors to think so too. Congratulations!"

"Thank you. For everything."

He wanted to take her into his arms and never let her go, and he was still weighing the consequences of such a public action, when Hattie walked to the front of the room.

All in good time, Morgan. All in good time.

For now, he escorted Kat to her chair while Judson did the same for Nell.

"Good morning, ladies." Hattie glanced at the front row where Morgan and Judson sat. "And our esteemed gentlemen, of course." She tittered and fiddled with her frilly collar before continuing. "Welcome to the May Wednesday luncheon of the Women for the Betterment of Cripple Creek. Most of you know Mr. Turner was scheduled to be our guest this month, but due to his mother's illness, he had to postpone his presentation." She motioned for Morgan to step forward, and he walked to the piano. "In Mr. Turner's stead, the new doctor in town, Dr. Morgan Cutshaw, has agreed to give us a piano concert."

The ladies were still clapping when Morgan struck the first chord of "Silver Threads Among the Gold." After several more songs, he finished "Love's Old Sweet Song" with Judson's vocal accompaniment. The ladies continued to applaud long after he played the last note. When Judson returned to Nell's side, Morgan looked out at Hattie.

"Before our intermission, I'd like to make an announcement, if you might indulge me."

She waved a gloved hand. "You go right ahead, Dr. Cutshaw."

He stood and cleared his throat. "Most of you know that I'm the new doctor in town. But you may not know that we have a distinguished writer in our midst." Kat flushed, and the room buzzed. "Kat, would you please join me?" He didn't have a plan for convincing her to come to the front of the room, and breathed a sigh of relief when she rose from her chair and walked toward him.

"Thank you." Instead of looking at him, she seemed to stare at the back wall. "I think it's important to celebrate new beginnings." The dozen or so women clapped. "Miss Kat Sinclair was kind enough to join me here today to support me, but now I want us to celebrate with Kat. She's just received an appointment as a new Woman Writer Out West for *Harper's Bazar*."

A wave of murmured approval swept through the room, followed by enthusiastic applause, and Hattie walked to the front of the room.

"Ladies, there's more concert to come," she said. "But first, we'll adjourn to the dining room to enjoy the mountains of refreshments you all brought." The gaggle of women hurried out of the room, chattering. Hattie waved a handkerchief at Morgan and Kat from the doorway, her smile warm and supportive. Judson and Nell remained in their chairs facing each other, engaged in a private conversation, which is what Morgan hoped he and Kat could do.

Morgan turned back toward Kat, who remained standing near the piano, her cheeks still pink.

"Thank you, Morgan." She took a step away from him.

"Wait," he said. "Would you mind remaining here…with me for a moment?"

Staying her steps, she looked up at him, her brows raised. "You wanted to speak to me about something else?"

Morgan bobbed his head, drawing in a deep breath. "I thought we could sort out your name issue."

She tucked her chin and raised a slender brow. "My what?"

"Your pen name. What name will you use on your stories?"

"My name—Kat Sinclair. Why? Do you think Katherine would be better suited for a professional byline?"

He shook his head. "I rather like the name Kat. But I thought you might want to use three names."

"Oh?"

"Many famous writers have three names. Gerard Manley Hopkins. Elizabeth Barrett Browning. Henry David Thoreau. Dante Gabriel Rossetti. Robert Louis Stevenson."

"All right, then." She raised her chin, a smile in her eyes. "What do you say about the name Kat Joyce Sinclair?"

He shook his head again, trying to keep a straight face.

"That's all I have." She shrugged her shoulders.

"I had something a little more poetic in mind." He tipped his head left, then right, as if he were weighing the thought. "See what you think of this: Kat Sinclair Cutshaw."

Her brown eyes pooled. She peeled off her gloves and stepped toward him. "It does have a writerly ring to it."

"I think so, but using that name does require a big commitment."

Her bottom lip quivering, she nodded. "I'm ready, Morgan." She laced her fingers with his, and he raised her hands to his lips and kissed them, her skin as soft as buckskin. He wanted nothing more than to lean in toward her, but he knew that kiss would have to wait for a more private moment.

"I love you, Kat," he said.

"And I love you, Morgan."

"Will you marry me?"

"Yes!" She squeezed his hand. "Yes. I will."

Miss Hattie was the first to clap. Until then, Morgan hadn't noticed that Nell and Judson were standing less than ten feet away from them. Smiling, they joined Hattie's applause as the women began to pour into the room.

Morgan leaned toward Kat and whispered, "To be continued." When she nodded, he led her back to her chair. The Women for the

Betterment of Cripple Creek cheered while the sisters hugged and he returned to the piano bench. "Ladies, I'd like to dedicate this next song to my fiancée, Miss Kat Sinclair." He looked out at her, rewarded by a smile that most definitely reached her eyes.

As he played the first few notes of "Home, Sweet Home," Morgan realized he'd finally let go of the past, and he was ready to embrace the new.

And as far as he was concerned, the sooner, the better.

FORTY-TWO

When the first wave of sunlight splashed across the bed and warmed Kat's face, her eyes popped open and she sat straight up. This was no ordinary day, and she still couldn't believe it.

"Oh no! Am I late?" Nell scrambled out of bed, her eyes half shut.

"No, the day just dawned." Kat tugged Nell's dressing gown, pulling her down to sit beside her on the bed.

"That's good news. I dreamed I slept the whole day long, and by the time I got to the altar, Judson had fallen asleep, and Reverend Taggart and everyone else had left."

"That's not as peculiar as the dream I've been having."

"Oh?" Nell tilted her head, her eyes wide.

"I dreamed I was getting married today too."

Giggling, Nell lightly pinched Kat's arm. "You're wide awake."

Kat nodded. "Actually, I feel more awake than I have in many months." Morgan's love and support had stirred her heart to love him when she thought it impossible to trust again. "I'm getting married today!" Kat squealed.

Nell sauntered over to the two white dresses that hung in the corner and pulled hers down. Holding it up in front of her, she spun around in slow motion. "Mrs. Judson Archer."

Nodding, Kat pulled hers down—Hattie's two-piece dress in silk mull—and did her own spin. "Kat Sinclair Cutshaw. Mrs. Morgan Cutshaw."

She hadn't imagined that Morgan would be able to top Judson's romantic proposal to Nell in Hattie's parlor, but he had indeed surpassed it. In a few heady moments, Kat had gone from wanting to strangle the man to a deep-seated desire to plant her lips on his and never remove them.

Their daily routine soon gave way to a flurry of activity. While Nell packed her things into her trunk, Kat stripped the bed. Construction would soon begin on Morgan's two-story house—their house—but she and Morgan would live here until its completion. She looked around the single-room dwelling. It would be Morgan sitting at the table for breakfast tomorrow. Morgan would shave at the washbowl and stoke the fire. He had already replaced the rope bed with a more comfortable one. The thought of being so near to him quickened her heart, and she suddenly found herself thankful for the cabin's coziness.

Less than an hour later, Hattie arrived at the cabin and turned the kitchen table into a hair salon. Moving from one head of hair to the other and back again, she hummed as she worked. When Hattie twisted and pinned Nell's hair, she hummed "Love's Old Sweet Song." For Kat, it was "Home, Sweet Home."

The Lord had accomplished more in their hearts in a month than Kat would've dreamed possible in a lifetime.

With everything else ready, Kat and Hattie helped Nell into her gown and shoes. Then it was her turn. When all the lacing and buttoning was done, she and her sister were both dressed and on their way to each other's weddings. Boney Hughes drove the carriage. Hattie sat beside him. Kat rode in the back with Nell.

Boney reined the horses down the hill toward Bennett, then spent a few moments twisting and preening his groomed beard. "Right pretty day for a wedding, don't you think?"

"The best. Especially splendid for a ceremony that's taking place in God's great outdoor cathedral on Tenderfoot Hill."

Boney Hughes parked the carriage at the end of a ribbon of muslin cloth laid down as a path on the hilltop. And as soon as he did, two miners dressed in clean overalls stepped up, ready to help them down. Kat recognized them both from her shotgun-wielding day. The unlikely men-in-waiting assisted Nell first and then gave Kat a hand down from the carriage.

"You might remember my two boys, Billy and Bobby, from the other day. They're a couple of your neighbors," Boney said.

"Your sons?" Kat shook her head.

"Yes ma'am. Two of the finest." Boney helped Hattie down from the carriage and escorted her up the path.

But it was the two men who stood slack-jawed at the far end of the fabric path that caused her and Nell to gasp. Both of their grooms stood stick-straight and proud, looking every bit like princes. But it was the tender love in Morgan's dew-kissed green eyes that quickened Kat's feet.

Even Cinderella would be jealous.

Holding her beloved's hand, Kat took in the panoramic view in front of her. God's handiwork on Tenderfoot Hill stirred Kat's heart to even deeper praise. Her heart overflowed with uncontainable joy and immeasurable thanksgiving as she looked into Morgan's eyes.

After they exchanged their vows, Judson immediately dipped Nell into a long passionate kiss. Morgan pulled Kat into his arms and gave her a kiss that would melt Cinderella's glass slippers. Then he whispered in her ear, "You, Mrs. Cutshaw, are in for an epic adventure."

He winked. Kat had already seen the amazing things God had done on her adventure so far, and she could hardly wait for the next chapter.

AUTHOR'S NOTE

The joy of reading and writing historical fiction involves more than merely being drawn into the characters and their stories, but also vicariously experiencing history in a compelling setting. While researching *Two Brides Too Many* in Cripple Creek, Colorado, I made several interesting historical discoveries.

One of those fun discoveries was the twist on the spelling for *Harper's Bazar*. If you're like me, you wanted to add another "a" after the "z," but until the November 1929 issue, the magazine was spelled with only two "a's." Also, *Harper's Bazar* is known for its careful focus on fashion and homemaking, but when I discovered that they also published fiction and essays for women during the late 1890s, I decided it would be the perfect fit for Kat's writings about women, for women.

In each of the Sinclair Sisters of Cripple Creek novels, you'll meet at least one real woman from Cripple Creek history. In *Two Brides Too Many*, Sister Mary Claver Coleman serves as the historical woman in my fictional tale. Sister Coleman was part of the Catholic Order of the Sisters of Mercy and was sent to Cripple Creek to establish the town's first general hospital.

I look forward to our time together in these stories.

May God make a way for you in your wilderness. May His wisdom gird you. May His dreams for you come true.

Mona Hodgson

ACKNOWLEDGMENTS

I liken writing a novel for publication to either birthing or building. So as not to offend any sensibilities here, I'll use the building metaphor. I could not have constructed this story without the selfless support and endless resources of capable and committed subcontractors who offered the blueprints and tools I needed to get the job done.

- Bob, my hubby—a.k.a. caregiver, researcher, walking encyclopedia, personal computer technician, and cook.
- Janet Kobobel Grant of Books & Such Literary Agency, my agent extraordinaire.
- DiAnn Mills, my ultra-dedicated critique partner and friend. She kept my tools sharp.
- Shannon Hill Marchese, my super-duper editor, and her strong editorial team who helped me add bricks and mortar, windows, and the finishing trim to the story.
- The entire WaterBrook Multnomah–Random House team—you all provided the foundation on which I build.
- Jeanine, Shirley, Debbie, Karen, June, Lauraine, Ann—my personal prayer team, and all who prayed for me during this construction project.
- My mom, June Gansberg, and my sisters, Cindy, Tammy, and Linda—your raised pompoms cheered on this contractor.
- Dr. Kirk Stetson, my extremely patient and bighearted medical information supplier.

- Jan Collins, Director, Cripple Creek District Museum, a generous purveyor of historical information.
- Vicki Smothers, a gracious and knowledgeable volunteer at the Pikes Peak Heritage Center in Cripple Creek, Colorado.
- Leon Drew, an ardent volunteer at the Outlaws and Lawmen Jail Museum in Cripple Creek.
- A gargantuan thank you to all of these listed, and to all who aren't, who had a part in the building of this novelist and this novel.

Dedicated to the Master Builder and Cornerstone, Jesus—the Way, the Truth, and the Life.

About the Author

MONA HODGSON is the author of twenty-eight children's books, including *Real Girls of the Bible: A Devotional* and the Princess Twins series. Her writing credits also include hundreds of poems, articles, and short stories in more than fifty different periodicals, including *Focus on the Family, Decision, The Upper Room, The Quiet Hour, Bible Advocate, Clubhouse Jr.,* and *Highlights for Children.* Mona speaks at women's retreats, schools, and writers conferences, and she was founding director of the Glorieta Christian Writers Conference. Mona is one of the four Gansberg sisters of Arizona. She and her husband of thirty-seven-plus years have two grown daughters, a son-in-law, three grandsons, and one granddaughter. To learn more about Mona, or to find readers guides for the Sinclair Sisters of Cripple Creek books, visit her Web site: www.monahodgson.com. You can find also Mona at www.twitter.com/monahodgson or www.facebook.com/mona.hodgson.